CONFUSION ASSAULTED TRINA, CLOUDING HER MIND

"Slate," she whispered, "I... right now I don't really know what I want..."

"You know." His mouth was gentle against hers, his tongue light and tantalizing. She shuddered as his lips left hers to follow a slow tormenting path across her face, pressing the throbbing pulse in her temple, the warm hollows of her ear. Reaching up, she urged his mouth to hers again, but the resistance she encountered made her eyes snap open.

"No, Trina," he said, "not this way. I want to hear you say it... tell me what you're feeling."

She hesitated briefly before responding softly, "You win, Slate—"

This time, Slate's interruption held anger. "It's not a case of winning, Trina. You're suggesting that if I win, you lose."

"It doesn't matter—"

"Damn! Don't do this to me, Trina. I don't want to be a victor here."

"But you are, Slate. You are..."

ABOUT THE AUTHOR

Elaine Barbieri is the bestselling author of seventeen novels, as well as a wife and mother to three grown children. Born in Paterson, New Jersey, she was employed as a secretary before striking out to write her first historical romance. *Race for Tomorrow* remains a special book to her because it is her only contemporary novel to date.

Elaine Barbieri

Race for Tomorrow

Harlequin Books

TORONTO • NEW YORK • LONDON
AMSTERDAM • PARIS • SYDNEY • HAMBURG
STOCKHOLM • ATHENS • TOKYO • MILAN
MADRID • WARSAW • BUDAPEST • AUCKLAND

If you purchased this book without a cover you should be aware that this book is stolen property. It was reported as "unsold and destroyed" to the publisher, and neither the author nor the publisher has received any payment for this "stripped book."

First publication August 1985

Second publication April 1993

ISBN 0-373-83243-5

Copyright © 1983 by Elaine Barbieri. All rights reserved. Except for use in any review, the reproduction or utilization of this work in whole or in part in any form by any electronic, mechanical or other means, now known or hereafter invented, including xerography, photocopying and recording, or in any information storage or retrieval system, is forbidden without the permission of the publisher, Harlequin Enterprises Limited, 225 Duncan Mill Road, Don Mills, Ontario, Canada M3B 3K9.

All the characters in this book have no existence outside the imagination of the author and have no relation whatsoever to anyone bearing the same name or names. They are not even distantly inspired by any individual known or unknown to the author, and all incidents are pure invention.

® are Trademarks registered in the United States Patent and Trademark Office and in other countries.

Printed in U.S.A.

With special thanks to my son, Mike, of 17A racing fame, for his technical advice on the sport of dirt-track racing; and for bringing me to a true appreciation of the sport.

CHAPTER ONE

"What a body!"

"Sure is terrific, isn't it?"

"Will you look at those curves! I haven't seen anything that good lookin' since..."

"Oh, come off it, will you!" Realizing her own was the lone dissenting voice in the male chorus of ardent admiration, Trina Mallory steeled herself against the verbal abuse she was certain would follow. The roar of modified cars, as they circled the track behind her on their hot laps, momentarily delayed a response to her remark. Pulling her tall, slender frame to its full height, Trina raised her chin defiantly and returned the glares of the small group of drivers assembled before her. As much as she liked them, their drooling praise had struck a particularly tender nerve and she was not about to allow them to ramble on unchallenged.

It was an unusually warm spring afternoon and she had just taken her own hot laps with the other sportsman drivers. Distinctly dissatisfied with her car's performance, she had pulled into the pits only moments before, and without taking time to remove her firesuit, had started in search of her brother. Frustration had made her oblivious to the heat, which was intensified by the heavy fireproof longjohns and coveralls required by law for all drivers. Instead, with her long curly black hair released from the crash helmet she had flung unceremoniously into her car, she had covered the rutted ground in long, graceful strides, only to come upon the pack of drivers who now eyed her with gratingly superior smirks.

Intriguing black eyes narrowing with disgust, she stood her ground as Tom Harper drawled, "Come on, Doc, take another look and try to put your jealousy aside." The knowing look on his face was even more annoying than his use of the irritating nickname that dogged her. Gritting her teeth, she surveyed him with a narrow gaze as he continued with a small smile, "You don't mean to tell me that isn't a fantastic body."

Trina was well aware that to these men, the fact that she was a woman almost negated her twenty-four years' experience at the track, not to mention her superior driving skills and notable ability as a mechanic. To Tom's remark she replied testily, "And if I said I didn't agree, you'd all say I'm jealous, is that right?"

"Well, we might not *say* it, but we'd sure as hell *think* it, sweetheart!"

Biff Martin's short interjection brought another round of snickers from the group, and realizing she didn't stand a chance as the only female against a tight group of chauvinistic males, Trina felt a familiar sense of frustration. Refusing to be intimidated, she continued in a deceptively lazy tone, "What's so great about her? A few good lines? She's kind of flashy for my taste. Other than that, I'd say she's just ordinary."

"Ordinary!" The tone of irritated impatience in Tom's voice gave Trina a brief flash of satisfaction as he continued with considerable heat, "Look, I couldn't afford that little baby any more than anyone else here, but I'm not too proud to admit she's a beauty!"

"That's a matter of opinion, and in my opinion, it's performance that counts, not a flashy exterior."

"You can bet your last dollar her performance will match her appearance...the best!"

The last came from behind the impromptu gathering and was delivered with an air of indisputable confidence. Turning at the sound of the unfamiliar voice, Trina directed her attention toward the man who had spoken as he moved forward to lean a well-muscled body casually against the fender of the car under discussion. Startling blue eyes roamed her face familiarly as he continued arrogantly, "She's nothing but the best, inside and out, 'Slim.' Just keep your eye on the next heat if you doubt what I'm saying."

"There's a colorful expression about putting your money where your mouth is, 'Stretch.'" Hesitating for a moment for effect, Trina felt satisfaction as a light flush transfused his face. "You do know that saying, I presume?"

Watching as his lips compressed in silent acknowledgment of her gibe, Trina attempted to control the heat rushing through her in reaction to his quick, raking glance. Not waiting for a reply, she turned with an air of cool composure she did not feel. Intensely aware that his eyes followed as she strode away, Trina felt her annoyance flare anew. Arrogant oaf! He could be no one else but Slater Montgomery. The track was buzzing with talk of Slater Montgomery's new car, Slater Montgomery's personal financial backing, Slater Montgomery's latest equipment... Slater Montgomery... Slater Montgomery... She was thoroughly sick of hearing his name.

Just what they needed—another big bucks racer. As if the competition wasn't tough enough already. It was difficult for privately financed owner-drivers to compete with those commercially financed, especially with the kind of money Slater Montgomery's company had. No wonder his car was fabulous. While Trina and her brother, Buck, sank every spare penny into their cars, he had only to make a telephone call or charge his expense account for anything he needed. And if all the stories she had heard weren't vastly exaggerated, he even had a formal pit crew to work on his car at the track!

Damn! How was it that dirt-track racing was still touted as the last remaining holdout against big money racers? Perhaps that had been true at one time, but the situation had changed dramatically since her dad's time when she and Buck had spent every weekend during racing season at the track as his pit crew.

A warm, happy feeling came over her at the memory. When most girls her age were spending time before the mirror testing out new hairdos and makeup, she had been working in the garage beside her father and brother on the car that was going to "make dirt-track racing history." Her mother had died when she was five, and she hardly remembered her. After her father was gone, leaving only Buck to take care of his fourteen-year-old sister, she had been perfectly content to continue spending her spare time with her head tucked under the hood of a car beside him.

She and Buck still functioned as crew chiefs for each other's cars. The rest of the crew was strictly volunteer and constantly changing, depending on who was free for the weekend. Not so with big shots like Slater Montgomery. It was rumored that he traveled with a fantastic rig...a van in which his car, a spare engine, numerous spare tires and his neatly uniformed crew traveled in comfort! And here she was with a twelve-year-old truck and a rusting trailer to tow her car, wearing a stained, two-year-old firesuit, searching for her crew chief...her own brother, who had problems of his own and didn't really need any of her grief.

Slater Montgomery...whose ego seemed to match his rather considerable bankroll! It was obvious he considered himself a big man with the ladies, too. If she were honest, she'd have to admit he probably had women falling all over him. Not that he was handsome...no...he wasn't conventionally handsome in the least. Quite the contrary. His features were bold, irregular, with light, peculiarly arresting blue eyes dominating a broad, sharply boned face. And that chin! She didn't need a second look to see the stubbornness indicated there! Sandy-haired with sun-weathered skin, he stood about six foot three at least...broad in the shoulder and chest, and more than adequate in other areas, as was apparent in tight, worn jeans that left little to a woman's imagination. He probably had to beat women off with a broom! No wonder he was so arrogant! Well, he wouldn't have to fight her off. As far as she was concerned, racing drivers could be great friends and amusing companions, but that was as far as it went.

Well, at least those big bucks wouldn't be competing with *her* on the track. She had considered herself lucky to scrape up enough money to finance a sportsman car. The larger-engined modified cars had been way out of her means. It had taken Buck years to financially work his way up to a modified, and even more time to free his painstakingly constructed car of the kinks that held him back from becoming points champion. He had been close last season, but breakdowns and a lack of funds had defeated him in the end. This year it was going to be different! Buck had a few good sponsors, and he had been putting the money to good use all winter. Yes, Buck was going to be the modified points champion this year, and she was going to end up in the money in the sportsman class. And to blazes with Slater Montgomery and all the drivers like him!

Suddenly spotting a familiar dark head at the parts booth, Trina frowned and hastened her step. There could be only one reason for the intensity of Buck's dark expression...a breakdown during warmup.

Trina's eyes were riveted on her brother's tense face. All other thoughts were forced from her mind by the apparent emergency, and she was oblivious to the interested male gazes that followed her. Without a trace of conceit, Trina was aware that most men found her extremely attractive. Above average in height, she had an elegantly slim, fashionable body that allowed her to supplement her income by occasionally modeling clothes. Her natural grace of movement indicated a coordination that undoubtedly contributed to her superior skill as a driver. Years of ballet classes had further developed this grace. But it was her delicate, almost doll-like features—her large, velvet-black, lushly fringed eyes—that seemed to snare the attention of the opposite sex. She had a strangely innocent, untouched beauty that was only enhanced by the fire that flared too often recently in her expressive eyes, and the impatience with which she accepted unwanted opinions and attentions.

She had long since passed the trial and error part of her life. Trina Mallory knew exactly what she wanted. She and Buck were dedicated to the same goal—to be full-time racing drivers—and neither of them would spare any effort in achieving it. It looked like Buck was closer than she: with the reputation he had already earned at Middlevale Raceway, he would definitely be in demand as a driver. His standing as points champion this season and a possible win in the Schaefer 200 at Syracuse in the fall would probably allow him to write his own ticket. But everything hinged on this season. It had to be a good one for him or he would be set back several years. He couldn't afford even one bad weekend...or one serious breakdown....

Shouting, to be heard over roaring engines, Trina gripped her brother's arm, jerking his attention to her worried face. "What happened, Buck?"

"The carburetor's acting up again! I knew I should've changed it, but I thought I had all the kinks worked out. It's a good thing I'm not scheduled to go out until the last heat. It'll be a tight squeeze, but I think I can get it fixed in time. That is," he continued, turning his attention back to the attendant still looking through boxes for parts, "if I can get some help from somebody who knows what he's doing!"

His brow still knit in a tight, irritable frown, he turned back in Trina's direction. His bearded, craggy face was the image of her father's. Intimidating in anger, it moved into warmly familiar lines of concern as his eyes touched on her face. "How's your car working, Trina?"

"I'm having a problem with the steering. I was all over the track in the turns and I think..."

"The problem isn't with your steering, and you know it. You shouldn't be racing with those tires. They're practically bald."

"Look, Buck, I didn't come here for a lecture...just some advice. Do you think..."

"You know very well what I think." Shaking his head, Buck mumbled under his breath, "If my credit wasn't already stretched to the limit, I'd go over to that tire truck right now and get you four new tires. I told you not to buy used tires."

"I bought the best I could afford, Buck." Pausing as his frown deepened, Trina felt a flash of remorse for her thoughtless response. She knew that somehow Buck seemed to feel he had failed her in not being able to help her financially with her car. She had tried to explain to him that that kind of thinking was unreasonable...that she was a grown woman and responsible for her own expenses. But Buck had taken care of her too long.

The momentary lapse in racing activity allowing her to speak in a more subdued tone, Trina squeezed his arm and smiled unexpectedly up into his worried face. "You know very well that you've raced countless times with tires in worse condition than mine. You're not trying to tell me that you don't think I could do as well as you did under the same conditions? You know I'm a better driver than you are, Buck!"

"Why, you little..." His face finally broke into a reluctant grin, and he shook his head in amused exasperation. "That'll be the day...when you're a better driver than I am. But I'll tell you something...." Lowering his head, he whispered confidentially into her ear, "You're a better driver than half the drivers at this track, and if anybody can make it with those tires, you can."

Turning away to accept the box held out to him by the clerk, Buck did not wait for a response. He returned his attention to her a few seconds later, saying briskly, "Come on, help me get this carburetor fixed and I'll see what I can do about your 'steering'."

Trina fell in beside him as he started back toward their cars. "That's all right," she said lightly with exaggerated confidence. "You don't have to bother, Buck. I'm so good, I'll win anyway...."

Laughing spontaneously as Buck threw a sharp glance in her direction, Trina concluded outrageously, "And I'll help you fix your carburetor, too."

"Trina..."

"All right...all right..."

A short distance away, Slater Montgomery nodded his head absentmindedly as the man beside him continued speaking. He was already occupied, following the progress of the two making rapid strides across the muddied pits. Intrigued, he had been unable to take his eyes from the long-legged brunette who had put him so solidly in his place just a short time earlier. Even in that baggy firesuit, she looked better to him than any woman he had seen in a long time. He had been startled at the intensity of his own reaction when she and the big, dark-haired driver at the parts booth had been speaking. The intimacy between them was obvious, and he had experienced an unreasonable sense of loss when she had slanted a teasing smile up into the big man's face.

They had stopped walking and seemed to be working between number 82, a red and white modified car, and number 013, a pink and purple sportsman model, and he realized they were helping each other. Again, there was that inexplicable sense of loss. He had noted instantly that her long-fingered hands had been bare...there had been no rings that would indicate her marital status, but the thought gave him little consolation. She would probably have removed them for the day with the expectation of working on her car.

He had found out that her name was Trina Mallory. He had also found out that despite the fact that the scene into which he had barged earlier had appeared to be the typical case of a group of male drivers putting down the lone female driver, it had instead been a case of good-natured teasing that had gotten a little out of hand.

"Are you listening to me, Slate?"

Not bothering to respond to his inquiry, Slater abruptly turned his intense gaze toward his annoyed crew chief and said, "Looks like our lady driver is pretty chummy with that big guy with the red and white modified."

"Yes, I guess she is."

Slater eyed the gray-haired mechanic with wry impatience. "Don't be coy, Bob. You and I both know that you know everything that goes on at this track. Do I have to pry it out of you word by word? Who is he, and what's the status between them?"

Amusement apparent on his face, the older man responded slowly, "I figured that being as I finally had your attention for a few minutes, I'd take advantage of it, but I can see you're in no mood to mince words."

"That's right, I'm in no mood to 'mince words.' Now, who is he, and what is he to Trina Mallory?"

Laughing openly, Bob Mitchell shook his head. "Don't snap my head off, Slate. You won't stand a chance with her anyway."

"Bob..."

"The big fellow's her brother."

Relief brought a smile to Slate's lips. It left suddenly as he questioned intently, "What makes you think I wouldn't stand a chance with her? I don't usually meet up with too much resistance."

Bob shook his head with a small laugh. Having been Slater Montgomery's crew chief off and on for the past three years while he played with the idea of racing, Bob had been witness to the way women reacted to Slate's rugged good looks. He still could not understand why Slate's casual treatment of women seemed to turn them on all the more. But this time it was going to be different if he set his sights on Trina Mallory. Raising his eyes to Slater's steady perusal, he insisted unrelentingly, "Don't waste your time on her, Slate. You don't stand a chance."

"Says you." Bob's attitude was beginning to get to him. "What makes you think Trina Mallory's so different?"

"Maybe you should ask yourself that question, Slate." Eyeing him with barely suppressed amusement, Bob continued, "But unless things have changed since the last time I was at this track, Trina won't date any of the drivers here. She just keeps it friendly...like she's one of the boys. She keeps her social life separate from the track."

"That's because she hasn't found a man here that interests her. But she's about to meet him."

"If you mean *you*, from what I heard she already met you, and she wasn't too impressed."

Taking a step forward, Slater clapped his hand on Bob's shoulder. His smile was confident. "That's where you're wrong, Bob...dead wrong."

CHAPTER TWO

THE ROAR OF REVVING engines was dulled only slightly by the ear plugs Trina had automatically inserted into her ears before donning her helmet. Strapped tightly into the seat of number 013, she gripped the steering wheel firmly with her gloved hands as she awaited the signal for the pace car to begin moving the cars onto the track. She was conscious of nothing but her own position—eleventh in a starting lineup of seventeen.

Shooting a quick glance to the car in the inside position beside her, she winced. Harvey Steele...she'd have to watch out for him. He always went squirrely in the turns. It had to be her luck to draw a spot beside him in the lineup! Her best bet was to put some space between them and to stay as far away from him as possible. The first couple of laps until the field could stretch out a little bit were going to be hairy, but if she could manage to get through them without Harvey damaging her car in any way, she would have a chance.

Tensing as the cars in front of her gradually began to move forward, Trina shifted gears and stepped lightly on the gas. Her eyes flashed toward the pits as the pace car began moving slowly around the track. Buck stood in the back of his pickup truck for a better view of the track. Realizing that her head was turned in his direction, he raised his fist in a confident sign of victory. Trina smiled, her shifting glance moving to catch another tall figure in the pits as they rounded the second turn. Sandy-blond hair glinting in the brilliant afternoon sun, Slater Montgomery saluted her briefly with a mocking expression as she drove past. The smile slowly faded from Trina's face. She could do without his silent sarcasm! Whatever she lacked in equipment, she would make up for in driving skill, and she'd show him! "Nothing but the best, inside and out..." What arrogance! If he drove as well as he bragged, he'd be a driver to watch. But somehow she doubted that he would.

The line of cars in front of her began rapidly accelerating, the powerful engines revving to a roar that shook the ground beneath them. The tight lineup was rounding the third turn when the pace car turned sharply off the track, and the lead car abruptly accelerated to racing speed. The green flag signaling the start of the race was raised and dropped as he passed underneath.

Adrenaline pumping through her veins, Trina accelerated sharply and moved the wheel in a deft movement that shot her expertly into the brief opening in front of her. The race had begun!

Minutes later, her arms aching with fatigue, Trina pulled into the pits and drove cautiously to her allotted spot. Despite the abominable heat, the dirt that gritted between her teeth and the perspiration that streamed down her temples, she was elated! Third! She had come in third! Not bad for a car with bald tires and a tired engine! She would be able to finance new tires before the end of the month, and then she'd really make her move in the points rating.

Pulling her car to a halt, Trina unbuckled her seatbelts and squeezed out of the car with the ease of long practice. She turned, jerked off her helmet and threw her arms exuberantly around Buck's brawny frame.

"How about that, Buck? I finished in the money, and without even one dent!"

Prying her arms loose, and obviously suppressing a smile, Buck raised his brow. "From the way you're jumping around, you'd think you came in first!"

Having no success as she attempted to shake his arm playfully, Trina narrowed her eyes with feigned menace. "Buck Mallory, you know very well I didn't stand a chance of winning with the condition of my tires! But I made third, and those points will keep me in contention! I'm telling you, dear brother, this is going to be the year for the Mallorys...the big one!"

An almost indefinable flicker moving across his features, Buck mumbled, "Maybe so, honey. We'll see after the modified feature race."

"What do you mean, 'maybe'?" Startled at his momentary lapse of confidence, Trina fixed an intense gaze on Buck's face. "I've never heard you use a 'maybe' in your life!"

"Well, maybe it's time for me to start. Did you ever consider that I might be getting tired of this uphill battle? I worked all winter on this car." Frustration obvious in his eyes, he continued heatedly, "And now the carburetor—"

"I thought we fixed it! The engine seemed to work well enough in the last heat."

"Sure, we fixed the carburetor this time, but next time, it'll be the timing chain, or the linkage, or some other thing that'll keep me broke the rest of the year."

"These setbacks didn't seem to bother you so much before. What happened to make you—"

"Nothing happened!"

The vehemence of Buck's response sent out a familiar warning signal. Frowning, Trina questioned in a softer voice, "What's the matter, Buck? Is Karen tired of waiting to get married?"

Buck's eyes jerked to her face in unspoken confirmation as he responded in an abruptly sharp tone, "It's this season or never, Trina."

Trina hesitated only a moment, her expression hardening. "That makes it simple, doesn't it, Buck? You're going to make it this season."

Jerking down the zipper of her firesuit, she pulled her arms out of the suffocating garment and tied the arms around her waist. In another quick movement she pulled off the heavy fireproof underwear top, leaving her with only the light sleeveless T-shirt she wore beneath. Her eyes level and direct she looked back into Buck's face. "Come on, let's check that engine again."

THE BRIGHT AFTERNOON SUN had dropped below the horizon as the full card of hot laps, qualifying heats, consolation races and feature races for the street stock and the sportsman car divisions had progressed. Tensely engrossed, Trina watched as modified cars thundered around the track for the feature race. Her vantage point was the back of the same pickup truck her brother had occupied as he had watched her a few races before, and it afforded her a perfect view of the track. Her eyes had not strayed from the roaring cars since the inception of the race. The modified feature race was always the final race of the evening, and for Trina the wait had been interminable.

Immediately after she and Buck had finished checking out his car, she had gone to the dressing room and stepped out of her fireproof coveralls. Stripping down to her underwear, she had sponged the grit of the track from her skin as best she could under the primitive conditions and had slipped into her jeans and a fresh T-shirt. Taking only a moment to apply a touch of makeup and brush the dirt from her hair, she had returned immediately to the pits, her heart in her throat. The normally pleasant tension of the approaching race had been magnified disturbingly by Buck's statement. He was so close to achieving his dream...so very close.

The track was flooded with brilliant, artificial light, lending an unreal quality to the event in progress. Starting tenth in a field of eighteen, Buck had not done too poorly in the draw. She had found it extremely difficult to oust the picture of Slate Montgomery's arrogant expression from her mind. Any consolation she'd felt, that as a new driver he would have to start at the back of the pack for the first two nights of racing, had not lasted for long. The ease with which the slick blue and white modified had passed the cars at the rear and advanced to the position of fifth had been frightening. The power of his engine was awesome!

The knot that had formed in her stomach tightened painfully as the gap gradually closed between Slate Montgomery's number 008 and the fourth position car. Gasping as Slate Montgomery moved into fourth with a sudden burst of speed, Trina closed her eyes in a brief, agonizing denial of reality. Buck had held the lead for the past four laps, and with four more laps to go, a win had seemed almost inevitable. Turning to shoot a frantic look at Bix Morley and Sid Lutton, their volunteer pit crew for the weekend, Trina saw the same tension reflected on their faces.

The blue and white 008 moved inexorably forward as the loudspeaker blared the progress of the race with rabid excitement. Feeling the edge of panic, Trina watched as Slater Montgomery edged into third position. Her heart thundered in her ears as he crept ever closer to the second place car. Abruptly, with startling speed, he moved into second place! Her eyes shooting to the red and white car in the lead, Trina realized the gap was slowly closing. The white flag waved wildly as Buck flashed past the starter's booth.

Turning to Bix, Trina shouted adamantly over the roar of engines, "Montgomery'll never make it past Buck! There's only one more lap!" Seeing something in Bix's expression that she refused to accept, Trina quickly returned her attention to the track.

There was no contest as far as the other cars were concerned. The race was clearly between Buck and Slate Montgomery. Unable to restrain herself any longer, Trina screamed into the ever increasing din of the crowd's roar, "Come on, Buck! Come on!"

Suddenly, almost instantly, Slate Montgomery snared the inside position beside Buck on the third turn as the two cars approached the final straightaway. Driving side by side they entered the final stretch. Her attention glued to the track, Trina watched with terror-filled eyes as Slater Montgomery's car moved momentarily sideways to tap Buck's rear wheel. The result was catastrophic, sending Buck's car careening wildly across the track! Unable to breathe as she watched the horrifying spectacle, Trina finally caught her breath as Buck regained control in a supreme demonstration of driving ability and maneuvered his car back on course.

But it was too late! Unable to bear the sight of the blue and white number 008 flashing across the finish line underneath the checkered flag, Trina closed her eyes. The results of the race blared loudly over the loudspeaker in confirmation. Slate Montgomery had won! Buck had come in a close second!

Turning away as the slick blue and white car pulled into the winner's circle to the adulation of the screaming crowd, Trina slowly walked to the end of the truckbed and jumped down. She had seen all she cared to see.

Walking over to the pits to wait for her brother's car to pull in, she knew he would be furiously angry at Slate Montgomery. A few moments later, she was proven right.

Seething with rage, Buck squeezed his broad body out of the car and turned to face her.

"He did it on purpose! The dirty, cheating—"

"Buck, calm down. It's over and done. There's another race tomorrow. You can give Slate Montgomery a good lesson in losing then."

"He tapped my wheel deliberately. It's the oldest trick in the book."

"No, Buck, he couldn't—"

"I know what I'm talking about, Trina. The second before he turned the wheel, Montgomery looked directly toward me. I knew what he was going to do before he did it, but it was too late to steer away from him!"

"Even if it's true, there's nothing you can do about it now, Buck. Just let things lie. You'll pick up a win tomorrow and then he can..."

Trina's voice trailed off as her brother strode away to confront Slate. As the blue and white number 008 moved slowly through the pits after the conclusion of the award ceremony, Buck Mallory stood solidly in its path, forcing it to an unceremonious halt. He walked to the driver's side of the car and looked down into Slater

Montgomery's questioning expression. His voice was low and threaded with anger.

"You didn't fool me with that little trick, Montgomery."

Returning his gaze without a change in expression, Slate responded coolly, "I accidentally tapped your wheel. I'm sorry, but the race is over, Mallory, and you lost. Let's leave it at that."

"You're right, it's too late to do anything about it today, but just a little word of warning, Montgomery. Don't try it again. I have too much invested in this game to let a hotshot like you push me out of the top spot with a few old tricks."

His eyes flicking briefly to Trina's face, Slate responded slowly. "Believe what you want, Mallory, but the fact is, as much as it might have looked that way, I didn't hit your car deliberately. And I don't expect to stay here and argue with you about it. The race is over."

True to his word, Slate Montgomery turned his attention away from Buck's flushed face, and stepped on the gas.

Watching until his car slipped into its slot at the other end of the pits, Trina jerked her gaze back to her brother's unrelenting expression. She had a distinct feeling that they had not heard the last of this.

LOUD DISCO MUSIC BLARED from the antiquated jukebox in the far corner of the room as a few couples gyrated to the energetic rhythm, but Trina was in no mood for The Last Pit Stop tonight. The long racing weekend with which Middlevale Raceway had opened the new season had seemed like an excellent idea to her when it had first been announced. After a long winter layoff, she had been anxious to test her car and sharpen her driving skill. A full card on Friday, with street stock, sportsman and modified cars racing; sportsman and modified cars on Saturday; and street stock cars on Sunday afternoon, had seemed like an excellent opportunity to pick up some points toward the track championship. But the weekend had turned into a nightmare with the addition of one unexpected element. Slater Montgomery.

Glancing surreptitiously at her wristwatch, Trina closed her eyes briefly in disbelief. Could it only have been an hour and fifteen minutes ago that they had arrived here? She was exhausted. Every muscle in her body ached, and she wished desperately she was back in the motel right now, soaking in a hot bath. But she was aware that her afternoon of racing was not the only cause for her discomfort. Her throbbing headache and the tension that squeezed at the back of her neck and moved painfully into her shoulders was due more to Buck's dark mood than her own physical exertion.

Shooting a quick glance toward Karen's worried face, Trina felt an unexpected pang of sympathy. She and Buck had been living together for over a year, and Trina had no doubt in her mind that the tiny blonde loved her brother without reservation. The speed with which she had come flying to Buck's side after his race, and the true concern reflected on her small, pleasant face despite her lack of enthusiasm for the sport of dirt-track racing, had been evidence of her devotion.

Buck had consumed far more than was his usual custom since arriving for their ritualistic visit to The Last Pit Stop. The small-town tavern was the unspoken meeting place for drivers each racing weekend. A lot of good racing information had been traded at the weathered wooden bar on which she now leaned. A lot of good memories were associated with this spot, too—her father's years in racing, Buck's first step into racing and the outrageous celebration they had held the night she had raced for the first time.

Trina's eyes moved casually to the doorway as it opened, her body coming to rigid attention as her eyes touched on the figure who hesitated briefly there. Slater Montgomery! He was obviously searching for someone, judging from the manner in which his eyes scanned the room. Her stomach knotted tensely as she shot a quick look toward Buck. Hopefully Montgomery wouldn't find the person he was looking for here.

Turning back to the bar, Trina made an attempt to catch up on the conversation progressing beside her when a surprisingly familiar voice sounded quietly in her ear.

"So this is where you've been hiding!" Directing the full force of his astoundingly bright blue eyes into hers, Slater Montgomery continued in an irritatingly intimate tone, "I stopped at your motel. The fellow at the desk said you were already out, so I knew you had to be in one of the local night spots. I didn't expect it to be this one, though."

Stifling her surprise at his statement, Trina responded in a controlled voice, "Oh? Doesn't this bar meet your standards? Then again, I should have realized...a man who prides himself in having 'nothing but the best' might find this old place a little common."

A spark of reciprocal anger flashed momentarily in his gaze the second before Slate moved slowly to situate himself beside her at the bar. Blocking her view of Buck with his broad shoulders, he turned to lean his elbow casually on the scarred surface, facing her squarely. His incredible eyes moved searchingly over her face.

"You know, it beats me why I spent the last hour searching every bar in this town for you. I don't think you truly appreciate all the trouble I went to, Trina Mallory."

"I think you're right. And I don't appreciate drivers who steal their wins with dirty tricks."

All trace of humor abruptly disappearing from his face, Slater Montgomery responded in a serious tone, "Look, I'd like to get one thing straight with you, Trina. I know the last few seconds of the modified race looked suspicious, and I suppose if I was your brother, I'd have gotten angry, too. But the truth is, I didn't hit your brother's car deliberately. My steering was beginning to get a little ragged near the end of that race. I tried to judge my distance from your brother's car when I pulled up alongside him. But the exact thing I was afraid might happen did happen, and I tapped his wheel. My pit crew is looking at the steering right now. Look, I couldn't care less if your brother doesn't choose to believe me, but I do want you to know that I had no control over what happened."

Damn him! He looked so sincere.... Unable to hold out against Slate's direct stare, but still unwilling to declare a truce, Trina offered with a raised brow, "You've been looking for me all over town just to tell me that? Or did you hope to give me a lesson on the 'very best' that should be put into a car?"

Having the good grace to wince at her second reminder of his rather boastful words earlier in the day, Slate shook his head. "All right, I deserved that. But I'll tell you something, sweetheart. If I ever give you a lesson, it won't be on the kind of equipment you should put in a car...."

Judging it best not to respond to his remark, Trina turned away from his perusal and downed the last of her drink. She had been nursing it for twenty minutes, certain that the last thing she needed to do was feed her headache with alcohol. She instantly regretted her lapse of caution.

"Bartender, give the lady another drink."

Her sharp response reflected the pain that continued to throb mercilessly in her temple.

"No, thank you. If I want another drink, I'll order it myself!"

Turning back to face him, Trina was startled by the light flush that transfused Slater Montgomery's face. She hadn't expected vulnerability from the extremely confident man who stood at her side. Startling her even more was the ring of sincerity in his low voice after he hesitated momentarily and began to speak.

"Look, Trina, somehow we started out on the wrong foot today. I've been regretting the smart remarks I made this morning all day. But I'm not retracting what I said, only the way I said it. I am driving with good equipment. Just about the best equipment available as a matter of fact, but that doesn't mean much once we're off the track, does it? What does mean something is the way I've been thinking about you all day. I'd like to get to know you better...much better...."

Meeting the intense line of his gaze and holding it unflinchingly despite the heady awareness that moved across her senses, Trina responded quietly, "But I'm not so sure I want to get to know you any better than I do now."

She was not prepared for the impatience that flashed momentarily in the brilliant eyes so close to hers, nor for her own speeding pulse as the hand that gripped her shoulder drew her closer.

"Don't be stubborn, Trina. The vibes between us are so potent that I have all I can do to keep in mind that we only met this morning." Gripping her chin gently, he raised her unrelenting gaze to his. When she did not respond to his statement, merely held his gaze with a coolness that belied the rapid pounding of her heart, he shook his head. A wry smile flickered across his lips. "So, you're trying to tell me with those big black eyes that I'm crazy...you don't feel any vibes. Well, I don't believe you."

Lowering his head unexpectedly, he pressed a gentle, lingering kiss against her mouth. The result was a surging response that efficiently erased her cool composure of a moment before. His voice was a soft challenge. "Now let me hear you deny it...."

Surprisingly incapable of speaking at that moment, Trina jumped at the unexpected sound of Buck's deep voice behind her.

"Take your hands off her, Montgomery."

The startled look on Slate's face indicated that he, too, had not sensed Buck's approach. A curtain dropped over the warmth in his eyes, leaving them cold as he turned to face Buck.

"This is none of your concern, Mallory. Trina and I—"

"It looks to me like Trina's been saying 'no' to you in just about every way she knows without coming right out and telling you to get lost. So if she's too polite to come right out with it, I'll say it for her. Get lost, Montgomery."

"I think your sister is old enough to speak for herself. She doesn't need you to put words in her mouth."

Buck was beginning to bristle. Casting an almost disbelieving glance between the two men, Trina began to bristle, too.

"I'll let you in on a little secret, boys. You're both right. I am old enough to think and talk for myself. I don't need anyone to explain about vibes, and I don't need anyone to act as my personal bodyguard."

She turned to face Slate, a new coldness in her voice. "Somehow you seem to have gotten the wrong impression. I don't know what I said or did to give you the impression that I'd be waiting for you to come to find me tonight. Believe me, nothing could be further from the truth. Maybe you think I should be flattered, but I'm really just annoyed. So I'll say it flat out. Thanks, but no thanks. I'm not interested."

Slate's expression was frank disbelief. He reached out to take her arm, pushing her annoyance the step up to anger. "Trina, you—"

Roughly thrusting Slate's hand from her arm, Buck did not allow her the opportunity for a reply. "You heard what Trina said, Montgomery."

Managing to suppress her resentment of Buck's interruption, Trina took his arm. "Come on, Buck. You've been saying you're going to buy me a drink all night long. I'm going to take you up on your offer now."

Not bothering to look back, Trina urged her brother toward the opposite end of the bar where Karen waited tensely. Positioning Buck subtly between Karen and herself, she motioned to the bartender.

"Jerry, about my drink. Buck's buying." She hesitated a moment before adding, "Make it a double!"

An unexpected smile flashed across her face as Trina turned back to Buck. "You know, I've always wanted to say that."

An hour later, Trina looked up surreptitiously from the position she'd maintained at her brother's side. It had been tense since Slate Montgomery had entered the bar. She had really expected him to leave after she and Buck had walked away, but he had merely turned back to the bar and ordered a drink. She was still extremely concious of the dark looks Buck occasionally sent in his direction. She had almost been relieved when Sally Griffin had slid coyly into the spot beside Slate that she had vacated.

Good old Sally. Not that she was so old...or so good for that matter. She was merely dependable. Young, extremely impressionable and well endowed with physical charms, she seemed determined to get herself a driver of her own to cheer for. And it was to that goal so many of the drivers owed their gratitude for the memorable hours she had provided them.

Shaking her head, Trina mumbled under her breath, "To each his own...." Sally seemed invincible; each aborted romance only seemed to add to her determination. It hadn't been like that for Trina. Spence Morgan had turned her off drivers for life. A sizzling romance for a year had slowly turned into the role of chief maid and hand holder for the big man. And, when Spence had gone on to better things, he had left her behind. Now, with the advantage of hindsight, she wondered how she could have allowed him to make such a fool of her. Well, however it had happened, it would not happen again. The experience had changed her. In all her dealings with men now, she was the person in charge, and that was the way it was going to stay!

Shooting another look toward the opposite end of the bar, Trina groaned inwardly. Sally was so *obvious*...it was a wonder that a man with Slater Montgomery's apparent experience could stomach her cloying appeal for his attentions. Fingering the small red barrette that held her long blond hair back from her face, Sally was staring into Slate's eyes with an expression of open invitation that was nauseating. Slate's arm moved to encircle Sally's waist and draw her close against his side and Trina turned away. Well, so much for vibes... The only problem was that she *had* felt those vibes that Slate had talked about, and a lot more than that when he had kissed her.

"Trina, how about a dance?"

The voice in her ear was unexpected. Trina turned around to Doug Frawley's pleasant face. A regular at the track, Doug was a part of Stitch Pierce's pit crew. She had known Doug for years and liked him immensely, but she didn't want to encourage him. His feelings were too plainly written in his open expression, and he was too nice a guy to string along when she had no feelings for him other than friendship. Her momentary hesitation started a small smile moving across his lips.

"Relax, honey. It's only a dance."

Unable to resist the appeal in his warm brown eyes, Trina smiled and slid her hand lightly into his as he led her onto the small, wooden square that passed for a dance floor. Finding herself wondering if Slate's eyes followed her onto the dance floor with Doug, Trina was suddenly ashamed of herself. Surely Doug deserved her undivided attention at least for the duration of a dance. Guilt forced extra warmth into her smile as Doug turned to take her into his arms.

Doug hesitated for a brief second, his own smile dimming momentarily as he slid his arms around her to pull her close. They were swaying absentmindedly to the slow rhythm when he finally spoke. His voice was husky, revealing. "Don't do that to me, Trina, honey. Don't invite me in if it's only temporary. I don't mind your keeping me out, if that's the way it has to be for you, but if I come in, I'm going to want to stay."

Not bothering with a denial, Trina pulled back far enough to look into the eyes almost level with hers. "I'm sorry, Doug. You're a great guy." In wordless apology, she kissed him lightly on the cheek.

"You missed, honey." Before she could avoid it, Doug pressed a light kiss on her parted lips. "There, I fixed it."

Without waiting for her response, Doug pulled her close again, choosing to remain silent for the remainder of the number.

The music stopped, and Trina felt a moment's regret. It had been pleasant in Doug's arms. He was so comfortable and safe.

"I enjoyed that, Doug. You're a great guy."

"Yeah, I know. You said that already. I wish you'd find a different way to express yourself. Maybe like this." Cupping her chin lightly, he touched his lips to hers once again. Her expression became wary and he shook his head in weary acceptance. "Dammit, Trina, do you have to be so cautious? Why can't you just relax with me for a while? It might turn out to be pleasant for both of us. You could just let me know when you've had enough. I might decide it would be worth the chance."

"You're contradicting yourself, Doug. Just a few minutes ago you warned me about letting you in."

"Me and my big mouth."

Doug's smile was looking decidedly forced by the time he returned her to the bar beside Buck. Reluctantly removing his arm from her waist, he leaned against the bar beside her. "I think I need a drink." Turning, he raised his hand to the bartender. "Jerry, give me another, will you?"

But Trina was no longer conscious of Doug's presence. She had raised her eyes, only to have Slater Montgomery's angry gaze catch and hold hers. A tight, contemptuous smile touched his mouth as he deliberately lowered his head toward Sally. Trina could almost feel the touch of his warm lips as they grazed Sally's ear in a quick, whispered sentence. She did not have to stretch her imagination far to wonder what he had said. Sally's reaction was all too revealing. A victorious smile on her face, Sally turned and slipped a possessive arm through his as he turned and started toward the door. Unwilling to admit to the sharp prick of an unnamed emotion that moved her lips into a tight, unsmiling line, Trina followed them with her eyes until they disappeared through the doorway.

Vibes... She gave a small, disgusted snort. In future she'd remember not to pay the slightest bit of attention to vibes.

HER HEAD was still throbbing. It was the same headache that had plagued her the previous evening and finally forced her to leave The Last Pit Stop. Doug had taken her back to the motel where most of the drivers had elected to stay, and had bidden her good-night with obvious restraint. The sadness in his eyes when she had turned into her room had only seemed to add fuel to the fierce pounding in her head. She had awakened from a fitful sleep in the morning to find the headache still with her.

Damn! It was all Slater Montgomery's fault that this weekend she had looked forward to since the beginning of the year had been spoiled! She was not accustomed to the luxury of staying the night at a motel after a hard day of racing. It was her and Buck's custom to leave the track as soon as the last race was over and drive home. The late, lengthy drive back to Ridgewood, New Jersey, had become an accepted part of their weekend ritual. But this particular weekend they had realized the folly of driving home only to return early the next morning for the early racing card. She had intended to fully enjoy the luxury of leaving the bed rumpled after she arose, and going out for a leisurely breakfast in a coffee shop filled with the smell of freshly brewed coffee and frying bacon.

Instead she had spent a fitful night, and had arisen tired and achy. Buck had eaten in a hurry, his mind set on rushing back to the motel so he could work on his car for a few hours before they had to report to the track. Feeling compelled to keep up with him, she had been totally unable to enjoy her breakfast, and had ended up leaving most of it on the plate.

Later, Buck had apologized, no doubt at Karen's insistence, for being inconsiderate. That was one thing she liked about Karen. With the appearance of a small, helpless kitten alongside Buck's hulking size, she managed to hold her own against his occasional ill temper, and had actually managed to influence him favorably in many areas of his life. Trina could not deny that Buck had a few rough corners that could use some smoothing, but for the past few years he had functioned as brother, father and best friend, and she loved him.

When he had first told her that he was going to be moving in with Karen, he had been riddled with guilt for leaving her alone. She had scoffed at his worries and told him not to let her hold him back from doing what he wanted to do.

Of course, she had missed him terribly, but at least she still saw him three nights a week. Buck used the double garage at the small house their father had left them, and they worked side by side on their cars. It was a camaraderie she treasured.

The sun was bright, the glare and heat a double threat to her aching head as she scanned the nearly empty track. The races would be starting in a couple of hours, and already other drivers had begun to filter into the pits. She had been there for an hour already. Buck had arrived shortly after her.

She was hot and uncomfortable, and reaching around behind her, Trina shook two aspirins from the bottle she had thrown carelessly onto the seat of her car. She picked up her coffee cup and washed them down with a small grimace. Cold coffee! Yuk! She pressed her long, slender fingers to the spot near her temple that pounded so incessantly, and massaged it gently. This weekend was definitely not turning out as she had expected. As a matter of fact, it was a nightmare!

"What's the matter, Trina? Your head still bothering you?"

Buck's concerned voice penetrated her numbed state. His expression was full of concern. He persisted in acting the mother hen when he thought it necessary, and she could not suppress a smile at the incongruity of the thought when looking at his great, hulking frame.

"Don't worry, mother, I'll be all right as soon as the aspirins take effect."

Annoyance replacing the concern in his dark eyes, Buck snapped, "Since you're so testy this morning, is it all right if I ask if you have everything straightened out with your car for this afternoon?"

"Touchy, touchy..." Smiling, Trina nodded her head. "Of course I've got everything straightened out. You know I always finish what I set out to do."

A flicker of suppressed amusement flashed across Buck's formerly tense expression. He growled without true anger, "You're so smart...."

Reaching out unexpectedly, he encircled her shoulders with his brawny arm and gave her a short hug. His gaze already intent on her car, he did not see the moistness that momentarily filled Trina's eyes. When he looked back to her again, his expression reflected his concern.

"I don't like to see you racing with those tires, Trina. They were bad enough when you came, but the track beat them to death yesterday. Today they're downright hazardous." Hesitating only a moment, he gestured toward the two men who sauntered leisurely toward them. "Sid...Bix, give me a hand, will you? We're going to switch tires."

"Switch tires?" Trina tensed apprehensively. "What do you mean, 'switch tires'?"

Ignoring her question, Buck grabbed the jack and dragged it toward his car as Trina trailed him doggedly. "What do you mean, 'switch tires,' Buck?"

Realizing that she had not misunderstood his meaning as he stooped to slip the jack under the front tire of the red and white number 82, Trina exclaimed angrily, "Oh, no you don't! I'm not going to take your tires! Are you crazy? You won't stand a chance of beating Slater Montgomery without decent tires!"

"The same goes for you, doesn't it, Trina? You won't stand a chance of competing without decent tires. I'm a better driver than you are. I can compensate."

"A better driver!" Her black eyes flashing, Trina pulled Buck's arm as he attempted to pump the jack. "Buck Mallory, if you try to put those tires on my car, I'll refuse to race!" At Buck's disbelieving glance, her eyes narrowed warningly. "I mean it, Buck. If I can't afford to race on my own, I won't race! You know how I feel about that! I've just about convinced Barlett's Service Station to sponsor me for those tires. Even if they don't come through, I'll be able to pay for them myself within a few weeks. So keep your hands off that jack!"

Angry, Buck shrugged off her restraining hand. "If you're determined to race with those baloney skins, go ahead. You always do what you want anyway!" Turning back toward the two men who stood hesitantly between the cars, he said gruffly, "Come on, I'll buy you some coffee. The hardhead, here, is too proud to accept help."

Watching the three men as they strode toward the refreshment stand, Trina released a small sigh and fought against the tightness in her throat. Buck would have sacrificed his chance to beat Slater Montgomery to keep her safe. She swallowed hard against the tears that threatened to overwhelm her. Suddenly disgusted with her emotional state the past two days, Trina shook her head. What was wrong with her? She was not a person given to outbursts of emotion. Raised in a male household, she had learned to hide the softer side of herself, and she wasn't at all pleased with her sudden transformation.

Trina shook her head, regretting the action a moment later as her head throbbed in reaction to the sudden movement. She was too tense, that was all... What she needed was to relax for a half hour, until she could beat this insistent headache. Determined that was exactly what she was going to do, Trina grabbed at the aluminum chaise folded in the back of the truck. Stretching it out between the two cars, she lay down and closed her eyes. She was going to get rid of her headache, and then she'd be her old self again.

The sun was warm against her skin, but it now felt like a pleasant warmth that dulled the ache in her tired muscles. She stretched out full length. Her worn jeans were soft and comfortable, despite their skin-hugging fit. She was glad she had disdained to wear a bra under her bright orange T-shirt. She didn't really need one, anyway. She was extremely slender, her breasts not overly large. Her muscle tone was such that she appeared much the same if she wore one or not, and today she chose not. She should have done this sooner, and she wouldn't have had such an annoying morning. Yes, she was feeling better already.... If only she could manage to evade those piercing blue eyes that seemed to haunt her mind....

Slate made his way slowly across the dusty clay surface of the pits, noting as he walked that the earth was still damp beneath the top layer of dirt. It would probably remain that way until the summer months when the ground would dry out to the point where dust clouds raised by the roaring cars would hang over the track like a persistent fog.

Well, at least Bob had found out the reason his car had begun to handle so poorly on the final stretch of the feature race the previous day. And with Tony and Marty's help, he had fixed the radius rods. The car should be in perfect working condition today.

Despite his resolve, Slate found himself taking the roundabout way to the spot where his car was parked...the roundabout way that would take him past the pink and purple number 013.

What was it about Trina Mallory that kept him off balance? He was honestly disgusted with himself. She had made it very clear that she didn't want anything to do with him. With any other woman he would have tipped his cap and walked away. Sally had been more than willing to provide balm for his wounded ego last night. It was too bad he hadn't been interested. He had to admit that he had been a bit surprised at himself when he had dropped Sally off at her motel and returned to help his crew with the car. It was too bad Trina hadn't been with him to see the condition of that radius rod. Maybe then she'd have believed what he'd said about...

There he went again.

Slate slowed his step as he neared the red and white number 82, his eyes glued to the car parked beside it. So, he had wasted his time...no one was there...not even the pit crew. Feeling a sharp sting of disappointment, Slate was about to turn away when his eyes touched on the aluminum lounge chair stretched between the two cars. His stomach did a peculiar flop as his eyes touched on Trina Mallory. She was obviously asleep, despite the occasional roars of engines being tested. Completely relaxed, a graceful arm flung above her head, she tore him apart with her beauty.

Almost without thought he moved to stand over her, then he crouched down beside her so he could see her more closely. That unbelievably curly black mane swirled around her face and shoulders in gleaming spirals. Black velvet eyes he remembered so well were covered, a lush fringe of lashes forming luxurious black fans against the smooth skin of her cheek. Her nose was small, straight, perfect...and her mouth... Her lips were slightly parted, revealing a trace of white teeth beneath. He could almost taste that mouth.... He longed to taste it. A trembling began inside him, and he tore his eyes away from her lips.

She slept like a child, completely abandoned to the dark nether world that held her tight in its grip. He was filled with a strange tenderness. But she was not a child. One slow sweep of her slim, sensuous proportions confirmed that thought. Despite her taller than average height, she was delicately boned...her shoulders narrow and gently curved. Her arms were thin and graceful, like those of a dancer. He remembered that she often gestured gracefully as she spoke, her long fingers with their well-shaped nails strangely titillating to his senses. His eyes moved slowly across her chest. It was obvious she wasn't wearing a bra, and he enjoyed seeing the outline of her small, firm breasts against the light material of her shirt. Her waist was minuscule, her hips trim. Her legs were long...incredibly long. He remembered her smooth, flawless stride, and his stomach did another flop. When had a woman's stride ever turned him on before?

His eyes slipped back to her face. The answer to that wasn't difficult. Everything about Trina Mallory turned him on...and on...and on. He could seem to think of little else. The fast approaching afternoon race had left his mind; a difficult fact to believe, considering it was his usual practice to allow nothing to interfere with his concentration on the day of a race. Concentration was essential, but today it was impossible.

She was stirring, her eyelids fluttering lightly. Unable to resist, he reached out and took a slender, gleaming curl in his hand. It was warm to the touch. His own eyes fluttered for the briefest second in a stringent battle against the desire coursing through his veins, but he was looking intently on her face as Trina awoke.

She was startled. Her eyes widened momentarily with fright, and Slate smiled.

Her heart was thundering in her chest! She hadn't expected to awaken to gaze into the same arresting blue eyes of which she had dreamed.

"Wh...what are you doing here? Where's Buck?" A trifle disoriented, Trina turned to search the immediate area before recalling that Buck, Bix and Sid had left for coffee.

"I don't know, and to tell you the truth, I really don't care, Trina." Observing the return of hostility into her eyes, Slate felt a flash of something akin to desperation. "Look, Trina, I came here to make peace with you..." That wasn't exactly true. He hadn't consciously set out to make peace with her. He had merely been driven by need....

Jerking her head so he would release the curl he held loosely between his fingers, Trina pulled herself to a sitting position and immediately stood up. In an efficient movement, she leaned over and flipped the chaise closed.

Bringing himself to a standing position as she did, Slate jammed his hands into the pockets of his jeans. It was the safest place for them, considering his urge to either pull her into his arms, or tighten those same hands around her neck. She was infuriating!

Turning back to face him after she leaned the chaise against the truck, she drew herself up straight and tall...like a soldier. Slate winced inwardly. Ready for battle...

"Look, Mr. Montgomery..." Trina hesitated, realizing how awkward the formality sounded.

Jumping efficiently into the gap, Slate interjected, "My name is Slate, Trina..."

"All right...Slate..." A peculiar flash of emotion seemed to flicker across his glance as she used his given name. A moment later his eyes reflected merely the same intoxicating brilliance as before, and deciding she had been mistaken, Trina continued quietly, despite the shakiness she felt inside, "Slate, this is beginning to get ridiculous. I'll be honest and admit I believe you when you say you hit Buck's car accidentally yesterday. But that's about as far as I can go. I'd appreciate it if you'd stay away from me and Buck...."

"Why?" His response was short and direct, taking her a little by surprise.

"Because Buck is still angry."

"Buck's angry with me...that's his problem. It has nothing to do with you and me."

"That's where you're wrong."

"Buck is a big boy. He doesn't need you to take his side. And, Trina, I don't want to fight with you."

His last simple statement took some of the sting out of her anger, but she was smarting nevertheless. "I don't expect you to understand what I feel for my brother, but since you're so persistent, I'll try to explain it. My brother and I are very close. Buck has a lot of pressure on him right now. He doesn't like you, whether his grievance is mistaken or not, and I don't want to add to his tension by—"

"You know I didn't deliberately try to run him off the track."

"I told you, whether you did or not doesn't matter much right now."

"It does to me. And if you were completely honest you'd have to admit that your brother is behaving illogically."

"And you have to admit it was a convenient time to have a problem with your steering, Slate. Your car was handling perfectly before...."

"I suppose it's never happened to you!"

"Never so conveniently."

A flush rose to Slate's face.

"Let's change the subject."

His gaze was intent on her face. His eyes moved as if irresistibly drawn to her mouth. He swallowed hard. His thoughts were so transparent that she flushed.

"Well, I geuss we can't discuss that subject." His expression lightened with a small smile, and Trina felt again the strong tug of his charisma. A little warning bell went off in her mind. This man was dangerous. He had a way of making her feel... No, she didn't want to think about the way she felt when he looked at her that way.

"Well, at least I can offer you the apology I owe you."

"Apology you owe me?"

"For yesterday...when I interrupted your little conversation with the boys...for writing you off as an attention-grabbing women's libber trying to show how good she was by entering a man's game."

"I take exception to that statement on THREE counts!" She was starting to get mad again, but she was forestalled by Slate's patient expression.

"And I apologize for them. You're obviously devoted to the sport, and you *are* an excellent driver."

"And this sport is no longer solely a man's game!"

He hesitated briefly, a small smile again curving his mouth. "I'll concede that point."

"Well! There may be hope for you yet!"

"Even if you do tend to go squirrely on the corners."

"Squirrely on the...! Who do you think you're talking to?"

She was too angry to see the grin Slate was unsuccessfully trying to hide. "Oh, come on, Trina. You were all over the place—"

"And if you had any brains, you'd see that skill had nothing to do with it!"

Slate's eyes shot immediately to her car. The smile dropped from his lips when he noticed the worn treads for the first time. "You're not going to use these tires this afternoon?"

"Oh, I'm not?"

"You're insane! They're not much better than..."

"Baloney skins..."

"So, if you know it, why aren't you doing something about it? Don't you value your life, lady?" He was starting to get angry again himself. How could she take such a chance with her safety? How could her brother allow her to?

"We don't all have big-time sponsors...or an open expense account."

All trace of amicability had disappeared from Trina's expression, and Slate groaned inwardly. What had started out as friendly teasing on his part had backfired, and it was obvious they were back where they had started. "There is such a thing as credit, Trina...."

"Yes, credit and I are old friends, but right now..." Pausing in midsentence, Trina looked momentarily incredulous. "Why am I explaining myself to you? I must be crazy!"

Furious with herself for having allowed the conversation to go so far into a personal vein, especially such a touchy one as her personal finances, Trina said tightly, "Get out of my way!"

In response to her command, Slate glared at her in frustration and impatience, his broad-shouldered frame efficiently blocking her only exit from between the cars. He was still searching his mind for the right thing to say to set things right again when Trina shoved unexpectedly at his chest. Her unanticipated action took Slate off guard and made him totter backward, allowing her the opportunity to storm past him in the direction of the refreshment stand.

Refusing to look back, Trina could almost feel the heat of his stare burning into her back. Let him glare all he wanted! It was none of his business how or when she raced! Shades of Spence Morgan! She had only met him yesterday, exchanged a few hostile words with him, and already he was telling her what to do...as if she had no brain of her own! Well, that would teach her to follow her instincts! And her instincts told her to stay away from Slater Montgomery!

TRINA CHECKED the leather-banded sports watch on her wrist. It was almost 11:30 A.M. Her gesture was picked up by the group of men surrounding her at the small table.

"Is it time to leave, Trina?"

She nodded, getting to her feet as the men seated around her began to rise. "It sure is. They'll be starting the hot laps soon, and I want to get a little time on that track before the race."

The past hour had been pleasant, and it had certainly served its purpose. Obviously having seen the exchange between Slate and herself, Doug had walked up to meet her as she had neared the refreshment stand. His eyes had searched her face assessingly, his expression telling her louder than words that she needed to be careful how much she told him about her conversation with Slater Montgomery.

His question had been easily anticipated. "Is Montgomery giving you a hard time, Trina?"

"It's nothing I can't handle, Doug. And *definitely* nothing I want you to step into."

She felt a moment's remorse for her harshness as Doug's mouth tightened visibly, then she smiled. "Come on, I'll buy you some coffee."

She had just slipped her arm through his when Bill Watson walked up and placed his arm casually around her shoulder. A veteran at the track, he was well liked by everyone. He had been a friend of her father, and appeared to take an almost paternal pride in her progress.

Bill's heavy gray mustache flicked upward as his smile widened. "Well, you're going to have to share Doug with us, Trina. We were all about to go for coffee at the little shop around the corner. There won't be much going on around here for a while, and I feel like giving my stomach a rest from the tar they serve here."

"Sounds fine to me!" She had turned back to Doug, extremely conscious of his irritation, and smiled. "Come on, Doug. Maybe I can pick up some pointers on driving from these old pros."

"About the only thing you'll pick up from these 'old pros' is fleas!" The men's laughter had cleared the frown from Doug's face and Trina had felt distinctly relieved.

Surrounded by friendly, familiar faces, Trina had felt her tension slowly slip away over the past hour. It was with a far more cheerful spring to her step that she entered the pits, only to come to a jarring halt as she neared her car.

"All right, what's this?" Her eyes swung to her brother's face as she waved toward the new tires on her car. "I told you I'd get new tires when I could afford them! Your credit is overextended anyway. How'd you manage this?"

"Wh...what are you talking about, Trina? I thought *you* had the tires put on the car."

His surprise was far too genuine to be feigned. Realizing Buck was not responsible, Trina shifted her biting gaze toward her pit crew.

"Hey, don't look at us, Trina," Bix disclaimed fervently. "We had nothing to do with it."

Completely puzzled, Trina turned toward Doug with a frown.

"Don't look at me, Trina. I was with you all the while, remember?"

"Then who could've...?"

Her eyes widened in sudden realization, and she turned sharply and began walking across the pits with her characteristically smooth, long-legged stride. Arriving seconds later beside the blue and white number 008, she addressed herself to the broad back bent over the engine.

"Did you have anything to do with those new tires on my car?"

There was no response as Slate continued working on his engine. Realizing she had indeed gained the attention of his smartly clad pit crew as they stared at her as if she was insane, she repeated heatedly, "I asked you, did you...?"

"My friends call me Slate, and I don't have time to talk to anyone but my friends right now." Responding without raising his head from the engine, Slate continued working, elevating Trina's ire to a volatile point.

"I'll repeat my question. Did you have anything to do with those new tires on my car, *Slate*?"

The broad back straightened slowly. A deep frown contorting his face, Slate turned toward her. "Don't be a fool, Trina. You couldn't race with those old tires! You'd get yourself killed."

"I've done fine with them so far."

"Don't be so pigheaded!"

"Look, I think there's something we should settle right now. Somehow you seem to have gotten the idea that it's perfectly okay for you to barge in and settle yourself in my life. Well, it isn't. And in case I haven't made myself clear, I'll spell it out for you. I don't need any handouts from you. I've been racing for the past four years without your help, and I don't need it now. So, if you'll be kind enough to return my own tires to me, you can keep those four pretty babies for yourself. You'll probably need them. Buck is going to run you all over that track this afternoon!"

No one needed to tell Trina she was starting to hit home with her attack. Slate's livid face was a clear reflection of his emotions. He responded in a carefully controlled voice, his eyes glaring into hers, a small muscle ticking in his cheek.

"Your old tires are gone. When the garbage truck came to pick up the debris from yesterday, I told them to take your old tires along with them. So the truth is, sweetheart, if you intend to race today, you're going to have to use the tires that are on your car." His tight expression unrelenting, Slate raised his hands to rest his tightly clenched fists on his hips. "Now, what's your answer? Do you want me to tell my crew to go over there and take those tires back off your car?" When she did not respond, but continued to stare at him with a blood-chilling gaze, he persisted, "Well, what's your answer? Hurry up! I haven't got time to waste!"

"You..." Momentarily at a loss for words, Trina's voice trailed off in exasperation.

"That answer is inadequate."

"You know I don't have any choice, don't you? If you think I'm going to give up this afternoon's race because of your high-handed actions, you're crazy!"

"I suppose that means you're going to use the tires." There was not even the hint of amusement in Slate's voice.

"And you can rest assured you'll get your money, too!"

"I'm not worried about the money, Trina." Slate's voice was beginning to sound weary.

"I should've realized that. You probably never had to worry about money a day in your life."

"Trina..."

Whatever it was he was starting to say, Trina did not stay to find out. In a swift movement she turned around and walked briskly back toward her car. As far as she was concerned, there was nothing more to say.

THE AIR HAD TURNED surprisingly chilly with the setting of the sun. Standing atop the bed of her pickup, Trina followed the narrowed field of cars as they continued thundering around the track. She was hardly conscious of the drop in temperature. She turned around as a light jacket was dropped over her shoulders, and shot Doug a small smile. She hadn't questioned the fact that Doug had come over to watch the modified feature race with her. Her mind had been too intent on the quickly changing positions of the blue and white 008, and the red and white 82.

Today had been supremely trying. She had been shaking with anger when she'd gone out on her hot laps. The presumption of the man! How dared he take such a liberty with her car? The fact that the car was handling beautifully in the corners and was holding the track better than it ever had, had not been balm enough to soothe her outraged pride. But even with her new tires, luck had been against her. Coming around the fourth turn on the tenth lap, she had been hit by Terry Sloan when his car had gone out of control with a broken steering box. Her damage hadn't been great, but enough to send her back to the pits. She had no doubt she would be ready to race again next week, and she had already determined she would make that race up with a win!

Somehow, she was almost glad the accident had happened. She didn't want to feel she owed her first win this season to Slate Montgomery! When she returned to the track next weekend, she wanted to be free and clear of obligation to Slate Montgomery. And she would be. She'd pay him back. When she went back to work on Monday, she'd ask Ingrid about the show Thursday night.

She had previously refused to model that night despite her need of the extra money. Somehow, earning her money modeling left her feeling less than satisfied. It was not the runway modeling to which she objected particularly. It was the followup. Moving between the tables in the elegant restaurants where the shows were inevitably conducted, turning this way and that for jaded glances always left her feeling demeaned. Especially when she knew she could not afford even the buttons on the high-priced garments she wore.

Now she would have to go to Ingrid and ask her if she could still use her in the show. Ingrid would be only too happy to get her, she was sure. She always sold far more of the garments that Trina modeled than she did any of the others. Ingrid had laughingly said that each woman believed the dresses she wore would make her look as slim and elegant as Trina. Ingrid said that most women spent the greater parts of their lives wanting a body like hers. Was that really true? All Trina had ever wanted was a winning car.

A loud crash snapped Trina's wandering mind back to the track. The green and white number 16 had spun out and become a standing target for the full herd! There were going to be a lot of cars taken out of the race in this crackup. With a relieved smile, she watched a few minutes later as the driver of the hapless number 16 slid out the window and shook himself off. His first concern for his car, he walked around it shaking his head, oblivious to the wreckers making their way toward him and the other cars presently knotted up into a tight ball of gleaming metal.

Trina's eyes moved quickly over the uninvolved cars. The red light had come on...full stop for the rest of the field...and there was Buck, in the clear. Relief swept her senses, but her eyes continued to search despite herself. Yes, there was Slate Montgomery. He was in the clear, too. The race wasn't half over, and he had already made his way from the back of the lineup to midpoint. Buck had been trading the lead with Cliff Deal in the earlier part of the race, but had just gained a substantial distance from him. Damn! The full stop would squeeze the pack—including Slate Montgomery—together, and would destroy Buck's advantage.

Trina's hands were damp with perspiration despite the night chill. Unable to move her eyes from the track, she had watched the laps count down. Two more laps to go, and the field was a replay of the previous day! Buck was in the lead, with Slater Montgomery fast closing in on him. Buck had to win...he had to win this time!

"What do you think, Doug?" She raised her eyes to Doug's intense expression. "Do you think Buck will be able to hold him off?"

Doug shook his head, his eyes more revealing than his words. "I don't know, Trina. Montgomery has a lot of power under his hood. Buck's going to have to go like hell to keep him off."

"He'll do it. I know he can. He has to...."

The white flag came down as Buck shot past the starter's stand. The last lap! Unable to speak...unable to move, Trina watched as the blue and white number 008 flashed past only seconds behind him. At Montgomery's present rate of speed, Buck wouldn't stand a chance of keeping his lead! Her heart in her throat, Trina watched the blue and white number 008 take the second turn tightly behind Buck. Oh, no! It was happening! Montgomery was overtaking Buck...passing him on the straightaway! Not wanting to believe her eyes, Trina saw her brother fall into a firm second place as Slate Montgomery's number 008 took the lead. But Buck wasn't giving up! Her nerves stretched to the breaking point, Trina saw her brother make a last valiant bid for first... He couldn't make it! But what was happening on the final turn? Slate Montgomery's car was going haywire across the track! He was completely out of control! A blowout! He had a blowout!

Her own wild screams joining with the crowd, Trina watched as Buck shot past Montgomery's car and took the checkered flag! He had won! Buck had won! Her eyes shifted automatically to the field. Slate Montgomery's car limped across the finish line...third! She was elated...ecstatic! Turning around, Trina threw her arms around Doug and squeezed as hard as she could.

"He won, Doug! He won!"

Not waiting for his response, Trina jumped down from the truckbed and ran toward the winner's circle. Her chest was heaving with exertion, her throat tight when she saw Buck's beaming smile. Catching her eye as he accepted the trophy, he waved it in her direction before getting into his car to drive back to the pits.

She was walking to her car when she caught Slate Montgomery looking at her from across the pits. He had seen her mad dash for the winner's circle and her elation. What could she say? He had lost, and she was glad.

CHAPTER THREE

IT HAD BEEN a long evening. The loud disco music which had predominated the jukebox selections earlier at The Last Pit Stop had faded to slower, more sentimental music. A country music singer was presently lamenting the loss of his "woman" and Trina felt a snicker slip across her lips. The poor fellow seemed to be making a good living off that "hard-hearted" woman. He had a lot to thank her for. She snickered again. She must have had too much to drink. She was starting to feel silly. No, not really silly, because that would imply a sensation of well-being.

She cast her eyes around the familiar dimness of The Last Pit Stop. A dullness had begun to overtake her mind. Buck had already left with Karen for the motel. He had been ecstatic about his win and had celebrated so heavily that he had been forced into a short night...or maybe a long one for that matter. Whatever, she was sure he was going to have a heavy head in the morning. Buck had had that celebration coming to him. He had worked long and hard.

But the nagging thought that the night might have been spent in an entirely different manner, if Slate Montgomery's car hadn't had a blowout in the last straightaway, would give her no rest. She would just have to force herself to remember that "if" was a very big word in dirt-track racing. Crashes, breakdowns and circumstances often took out the best driver along with the most inexperienced. Hadn't it been that way for her this afternoon? And she definitely considered herself one of the best drivers in the sportsman class at Middlevale Raceway.

But if she were to be honest, the letdown she felt had very little to do with her loss. Rather, it was the picture of the wild kiss with which Sally Griffin had rewarded Slate's third place that stuck in her mind, and the possessive way she had held on to his arm as he had been crowded with well-wishers. She had to admit she was surprised at his reaction. She would have thought a man of his age—he had to be at least thirty-four—and experience would find Sally too immature, too...

Oh, damn! Talk about "dog in the manger"! Just because *she* didn't want him didn't mean some other woman couldn't have him. She was going to be glad when they went home tomorrow afternoon. She needed to get back onto her own ground so she could put everything in its proper perspective.

And she needed to put some distance between herself and Doug Frawley, too. It was too bad she couldn't make herself feel the same way about Doug that he obviously felt about her. Her eyes unconsciously following her thoughts, Trina looked toward the jukebox where Doug was selecting some recordings. Just over medium height, slender, with straight brown hair and honest brown eyes, he was really an attractive man. He ran a small service station that made him his own boss and gave him a better than decent living. He always laughed about taking a busman's holiday when he came to the track as a part of Stitch Pierce's crew—it was, after all, exactly what he did every day. But there was no magic when Doug was near, or when he took her into his arms...not even one tenth of the "vibes" that seemed to electrify the air when she and Slate were within sparring distance.

She didn't know how he had done it, but Slate Montgomery had managed to put his mark on her this weekend. Somehow the friendly camaraderie at The Last Pit Stop and Doug's patient devotion just didn't work in eradicating that hard-boned face from her mind....

Trina shifted her weight on the soft, backless bar stool. The drone of conversation around the bar continued, punctuated by occasional shouts of laughter. She was starting to get restless and wanted to leave. Doug had already volunteered to drive her back, although she hadn't formally accepted his offer. Despite her resolve, she seemed destined to use Doug this weekend. It was unfair, but she had little choice.

Trina's eyes shifted again to the jukebox where Doug still stood. He was talking with Helen Carter. Helen always made her feel like an amazon when she stood beside her. Helen wasn't more than five feet tall, but beside Doug she looked just right. It was obvious Helen thought she did, too, but it didn't look like Doug was buying. She wished he would...

Her eyes trailed lazily away, scanning the room carelessly. The conversations on either side of her couldn't seem to hold her interest, and she shrugged her shoulders unconsciously. She supposed she had just about worn out her small talk for the night. All she could think about right now was making up for the sleep she had lost last night. The thought was becoming more and more appealing, but she hesitated to interrupt Doug and Helen when Helen was obviously on a roll.

Trina's eyes moved casually to the doorway as it opened, her body coming to rigid attention as her eyes touched on the figure who hesitated briefly there. Slater Montgomery. His eyes moved directly to the spot she had occupied at the bar the previous night, which was now filled by a rather flashy blonde. He had not yet seen her in the dark corner where the force of the early crowd had pressed her, allowing her the opportunity to study him more closely.

She had to admit, in his immaculate jeans and a Western shirt that fit his muscular torso far too well to have come off the rack, he was a fine-looking man. She reaffirmed her earlier judgement. He had to be thirty-three or thirty-four years old at least. She liked the way he moved...the well-honed physique that looked surprisingly like the result of good, honest exercise or toil instead of the tight, bulging muscles she had come to associate with the current preoccupation with physical fitness machines. Yes, his muscles looked mature, well used.

She hadn't realized how very tall he was. She liked tall men. She had an aversion to standing eye-to-eye with a man, or worse yet, looking down at him; with her height that was more often the case than not. Her stomach did a little flip as he shifted his broad frame, and she fought to stifle her reaction to his blatant male magnetism. With slow deliberation she averted her gaze. She wasn't doing herself any good gawking.

Trina did not have to look up to identify the person whose hand closed on her shoulder a few minutes later. How was it that his touch already seemed familiar?

"Trina..."

She turned slowly, a light color flooding her face. "What are you doing here? I thought you didn't like this place. And where's Sally?"

"I didn't say I didn't like this place, Trina. That was your idea. And since you asked, I took Sally home."

Shooting a quick glance at her watch, Trina mumbled, "It must be later than I thought."

"Yes, it is."

"It's only eleven-thirty." Hesitating a moment, she continued with an expression of exaggerated disbelief, "You don't mean to tell me Sally has a curfew? No, that's impossible...."

"Pull in your claws, Trina..."

Chafing at the inference, Trina inhaled sharply and looked directly into the liquid blue eyes that seemed to consume her. "I don't like being told what to say or do."

Suddenly disgusted with the realization that they had barely spoken a dozen words, and were already at odds, Trina turned back to the bar and directed her attention to the TV that had been playing, totally ignored, most of the evening.

"Trina..."

When the soft summons did not draw her back in his direction, Slate cupped her chin gently with his palm and turned her toward him again. "I took her home, Trina, because it suddenly occurred to me I was wasting my time trying to enjoy myself with Sally when there was only one person I wanted to be with tonight."

"And that person is me..."

Ignoring her sarcastic tone, Slate smiled. "That's what I've been trying to tell you."

"Oh, it is? Funny...I thought you were trying to tell me how I should act with my brother...the kind of equipment I should use when I race...that I was a fool, pigheaded."

"Well, you are pigheaded."

Ignoring the teasing smile accompanying his remark, Trina nodded. "I'm glad I wasn't imagining all that."

Slate's hand was caressing her shoulder, sending little waves of pleasure down her spine. He was looking into her eyes and he wasn't smiling anymore.

"Dance with me, Trina."

That same warning bell sounded again in her mind, causing her to break contact with Slate's gaze. She raised her glass absentmindedly to her lips, realizing belatedly that it was almost empty. She was still holding the empty glass when Slate reached up and took it from her hand.

"Come on, dance with me. You know you want to."

"And now you're telling me what I'm thinking.... How did you manage this insight on such short acquaintance, Slate?"

"You're hedging."

"No, I'm not. Didn't it ever occur to you that I might not want to dance with you?"

"It occurred to me, but I didn't consider it for more than a second. Not when you look at me the way you do...or maybe I should say, attempt not to look at me..."

"You have colossal conceit, Slate Montgomery."

"And you're still being pigheaded. Come on."

Tugging gently at her hand, Slate turned her around and eased her off the stool. She began to weave her way through the tables, aware that Slate followed close behind her. The startled expression on Doug's face as he glanced up in time to see Slate's arms closing around her caused a little niggle of conscience. But it soon disappeared in the wake of the tidal wave of sensations she began to experience as Slate drew her close against him. Trina knew from the small, inarticulate groan that escaped his lips that Slate experienced much the same, and she felt a small tremor of panic.

Drawing himself back, Slate gave her a shaky smile and noted her bemused expression. "And you were going to let your pigheadedness rob us of this?"

"I think I've had enough of your references to my pigheadedness, Slate." Trina's response, typical but without the usual tartness, succeeded in broadening Slate's smile.

"You are a feisty little witch."

"And nobody's ever called me 'little' before...."

"So tonight's a first."

Conversation suffered under the assault of the emotions that coursed between them. The music was almost forgotten in the wealth of feeling that flooded Trina's senses. His body was warm against hers, tantalizing. She could not remember ever experiencing such a violent reaction to a man before. Being in Slater Montgomery's arms was like being in the eye of the hurricane...the intoxicating, velvet softness holding her helpless, unable to free herself or fight against the oncoming tumult destined to follow.

Unable to speak and unaware that her clear, black eyes reflected her sense of closeness to him, Trina looked up into his open expression. The mingling of their glances brightened the flame smoldering in his light eyes, and his arms tightened around her, pulling her closer against the hard, lean length of his body.

The music came to a slow, sensuous halt and Slate separated himself from her with obvious reluctance.

Ignoring the fact that most couples on the floor had hesitated only briefly, choosing to continue dancing as an old Johnny Mathis favorite began, Slate turned and led her in a direct line to a vacant booth in the corner. Seating her without a word, he turned and motioned to the waitress. He sat beside her, the planes of his face tight with restraint when the drinks arrived. He reached for his drink with an air of desperation and, taking a long swallow, finally turned to face her again. He gave a small, self-derisive laugh as his hand moved to cover hers.

"Would it sound trite to say 'I needed that'? Because I did." When she remained silent, he shook his head. "Say something, Trina. You're not making it easy for me. I'm trying to behave myself. I decided before I came looking for you tonight that I'd made enough mistakes with you...that most of the trouble between us was a result of my coming on too strong. I was reacting, not thinking, and I apologize. I should have realized that you wouldn't have gotten as far as you have in a male dominated game if you weren't independent and determined. I can see that you've earned the respect of the other drivers here, even if they do like to tease you at times. I can't really blame them.... You take the bait so easily and come out fighting."

"Slate, I don't know what you're trying to say."

"I'm trying to say that I want us to get to know each other better. This thing between your brother and me...it has nothing to do with us...the way I feel when I look at you...."

Trina was beginning to feel the edge of panic. She had all but lost the desire to fight the heady feelings overwhelming her. She took a swallow of her drink, and then another. It was cold and refreshing. She took another sip, but its fiery bite did little to calm the trembling that had begun deep inside her. Oh, she knew only too well what he meant when he said, "the way I feel when I look at you...."

"Trina, do you understand what I'm trying to say?"

His expressive eyes intent on hers, Slate reached up to touch her cheek. The simple gesture increased the fluttering of confusion inside her. She swallowed tightly and took a deep breath in an attempt to shake off the haze that had begun to settle on her mind.

"Yes, I understand, Slate. But I think we're getting ahead of ourselves. We're reacting purely physically."

"Don't I know it."

At his teasing, Trina shot him a small frown, then continued, "The truth is, if you got to know me, you probably wouldn't like me at all. You're right, you know, when you say I'm pigheaded. Buck will tell you that, and anybody else you care to ask at the track. I've had to be to survive. Even Ingrid says I'm stubborn, and coming from her—"

"Who's Ingrid?"

"My boss. She owns the boutique I manage."

"Boutique!"

Slate's reaction was far too typical not to stir a familiar annoyance and Trina raised her brow in mock surprise. "What's the matter? Seem out of character for a grease monkey? What did you think I do for a living? Work as a mechanic?"

"Trina...that chip on your shoulder is showing again. So I'm surprised. I guess I expected a more common occupation...like a secretary, or a..."

"Please, spare me. I'm a person who doesn't like to take orders. How long do you think I'd last as a secretary?"

He was laughing. "I guess you're right."

But Trina wasn't laughing. Instead she studied his face, her eyes moving over the stubby brown lashes that rimmed his extraordinary blue eyes.

"What made you decide to race at Middlevale, Slate?"

Her direct question seemed to startle him momentarily. "Why am I racing at Middlevale?"

"That's what I asked."

"For the usual reasons.... I enjoy racing. It's a real kick. And strange as it may seem, it helps me relax from the tension of my job."

"Your job? You mean being head of Wright-Montgomery Precision Tooling? I didn't think an owner of a company had to account to anyone...other than his co-owner."

Slate looked surprised for the second time. "You seem to know a lot about me."

"And so does everyone else at the track...have that information, I mean. Didn't you know you were the main topic of conversation when you pulled in with that sensational rig?"

"I thought you weren't impressed with my equipment."

Realizing she had inadvertently trapped herself, Trina returned his steady perusal. Lifting her chin unconsciously she nodded. "You know very well you have terrific racing equipment. I just don't think that it'll give you the winning edge. I think Buck proved that today."

"Just because I had a blowout..."

"Yes, your 'winning equipment' failed you, didn't it?" Taking refuge in conversation, Trina pressed on.

"So, you think you're going to be points champion at Middlevale."

"I never said that, but since you brought it up...yes, I think I've got the car and the talent to do it. And knowing myself, I won't quit until I make it." Slate's eyes narrowed assessingly as he waited for Trina's response.

"And if you make it, what then?"

"Then? I don't know. I suppose other than being pretty pleased, I'd just continue racing until I got tired of it and..."

Trina's wry smile brought an abrupt halt to his statement. Somehow he had managed to confirm her less than complimentary opinion of him.

"Why? What would you do with the championship?"

Trina shrugged. "If I ever get it, I'll let you know."

Lapsing into silence, Trina raised her glass to her lips and drained its contents. She was confused. Her brief conversation with Slate had just proved how far apart they were in thinking. Buck and she had a dedication to racing, but for Slate the sport was just a temporary pastime. She had always abhorred that attitude in a driver. So why was it her attraction to Slate hadn't dimmed in the least? If anything, she was more stirred than ever by his unrelenting perusal, the way his big hand dwarfed hers as he held it warmly, the tip of his thumb caressing her wrist with a sensitive touch.

She was becoming more confused by the minute. Her frustration showed in her eyes, and Slate frowned as he reached up to trail his finger down her cheek and run it sensuously across the surface of her bottom lip.

She could feel the tremor that shook his body the moment before he offered huskily, "Well, at least we've come to an agreement on something. You're pig-headed...excuse me, stubborn. And I'm persistent."

Slate took a deep, shaky breath. Rising to his feet, he reached down and drew her up beside him. "I think we've talked enough for now. I get the feeling we should do our talking in short doses or we'll be in trouble again." He attempted a smile. "Come on, let's dance. I want to hold you."

Trina nodded and followed the path he cut through the crowded room. He was right. They agreed on one thing. He wanted to hold her, and she wanted to feel his arms around her.

Within a few moments she was in his arms. Giving herself up to the magic of his touch, Trina released a soft, inadvertent sigh as he drew her closer still. Oh, she was tired of trying to reason with the way she felt. She just wanted to enjoy....

His arm was a tight band around her waist as he raised his hand to cup her cheek. Still swaying to the music, uncaring of onlookers, Slate lowered his mouth to hers.

Trina no longer had any thought of suppressing her reaction to his kiss. Indeed, she was incapable of thought as the firm mouth, tantalizingly gentle as it touched hers, slowly inexorably tuned out the world around them with its complete possession. Finally drawing his mouth away, Slate drew her closer, his body flush against hers, locking her in a breathtaking embrace, as their feet moved unconsciously to the music. Her arms wrapped securely around Slate's neck, she could feel his warm breath against her hair, the heady sensation of her breasts pressed intimately close against his chest. She felt small, warm, protected yet overwhelmed by his strength. Her body was aglow with the feelings come to life within her. Her lips were pressed against the broad column of his throat. She breathed in the clean, male scent of his skin, a new electricity rushing through her veins as she moved her tongue to taste the smooth surface.

The first touch of her tongue sent a violent tremor through his body. Slate crushed her closer still, his hand moving to tangle in the length of black, unruly curls that rested against her shoulders. She was intoxicating, and he was drunk on the sensations she evoked within him.

Their bodies, pressed close together, continued to move in unison to the sensuous rhythm of the music that neither consciously heard. Trina had given herself completely to the glory of the moment; was conscious only of the heavy pounding of Slate's heart echoing against her own; the urgent strain of the strong arms that held her close; and the tremor in his voice as he drew back and looked intently into her eyes.

"Trina...this...this isn't any good.... Neither of us needs this torture. What we need is to be alone for a little while, just the two of us. Will you come with me...now?"

A small frown appeared between her slender brows, and Slate knew a moment of panic. "Trina, I want to be with you. You want it, too. You know you do. We're wasting time. We've wasted too much time already...." His lips touched hers lightly, fleetingly.

Pressed so intimately against him, Trina could feel the swell of his desire. The need that burned within her was deep and compelling, and all her excuses paled before it. For the first time in her life she was past reasoning. Maybe it was time...time to act on desire. Perhaps then the driving force within her would dissipate and allow a return to sanity.

"Trina..."

Slate's voice was a low plea that carried the agony of her hesitation only too clearly.

"All right, Slate."

Slate stopped still for a moment, his brilliant eyes searching hers. Reading the confirmation he sought there, he released her. His expression tense, he took her firmly by the hand and led her off the dance floor. He made a rapid, winding path through the surrounding tables toward the bar. Holding tight to her hand, he reached into his pocket with his other hand and slapped down some bills.

For the first time in what seemed a long while, Trina remembered Doug. She glanced quickly to the spot where she had last seen him talking to Helen. He was not there. She scanned the room quickly, holding back as Slate began to urge her toward the doorway.

His eyes shot to her face. "What's wrong, Trina?"

"Doug...I forgot about Doug." Her face flushed warmly. "He offered to drive me back to the motel."

Not bothering to respond directly to her statement, Slate turned toward Bill Watson. The old man eyed him assessingly, his brow furrowed with concern. "Bill, tell Doug he won't have to bother taking Trina home. I'll take care of it."

"Trina, honey." Bill spoke slowly and softly, watching her face carefully, "Are you sure you don't want to wait for Doug? He probably only stepped out for a minute. You know he wouldn't leave if he told you he'd take you home."

Trina's flush deepened. "No, that's all right. Slate will take me home, Bill. Tell Doug I appreciate his offer of a ride, and I'll see him tomorrow." Certain all the eyes at the bar were turned in their direction, Trina turned back to Slate. "Let's go, Slate."

The night air was cool and refreshing and the effect of it hitting her lungs made Trina waver uncertainly as they walked across the dark parking lot. His hand was firm on her arm as Slate steered her toward his Porsche. He opened the door, waiting until she had settled inside before he closed it securely. A moment later he opened the door on the driver's side and slid in. In a quick, sweeping movement, he gathered Trina into his arms. His kiss was slow, deliberate. They were both trembling when he finally drew his mouth from hers.

Releasing her, Slate turned the key in the ignition, and without another word shifted the car into gear and stepped on the gas.

THE MOTEL DOOR was closing behind her when Trina began to have true misgivings. This definitely wasn't her speed. She had been off kilter, unable to think clearly with Slate holding her in his arms. Now was the time to tell Slate she had made a mistake. She wanted no part of a one night stand....

"No, Trina, I won't let you back out now...not without a fight."

Trina's dark eyes snapped up to meet Slate's intense gaze as he offered in explanation, "I could see it coming. You don't have to tell me you don't usually do this kind of thing. It's written all over your face." Reaching up, Slate smoothed her hair back from her temples, unconsciously marvelling at the way the black wisps curled around his fingers. "But this is different." She winced at his words, and a revealing flush swept Slate's face. "I'm not handing you a line, Trina."

Trina's expression was disbelieving as Slate continued, a trace of anger in his voice, "Do you really think I'd have shown up looking for you tonight, if I didn't think we could have something special?" Her dubious expression finally brought his words to a halt. Expelling a short breath, he pulled her back into his arms.

"Did you forget what it was like when you're in my arms, Trina? I haven't. I'm just as sure now as I was before we walked through that door that we'll be good together. And I know one thing. I want you, Trina. And you want me, now...just as much."

Confusion began to assault Trina's brain. Her mind was cloudy, her heart thundering in her ears. "Slate, I...right now I don't really know what I want...."

"You know." His mouth was gentle against hers, his tongue drawing a light, tantalizing line across its trembling surface. She shuddered as his lips followed a slow, tormenting path across her cheek, pressing kisses on her fluttering eyelids, the throbbing pulse in her temple, the warm hollows of her ear. Slowly he returned to her mouth to circle it in light, fleeting kisses. Her trembling was increasing. She could take no more. Reaching up, Trina curled her hand around the back of Slate's neck to urge his mouth against hers. She met with unexpected resistance that snapped her eyes open to Slate's impassioned gaze.

"No, Trina, not this way. I want to hear you say it...tell me what you're feeling."

Momentarily stricken, Trina made an attempt to control her trembling lips. If she'd had a choice, she knew she would have vehemently denied Slate the words he sought. But she'd had no choice since the moment he had taken her again into his arms. With a supreme effort to regain her composure, Trina hesitated only briefly before responding softly, "You win, Slate..."

Slate's interruption held a thread of anger. "It's not a matter of winning, Trina. You're suggesting that if I win, you lose. It isn't that way."

"It doesn't matter...."

"It does."

"Whatever way it is, I do want you, Slate."

Stiffening spontaneously as she spoke, Slate whispered low in return, "Don't do this to me, Trina. I don't want to be a victor here."

"But you are, Slate...."

Tangling her long fingers in the back of his hair, Trina urged his mouth to hers. She sensed she was approaching the last remnant of his resistance and moved her body subtly against him. Her warm tongue flicked out to taste his lips, and she felt the deep shudder that shook him. She pressed her mouth to his, moving it slowly, the taste of him exciting a fervor for more. His muffled groan was simultaneous with his total surrender. Holding her tight against him, he accepted her at last, his mumbled words the last concession to his reluctance. "Damn you, Trina."

There was no more time for words. Mouths and bodies blended, welded together by the heat of their mutual hunger. Consumed by the ragged emotions searing her senses, Trina strained against him. Her hands moved in Slate's heavy sun-streaked hair, caressed the back of his neck. She clutched him nearer, her hands roaming his back, the taut muscles rippling beneath her palms inflaming her desire. His mouth ravaged hers, and she gloried in his possession of her.

She was trembling wildly when Slate abruptly pushed her away, his hands holding her firmly at a distance.

"Don't look at me like that, Trina." Unaware her need was clearly reflected in her eyes, Trina held Slate's smouldering gaze as he moved a wide palm to her cheek. She could see he was trembling, too, the hard planes of his face tense with restrained passion. "We're going too fast...I don't want it to be that way between us."

His words were unexpected and brought a small frown to Trina's brow. "Slate..."

"Do you know how beautiful you are, Trina? You're frowning..." He gave a small snort. "You don't believe me, do you? You think I'm handing you a line again.... I'm not. I've wanted to touch your face like this from the first moment I saw you." He slid his hand into her hair. "Your hair...I don't think I've ever seen anything like it. It's so black...vibrant almost."

He slid his hand to her shoulder, moving it to follow the scooped neckline of her shirt to the small yellow pearl buttons fastening its front. As he undid the first one, his eyes moved back momentarily to hers. "I've been dreaming of doing this. This morning...when you were sleeping on that chaise between the cars...I wanted to touch you. I didn't think I could ever desire you any more than I did then...but I was wrong...." He had come to the last button. He separated the front, a small muscle tensing in his cheek as he realized she did indeed not wear a bra.

He slid the light garment from her shoulders and dropped his hands to his sides. Swallowing convulsively, he stepped back under tenuous control as he allowed his eyes to move over the soft slope of her shoulders, the slender length of her arms, and finally to her small, well shaped breasts.

Startlingly, there was a moistness in the eyes he raised to hers. "Your breasts are beautiful. I knew they would be...just like you...."

Uncertain how much more she could stand, Trina raised shaky hands to the button on her jeans.

"No, not yet." Slate's low entreaty snapped her eyes to his. He was working at the buttons of his own shirt, and in a moment had stripped it away. He reached out and took her in his arms, a low laugh sounding in his throat as their flesh met. "This feels so good." His hands caressed her bared back, moving to slip up her side to cup a small, rounded breast. He fondled it gently, his finger tracing the darkened areola teasingly. His eyes held hers, revelling as he saw the flame of desire burn brightly in the dark depths.

His hand slipped to the fastening on her jeans. Quickly undoing the snap, he slid down the zipper, his hand following its descent into the silky curls beneath in a sensuous caress. Releasing her, he bent to slip the jeans off her narrow hips and down the slender length of her legs, leaving only her pink, lace-trimmed bikini. Carefully lifting each of her slender feet in its turn, he picked up the jeans and tossed them onto the chair in the corner.

Taking her trembling hands in his, he placed them at his waist. Passion colored his voice with hoarseness. "Undress me, Trina."

He need not have instructed her. She wanted nothing more than to feel Slate pressed against her, his body fitted intimately to hers. But in the end it was he who undid the clasp and slipped the tight-fitting jeans from his body. Her shaking hands were unable to accomplish the small task. Alarmed by the sensations overwhelming her, Trina raised her hand to her eyes, only to feel herself suddenly swept up into powerful arms and carried bodily the few steps to the bed. His eyes intent on hers, Slate lowered her slowly until her body touched the soft surface.

In a moment the last wisp of clothing had been removed and Slate had moved to lie atop her, his mouth slowly covering hers, his hands roaming her body, soothing, titilating.

She strove desperately to restrain the kaleidoscope of emotions running wild within her. Clutching him tight against her in an effort to restrain the relentless, loving assault, Trina gasped tightly, "Slate...please..."

"Do you want me, Trina?" Waiting a moment for a response that did not come, he persisted, "I need to hear you say it. Answer me, Trina. Tell me."

Her heart was pounding, her breath coming in short gasps. She didn't want to talk. She wanted only to feel Slate inside her, to know the beauty of his body joined to hers.

"Trina...answer me..."

Her response was a hoarse rasp. "What do you want me to say...?"

"I want you to tell me that you want me."

"Can't you tell, Slate?"

"I want to hear the words.... Say the words, Trina."

"All right...I want you, Slate."

He entered her body, plunging deeply, the sound of her hoarse declaration sending his pulses pounding. "Say it again..."

"I want you."

"Again..."

"I want you."

"Again...Oh, God, Trina...."

Culmination came in a soaring blaze of color, holding them at the summit of its glory for long, rapturous moments of searing climax. A breathless silence followed in which neither dared to speak.

Still lying atop her, Slate raised his head to press a light kiss against the closed lids that fluttered under his lips. Finally moving to the bed beside her, he drew her wordlessly into the circle of his arms.

His lips resting against the black, silky ringlets which edged her forehead, he whispered in a voice shaken with emotion, "This is just the beginning for us, Trina...a beautiful beginning...."

THE RAYS of the early morning sun were bright against the pale-blue drapes that covered the window. Squinting against the glare, Trina raised herself slowly on her arm. She was momentarily disoriented as her eyes flicked around the unfamiliar room. Her gaze shifted to the bed beside her, touched on Slate's broad back, and vivid memory returned. Her face flushing with color, Trina's eyes dropped closed in an effort to shut out total recall.

Finally opening her eyes again, she allowed her gaze to move over Slate's tousled sun-streaked hair, the bold planes of his face. He looked so different in sleep, his features almost unfamiliar. Yet she could remember so well the texture of his heavy hair between her fingers, the touch of his hands, the taste of his skin. Her flush darkened. She had had too much to drink last night, and her emotions had gained control. But the light of day had a harsh way of dealing with truth. And the truth was that she knew Slate's intimate touch far better than she knew Slate. Trina frowned. The truth was decidedly uncomfortable.

Not ready to face that truth while she lay beside him, Trina moved quietly to the edge of the bed and rose to her feet. A sharp pain pounded unexpectedly at the top of her head, forcing her to grasp her temples tightly in an attempt to still the savage throbbing. Satisfied at last that her head would indeed remain attached if she released it, she snatched at her clothes and walked silently toward the bathroom.

She closed the door behind her, unexpectedly facing her own naked reflection in the floor-length mirror attached to it. Pulling herself to attention, she whispered to her reflection, "Well, this is a first you don't want to mark in your memory."

Her face reddened again. She had to get away, before Slate woke up. It had been difficult enough to face herself. It would be impossible to face Slate Montgomery's knowing gaze.

She was hurriedly dressing when a small article on the vanity caught her eye. She picked up the slender red barrette and almost laughed aloud. Good old Sally. Good old Sally had probably stood in this same spot yesterday morning, assessing herself in this same mirror.

Treacherous recall returned Slate's voice to her mind. "It's different with us, Trina...." She turned the red barrette out of her palm with distaste.

Yes, it had been "different" between Slate and her...just as it had doubtless been "different" between him and Sally, and would be "different" for him again with his next woman. Harsh reality cutting her deeply, Trina finished dressing and quietly pulled open the bathroom door.

Her eyes shot toward the bed. Slate was breathing deeply and heavily in sleep, and she felt a familiar warmth assail her. She swallowed convulsively. The knowledge that she had been a fool was made even more painful by the fact that her attempt to exorcise her desire for him had not worked. If anything, it had only served to allow her to become more completely immersed in the emotions she had originally sought to purge. Nothing had changed since yesterday...nothing except her own opinion of herself.

She had allowed herself to be swayed by her emotions only once before. The result had been a disaster. It would not happen again. No, once had been enough....more than enough.

A few moments later she was walking rapidly up the sunny street toward her own motel. She was thankful there was no one around. She needed no witnesses to her stupidity.

A few minutes later, still slightly breathless from her rapid walk, Trina inserted the key into the lock and opened her motel room door. She slipped quickly inside and pulled the door shut behind her, leaning back against its cool surface. Yes, she needed to be back on her home ground where she could regain her perspective.

Her head was still throbbing. Her clothes were damp with perspiration. She was distinctly uncomfortable; she needed a shower. But more disturbing than her physical discomfort was the fact that the scent of Slater Montgomery, the stirring masculine fragrance of his skin, was still in her nostrils, teasing her...reminding her. She needed to be free of the thought and scent of him.

A light, rapid knock on the door broke into Trina's thoughts. Her head jerked to the side, her brows drawing into a frown as she tensed.

"Who is it?"

"It's me, Trina. Karen. Open up."

Uncertain if she was relieved or disappointed, Trina stepped back and pulled open the door. Karen's disturbed brown-eyed gaze met hers.

"Buck's got a head the size of the planet Venus this morning, Trina. He doesn't want to stay for the stock-car races this afternoon. We're going to be leaving...."

Relieved at the excuse for an immediate escape from her tormenting circumstances, Trina responded quickly, "I don't feel like staying either, Karen. I'll leave with you if you can wait another fifteen minutes while I take a shower and get my things together."

"It'll take Buck that long to make it out to the truck." A small smile flicked across Karen's pert face. She added with a shake of her head, "But he's a bear this morning. You'd better not keep him waiting."

"Don't worry, I won't."

Within minutes Trina was in the shower and out. Her skin still damp, she gave a last quick glance around the room before snatching up her bag and making for the door. She glanced cautiously out the doorway before emerging. She was disgusted with her own sense of stealth. Slater Montgomery had doubtless risen by now, and seeing her gone, had dismissed her from his mind as easily as he had dismissed Sally the night before.

Frowning, Trina stepped out into the bright sunshine. She nodded as Buck motioned impatiently from the cab of his truck. Moving wordlessly toward her ancient rig, she unlocked the door of the cab, slung her bag inside and slid into the seat. The old engine roared to life beneath her. Relieved, she turned the wheel to follow behind Buck's rapid departure from the lot.

CHAPTER FOUR

DETERMINATION WAS EVIDENT in the unsmiling planes of her face as Trina pulled her car into the parking lot beside Ingrid's Boutique and withdrew her key from the ignition. She had done a lot of thinking since her arrival home from the races yesterday. Her telephone had been silent all day. Not that she had really expected Slate to call. Her departure from the motel had been an explicit statement of her attitude about the night they had spent together.

But away from Slate's influence, during the long day after she had returned home, Trina had done some thinking. She disliked being beholden to anyone. She had decided long before that she would depend upon no one but legitimate sponsors and herself in order to get her racing ambitions off the ground. Her conscience...her natural independence...would allow it to be no other way.

Those tires... Now she had the job of raising five hundred dollars for the tires Slate had put on her car. Trina shook her head. What Slate really deserved was to get stuck for the money, although he probably would never miss it. No, it was a matter of pride that she pay him back...the next time she saw him.

Trina reached into her purse with a frown and pulled out her checkbook, marvelling as she did at the futile effort. No amount of checking would transform those three hundred and fifty dollars to five hundred. Damn! Her weekly paycheck was already earmarked for other bills that could not wait. She couldn't even squeeze another dollar out of it toward the five hundred. There was no choice but to ask Ingrid if she still wanted her for Thursday afternoon's show. Trina had been a fool to turn down an opportunity to make extra money in the first place.

Taking the precaution to lock the door of her tired old Mustang, Trina turned and started across the lot. She shot an absentminded smile toward the friendly attendant and turned toward the small boutique.

Ingrid's Boutique was located at the end of a row of unostentatious stores in the affluent town of Ridgewood, New Jersey. Three years before, she had wandered into it with Monica Storms. Knowing Monica's background, Trina should have realized immediately she could not afford to buy anything in the shops Monica frequented. But differences in financial situations were all but eliminated in the dancing school they had both attended from early childhood, and long years after the lessons had stopped, their friendship had continued. She could still remember her initial shock at the prices on the tags of the dresses Monica had convinced her to try on, and her embarrassment when she realized she would never be able to afford any of the exquisitely tailored garments.

But Ingrid, the shop's owner, had been impressed with Trina's tall, slender proportions and had commented several times on how well Trina displayed her sophisticated styles. When Trina had finally confessed to Ingrid that Monica was the only potential customer and that, not only was she unable to afford the dresses, she did not even have a job at the time, Ingrid had offered her a position within the store.

Now, three years later, the job that had begun as temporary had grown along with Ingrid's reputation as a couturier. Trina now managed the boutique, her business-school training in accounting being put to good use as she freed Ingrid from all aspects of the business except buying trips. Ingrid was now allowed the freedom to come and go as she pleased in the successful shop, which suited her just fine.

The one facet over which Ingrid had retained complete control was the promotional shows she periodically gave in posh restaurants in and around the affluent suburb. Luncheon and dinner shows were an innovation of Ingrid's that had become quite popular. Each individual model was introduced and the fashion she wore described as she entered the dining area of the restaurant from a small runway. Then, the models circulated between the tables for closer inspection by the diners. The shows were usually announced a few weeks in advance and were well attended by wealthy matrons in the area who could be depended upon to spend heavily.

Efficient in every aspect of her business, Ingrid had noted that the garments Trina modeled were usually more successful than the others. In the hope of encouraging Trina to continue modeling in her shows instead of working behind the scenes as she preferred, Ingrid had offered her a commission on the sales of the garments she modeled. As a result, the shows had proven extremely profitable for Trina as well as Ingrid.

But Trina had an intense dislike of parading between the tables, smilingly answering questions regarding the garments, turning this way and that to the whims of potential customers. She could not understand how the clothes she wore were so successful when she modeled them so begrudgingly. She was certain her attitude would begin to show, and not wishing to hinder Ingrid's success, she had declined Ingrid's offer to model in the next show.

But the situation had changed. Now, she could not afford to pass up the opportunity for some very necessary cash. The flat fee of fifty dollars for modeling, plus the possible commission she could earn would be a long stop toward the one hundred fifty dollars she was short. In any case, she needed every dollar she could get.

Her step slowed as she neared the entrance to the boutique. Trina took a deep breath. Damn that Slate Montgomery for his haunting blue eyes, *and* for getting her into this whole mess!

When she approached Ingrid with her change of mind, her employer was delighted.

"But of course, Trina! It is never too late for you to model in my shows!"

Ingrid's softly accented English was precise, her pretty features reflecting true delight as she clasped her hands together in a characteristic show of pleasure. Ingrid Bolsmar with her petite figure carefully controlled was truly the classic picture of the successful couturier. Her carefully maintained blond hair was always perfectly coiffed, and her small-featured face still startlingly attractive despite her fifty-odd years. She displayed a natural enthusiasm and talent for fabrics and style, which her customers valued. Her instinct was faultless, her taste impeccable, and she could be relied upon completely not to sacrifice good taste in order to pad her pocketbook.

"Thanks, Ingrid. If I didn't need the money so urgently, I wouldn't change my mind at the last minute like this."

"Trina, dear, I am a businesswoman, and having you model in my shows is good business. I am not merely accommodating a friend. You should know I would not miss an opportunity to increase my profits. But..." Her lightly lined face showed a trace of concern as she continued quietly, "I dislike seeing necessity force you to model. The racing...it did not go well this weekend?"

Unable to restrain a smile at Ingrid's polite inquiry, Trina shook her head. Ingrid often expressed disapproval of her racing ambitions, but she was still concerned about Trina's happiness.

"Oh, it went pretty well. But as usual it's doing a good job of eating up my financial resources. Tires are expensive."

Ingrid shook her head expressively. "You will never get out of this sport financially what you put into it, my dear. You're wasting your youth on a fruitless ambition.... But, since your need keeps you here, improving my profits, I suppose I cannot complain."

Her doll-like face now smiling brightly, Ingrid beckoned toward the back of the store. "Well, that is enough of my sermons for today. Come, we will pick out the ensembles you will wear before the store opens. The blue linen suit...it will be perfect for you! And the white strapless gown...the one with the black beading...you will be stunning in it." Her expression beaming even more, Ingrid smiled broadly. "Oh, my dear, you have made my day!"

Following closely behind the small woman who made her way to the rear of the store, Trina shook her head and laughed lightly. "Ingrid, it takes so little to make you happy!"

TRINA'S NERVES were on edge as she turned the wheel of her rig sharply into the pits. It had been a long week, punctuated by endless annoyances. She truly could not understand her impatience. The repairs and standard maintenance on her car had gone smoothly. She had encountered only one problem with the carburetor, and with Buck's assistance she had handled it without too much hassle. The show had gone exceedingly well. True to Ingrid's predictions, the ensembles she had worn had almost all sold, and her fee for that afternoon's work had been more than ample to make up the five hundred dollars she needed. She had already written out a check payable to Slate Montgomery, and all that remained was to find him and deliver it.

Yes, that was what was on her mind, she was sure—the unfinished business between them. She had come to terms with herself as far as her own personal reaction to Slate went. After all, she was a normal woman, and she had allowed no one an intimate part in her life since Spence. Oh, she dated occasionally, and smilingly accepted Doug's frequent visits to "help her work on her car," but there had been nothing serious. She had firmly turned down all outright and intimated offers.

She shook her head. She had really set herself up for someone like Slate, and he had handled the personal magnetism between them like a master. She couldn't really blame him. She had made the mistake of presenting herself as a challenge to him. Well, he had met that challenge, and the rest was history.

She'd return the money for the tires, and maybe then she'd be able to get her mind back on track. The only problem was that Slate had awakened feelings long dormant inside her. She was beginning to feel vulnerable again, and she didn't like it. Her reaction to Slate Montgomery had been totally out of character for her. She was still embarrassed by her complete abandon when she had been in his arms. Even with Spence, she had never been so completely overwhelmed, so lost in a man's arms. But she had decided to write off the night she and Slate had spent together as a moment of weakness—a weakness to which she did not intend to succumb again.

Turning her wheel sharply as Buck's rig came to a halt beside the long line of rigs already assembled in the pits, Trina pulled in beside him. It was only four o'clock, and already the pits were half filled. Since warm-ups didn't start until six, that was a pretty healthy showing. Trina gave a quick glance down the row of parked vehicles, her eyes coming to rest momentarily on the large blue and white rig at the far end of the pits. So he was here already.... Suddenly irritated by her covert surveillance, Trina jerked open the door to her truck and stepped down.

The warm, humid breeze that lifted her hair momentarily did little to relieve her discomfort. Her thin T-shirt and jeans were glued to her body with perspiration. Her long, unruly curls stuck to the back of her neck. She was stiff and uncomfortable after the long ride from Ridgewood. Slipping her hands under her hair, she lifted the curling mass to allow the warm breeze to cool her neck as she arched her back and stretched.

A prickling at the back of her neck—a warning—caused her to turn in time to catch Slate's intense stare. Startled, Trina was unable to react before his eyes became suddenly cold and he averted his gaze. His only acknowledgement of her presence had been a short, indifferent nod.

More shaken than she wished to admit, Trina swore softly under her breath and, turning, walked swiftly toward Buck and Karen. No, it was not the time to approach Slate with the check now. She needed to be in complete control of herself...as cool and unaffected as he apparently was in her presence. She would not give him even the smallest edge. Damn, she couldn't wait until the check was in his hands and everything was settled.

An hour later, Trina sighed with exasperation as she straightened up and pushed herself back from the engine of her car. The sun was unrelenting, and she was certain she was on the way to complete dehydration. She couldn't stand it another minute.

She turned toward the car beside hers. "What do you say we break for a while, Buck? I'm starved, and I can't take this sun a minute longer."

Karen interjected quietly from her position on the aluminum chair between the two cars, "I've been telling him the same thing for the past twenty minutes, Trina, but you know how stubborn he is about checking out the car before he does anything...."

Not for the first time, Trina felt a spark of compassion for Karen's plight. It had to be hard for someone who had not the slightest interest in engines and driving to spend the greater part of her day listening to conversations that centered on torque, compression, gears, and the latest silicone spray that would give a racing engine a greater advantage. And as much as she loved Buck, at times she felt his impatience with Karen's lack of interest a bit unfair.

Buck turned slowly and looked in Karen's direction. The dark eyes that focused on Karen's small frown squinted momentarily before he drawled, "I thought I was doing you a favor, honey. Didn't you tell me just this morning that you were determined to lose a few pounds you had put on in the—"

"Buck!" Her eyes jerking to Trina with embarrassment, Karen stood up and self-consciously ran her hands over the rounded curve of her buttocks. "I'm beginning to think I can't tell you *anything* in confidence! You blurt everything out in front of your sister like a..."

The suppressed amusement lurking in Buck's dark eyes became more apparent as Karen became more flustered. Walking the few steps to her side, he slung a brawny arm around Karen's narrow shoulders, the comparison between his hulking frame and her tiny proportions more pronounced as he lowered his head to her ear and commented in a stage whisper, "I told you, sweetheart, as far as I'm concerned, you have the sweetest little—"

A sharp poke from Karen's elbow brought an abrupt end to Buck's statement, and a small smile to his lips as he turned once again in Trina's direction. "Okay, Trina. Looks like Karen's had it, too, for a while. My car checks out perfectly anyway. What about yours?"

"Right now my car's in better shape than I am. Come on, let's get out of here for a little while. Air conditioning will do me just about as much good as food right now."

"Sounds fine with me!" Stopping only a minute to motion Sid and Bix to join them as he wiped the grease off his hands, Buck fell in beside Trina as she started toward the narrow exit from the track. His smile stretching wider, Buck commented as he glanced at Trina's spotless, well-tended hands, "Nobody'd ever take you for a grease monkey with those hands, Trina. Maybe I should start wearing surgical gloves, too."

Shooting his broad, callused hands a quick, skeptical glance, Trina offered with smiling sarcasm, "Yes, it really is a shame to spoil those delicate lily-whites."

Buck's snicker widened her smile. Suddenly Trina became aware that Slate Montgomery and his crew were approaching the gate from the opposite direction. Her heart immediately began an accelerated beat, cresting to a thunder in her ears as they all seemed to reach the gate at the same time. Extremely aware that Slate and his crew had fallen in behind them, Trina toyed with the thought of completely ignoring his presence, before pride assumed control. After all, there was no reason she shouldn't speak to him. They hadn't parted in anger. They had just parted...or rather, she had. She'd never have a better chance than now...in the presence of others...to return the money without unnecessary small talk.

Buck, Karen and the crew had moved in front of her in line in order to talk to several old-timers ahead of them, and extremely conscious of the fact that Slate now stood directly behind her, Trina took a deep breath and turned a casual smile into his face.

"Hello, Slate. Looks like we're going to have a good showing today."

The cold indifference in Slate's gaze painfully tightened the knot that had formed in her stomach. Infuriated at her own intense reaction, Trina managed to maintain a casual facade as she reached into her pocket, withdrew the folded check, and slipped it into his hand.

"I'm glad I had the opportunity to see you before the races start. I wanted to make sure everything was squared away between us."

His indifferent expression tightened into a frown as Slate unfolded the check. The look he shot back to her a few seconds later was tight with anger. Gripping her elbow powerfully, he unexpectedly moved her forward, past the slowly moving line and through the gate.

Unable to free herself from his grip without making a scene, Trina managed a stiff smile through which she muttered, "What do you think you're doing? Let me go, Slate!"

Slate continued to propel her forward, his long stride forcing her to a pace just short of a run in order to keep up with him. Jerking her into a driveway between two stores, his broad back blocking them from curious onlookers, he held the check up in front of her face and demanded sharply, "What the hell is this?"

Trina responded heatedly, infuriated by his high-handed manner. "It's the money for the tires you put on my car. What did you think it was?"

A sarcastic sneer twisted Slate's lips. "I thought it might be a token of your esteem for the night we spent together last weekend."

A rapid flush suffused her face. "You have a rather high opinion of yourself, don't you? That's a pretty big check for the kind of service you're talking about."

"It was worth every penny of it, and you know it."

The heat in the blue eyes holding her gaze stirred memories Trina preferred to suppress. Unwilling to allow him to see his effect on her, Trina dropped her eyes momentarily, only to feel his hand unceremoniously jam the check into the pocket of her jeans. Her eyes jerked back to his face. She attempted to remove the check but the clamping of Slate's huge hand on her wrist stayed her effort.

"What are you doing?" Trina attempted to retrieve the check as she spoke, only to feel his grip tighten painfully. "You're hurting me. Let go of my wrist!"

Slate was alarmingly close. His chest was beginning to heave in agitation, but the heat of her own anger helped her ignore the danger signals in his eyes.

"I said let me go! And take this check—"

"Forget the check, Trina. I've been paid already."

Stiffening at the insult, Trina held his mocking gaze with her own until she was capable of speech.

"I don't pay for my equipment with my body, and I resent the implication—"

"Oh, do you? But last week I was the one you left in that motel like a used-up whore!"

Intensely aware of the strength of his body so intimately close, Trina managed sarcastically, "I didn't realize you were so sensitive. Anyway, last weekend is old news as far as I'm concerned." Managing to jerk her hand free of his grasp, Trina stuffed the check into the pocket of his shirt. "And as far as I'm concerned, this squares everything between us."

Her eyes were still boldly holding his when a small flicker moved across Slate's expression. Slowly taking the check from his shirt pocket, Slate held it motionless in his hand as his gaze trailed gradually from her eyes to the curve of her cheek, along the line of her jaw, coming to settle on her mouth. Mesmerized by his gaze, Trina stood rigidly as Slate lowered his hand to tuck the check deep into the pocket of her tight jeans, his hand remaining intimately against her body as he whispered, "I told you, I don't want this check. I don't want money from you, Trina."

Pushing the check deeper into her pocket, Slate turned and walked away.

THE SUN had long since dropped from the horizon, but the heat of the day had not dissipated in the slightest. Squinting through a visor covered with a thin layer of dust, Trina assessed the long line of cars revving their engines in front of her. Twentieth in a field of twenty-four! Of all the luck! Why couldn't she have drawn a position closer to the front? It seemed she was destined to earn her wins the hard way. And it *would* be a win tonight.... She was determined!

The pace car was moving slowly into motion, drawing the double line of cars onto the track as Trina's mind raced anxiously. She only had two real competitors in this race, Charlie Strong and Wally Tierney. Charlie had been points champion the previous year, with Wally running a close second. She didn't want to remember her position in the points race last year. Engine problems resulting from parts fatigue had done her in, but she had done extensive repairs over the winter and her engine was in good shape. She now had excellent tires.... Suppressing her irritation at the memory of the way she had gotten them, Trina forced her mind back to the race.

The tight line of cars was circling the track, approaching the far stretch when the pace car dropped off into the pits. Her eyes flashing to the pole in the third turn, Trina felt the first burst of adrenaline shoot into her veins as the yellow caution lights went out. Leaning heavily on the accelerator, she followed the pack as it rounded the third turn. Her eyes were fixed on the cars ahead of her as she sought the break she needed. She didn't have to look to the starter to see the green flag waving them forward; the sudden lunge of the pack was all the indication she needed. Trina stepped on the gas and surged into the tightly closing stream of cars. Lap number one had begun!

Oblivious to the roar of engines surrounding her, Trina gripped the wheel as she made a bid to pass the gold and white number 43 ahead of her. Unable to take him on the inside for the last two laps, Trina had been forced to go to the outside, aware of the danger of its soft, slippery surface.

She had progressed diligently up through the pack for the first harrowing laps. She had no indication of the time remaining in the race. Her general calculations led her to believe they had passed at least ten of the allotted fifteen laps, and if that was the case, she was extremely satisfied with the progress of her race so far. Five laps remaining and five cars ahead of her.... The toughest part of the race had been weaving through the pack to attain a position where she might be free to use speed as freely as she used her maneuverability. She need only get in front of number 43 and then she would be in the clear.

A caution light... Automatically stepping on the brake as the field slowed, Trina passed the maroon and yellow number 15 which had smashed against the fence in the fourth turn. A quick glance in its direction brought a smile to her face. Jim Steed was out of his car and kneeling beside it in an attempt to estimate the extent of the damage even as the tow truck pulled up alongside. She felt a flash of compassion. The position of his wheels looked bad...broken axle....

Well, Jim's bad luck had been her good luck. The caution light had squeezed the remaining cars together, eliminating the lead the two front runners had gained while she had been weaving her way through the pack. The race was more than half over, demanding a single-file status as they prepared to resume the race. Once again, the cars approached the caution lights, which suddenly turned off. Immediate acceleration and a quick maneuver allowed her to surge ahead of number 43 and into fourth position! Trina was elated, an elation that soared higher as the third position car took the corner too fast and spun wildly out of control. Speeding past his careening car, Trina realized he would be well back in the pack before he gained control!

There were only two cars ahead of her now...Charlie and Wally, just as she had expected. Three laps.... If she was right, she had three laps remaining in which to...

A flickering red light caught her attention on the dash.... Overheating...she was beginning to overheat! The light flashed off and Trina felt a rush of hope. If only she could last it out....

Trina roared past the starter's booth. Two flags held horizontally, side by side...the signal for two more laps.... She needed to maintain full power for only two more laps....

Grim with determination, Trina pressed her foot to the floor in a vain bid to overtake Wally's number 23 on the straightaway. It was no good! There was only one way she was going to overcome these two front runners! Keeping close to Wally's tail, Trina stayed tight to the inside as she approached the third turn. Edging closer, ever closer, she waited for the first indication that Wally was beginning to reduce speed for the turn. All her senses concentrating on the timing needed, Trina stepped on the gas at the exact second Wally applied the first touch of the brake. With a slight turn of the wheel, she shot forward, passing him on the inside, straining, even as she did, to avoid the spin into which the car seemed fated to plunge.

She had done it! There was now only one car ahead of her! One more to pass! The red light on the dash was now almost steady. Her engine could not take much more of this abuse without overheating and failure! The white flag waved as she passed the starter's booth! One more lap...

Charlie Strong was racing free and clear ahead of her. She couldn't hope to take him on the outside. She didn't have the engine to outpower him. The red light was constant on her dash. Perspiration streaming down her temples, Trina made her decision. Her foot jammed to the floor, Trina stayed tight to the inside of the track in the back straightaway. Two more turns and it was the final straightaway. It was now or never....

Unwilling to give ground even as the two cars moved into the third turn, Trina kept her foot to the floor, her heart pounding as the wheel pulled and tore at the muscles in her arms. But she would not give in! Then, they were side by side, Trina on the inside, the perfect position.... The fourth turn and Trina strained at the pull of the wheel... No, she couldn't give....

Charlie's number 61 dropped back in the final moments of the turn. She was in front...out in the clear! Although her leg trembled under the strain, Trina kept the accelerator jammed to the floor and suddenly realized she was alone...by herself...uncontested as she roared up the final straightaway. Above her head the checkered flag waved victoriously. She had won!

TRINA STRIPPED the greasy surgical gloves from her hands and, stepping back from her engine, brushed her hair from her forehead. She breathed a deep sigh of relief. There had been no major damage to her car as a result of the chance she had taken during the feature race. After a few minor repairs and the usual weekly maintenance, she'd be ready to race again next week.

She raised her head, her eyes scanning the track around her as the announcer continued to call the modified feature race already in progress. Her ears catching on a familiar name, Trina jumped up onto the bed of her truck and sought out the placement of the cars. How many laps had progressed ... four ... five ... and already Slate and Buck were battling each other on their way through the pack. Even at a distance, the hostility between the drivers of the red and white 82 and the blue and white 008 was evident. Maneuvering in and out through the field of cars, their powerful engines easily outperforming the lagging cars around them, each refused to allow the other to gain even the slightest advantage before a desperate, all-out fight to assume the lead.

An anxious perspiration began to form on Trina's brow. She didn't like such an intense display. The announcer's voice blared over the loudspeaker again, commenting on the grudge that seemed to have developed between Mallory and Montgomery. The gasp of the crowd echoed her own as 82 swerved, forcing 008 to the outside of the track. Trina groaned. Buck had accomplished a tricky but effective maneuver that had forced Slate back two spots.

Eighteen laps down...two more to go, and the race was entirely between Buck and Slate. Trina, uncertain if she could stand the strain much longer, felt herself torn between the two cars that had been exchanging the lead constantly for the past three laps. Anxiety took control of her, and she felt neither elation nor despair when either of the two assumed the lead. She was confused. She just wanted this race to be over—safely over at last.

The fourth and final turn! The roaring cars forced their last burst of speed as the crowd rose to its feet. Numbers 008 and 82 were side by side up the final straightaway when a miss in the engine of the red and white 82 caused an almost imperceptible hesitation. But that minute fraction of a second was all that was needed! Surging ahead, 008 took the lead! Buck had no time to make up his loss. Unable to put a name to the emotion that choked her throat, Trina watched breathlessly as Slater Montgomery's 008 roared past the starter's stand to take the checkered flag.

TRINA SQUINTED at the dark road ahead of her. It seemed she had been following the red taillights of Buck's trailer for an eternity as they headed home. No, she had not needed to feign fatigue to avoid the expected celebration of her win at The Last Pit Stop. She was truly exhausted. Buck's disappointment had not been conducive to a celebration, either, despite the fact that she knew he was truly proud of her win. The smile on his face when she had returned to the pits from the winner's circle had said it all.

But only a few minutes later she had turned to catch Slate Montgomery's expression as he had glared in her direction from across the pits. Trina had been surprised to see anger reflected there...not joy. Damn! What did she care if Slater Montgomery didn't share her happiness over her win?

Buck's trailer made the final turn onto May Street, and emitting a sigh, she turned her wheel to follow. Before she could pull her truck to a stop, Buck was already out, unhooking his trailer. Trina frowned. Buck was so disgusted that he wasn't even going to take the time to get his car into the garage before he left for home tonight. Well, it was just as well. She was too tired to do anything tonight, either.

Trina managed a small smile as her brother's tall figure turned toward her.

"Not going to put the car in the garage tonight, Buck?"

"The way I feel right now, I couldn't care less if I ever see that steel monster again!"

"Sure..." Reaching out as she walked to his side, Trina patted her brother's broad shoulder with exaggerated commiseration. "I've heard that song before. Knowing you, you'll be back here to work on that car before I get a chance to get out of bed tomorrow morning."

Not bothering to respond, Buck mumbled a quick good-night and, taking Karen's arm, steered her toward the truck. Waiting only until Trina had opened the front door and stepped inside the house, Buck pulled out of the driveway and within a few minutes had disappeared down the road.

Trina made sure to lock the door behind her and headed for the kitchen. It looked like Buck had the best idea tonight, after all. And as soon as she got something to drink, she was going to go straight to bed and do her best to forget the whole irritating day. She frowned as she pulled open the refrigerator door and reached for the milk carton. She shook her head. The way she was acting, no one would believe she'd won today! Hardly able to comprehend her own depressed state, Trina poured herself a glass of milk.

The doorbell sounded in the silent house. Buck must have forgotten something.

She started toward the front door, her voice calling out casually as she reached for the knob, "I don't know, Buck. You must be getting old! You never used to forget..."

Trina's words died on her lips as she jerked open the door and a familiar pair of direct blue eyes met her glance.

"You! What are you doing here?" Conscious of the trembling beginning deep inside her, Trina met Slate Montgomery's unsmiling expression with a deep frown.

"We have to talk, Trina. I thought I might be able to get a chance at The Last Pit Stop after the races.... It's a good thing I noticed Buck packing up early or I wouldn't have seen you leave...."

"Yes, that would have been a loss, wouldn't it?"

Trina's sarcasm did not go unnoticed, but preferring to ignore it, Slate continued, "Well, aren't you going to ask me in?"

"No."

"Trina..."

"No. We don't have anything to discuss. Oh, wait...yes we do at that." Withdrawing the tattered check from the pocket of her jeans, where it had been most of the day, Trina held it out toward him. "You've obviously changed your mind about accepting this. I'm glad you're not being stubborn."

"No, I've decided there's nothing to gain in being stubborn, Trina." His gaze direct and penetrating, Slate shifted his tall frame uncomfortably in the doorway. "But neither do I intend to take that ragged check to my bank to be cashed. Is it asking too much for you to write me out another one?"

A bit annoyed by the request, Trina hesitated as she considered the check's tatty condition. "No...I guess I can write you out another one. I'm sorry. I didn't realize you were so fussy or I would've had it sealed in plastic.... Come in."

Hesitating as she scanned the room for the location of her purse, Trina was aware of Slate's quick perusal of the small, comfortable living room. The furnishings were old...the same she and Buck had grown up with, but they were comfortable...a part of her. Her Dad, Buck and she had moved to this house, in one of the more modest sections of Ridgewood, shortly after her mother's death. Her dad had left the house to them when he had died, and Trina and Buck had continued to live there. At this point in time, she truly felt it was home. She had dreams of being successful in racing, buying out Buck's interest in the house, and restoring it to its original beauty. But so far, her dreams had been just that...dreams.

The large two-car garage adjoining the house was perfect for their needs, and the neighbors were accustomed to the Mallory family's involvement in racing. They were extremely indulgent, and both Buck and Trina appreciated them. If it was up to her, she would never move.

Realizing she had left her purse in the kitchen, Trina left Slate standing near the door as she started in that direction. "I'll get my checkbook."

The kitchen was small, too small to hide something of her purse's proportions, and Trina stopped momentarily. Where was it? She specifically remembered carrying it in when she came for her milk...oh, there, on the floor beside the refrigerator.... Trina had snatched it up and turned back toward the living room, when she realized Slate was standing in the doorway behind her.

His broad frame seemed to shrink the already small room.

Trina withdrew the checkbook from her bag, annoyed at the trembling of her hands. Why did this man knock her off balance so? Damn! She wished he had stayed in the living room. It was larger...easier to maintain space between them. Realizing her writing was close to illegible, Trina rewrote the check. She stepped back and held it out to him.

Slate had advanced into the room as she was writing, and now stood an arm's length from her. Extremely aware that the check shook revealingly in her hand, Trina laid it on the table beside them. Swallowing tightly, she raised her eyes to Slate's face. The anger of the afternoon had faded from his expression, leaving it sober and unrevealing. She was intensely aware of the way his eyes caressed her face. He took a step closer, and Trina took another step backward, stopping short as her back touched the stove.

A small smile broke across Slate's lips. "What are you going to do now, Trina? You can't run any farther."

"Don't flatter yourself, Slate. I don't have to run away from you."

"Then what would you call what you did last weekend?"

"As far as I was concerned, the evening's entertainment was over. I didn't realize you expected me to hang around for a long farewell."

"You're a liar, Trina." Slate's broad hands clamped on her shoulders. "Stop acting. You know it's special between us. What happened? What were you afraid of?"

"I'm not afraid of anything.... I just opened my eyes and saw myself and the whole situation more clearly without alcohol and romantic music clouding my vision."

"Are you trying to say you were drunk? You weren't."

"No, my resistance was just lowered a little, that's all."

"So what's your excuse now? You're trembling.... It's not because you're afraid of me—afraid of what I might force you to do. Because you and I both know I'd never force you." He hesitated. When she made no response, he drew her toward him. "Trina..." He slid his arms around her and held her close. "I was furious when I woke up and you were gone. At first I thought you were in the shower, or had gone for coffee. When I finally went to your motel and found out you had left, I couldn't believe it.

"'Why?' I kept asking myself, 'Why?' And then I got mad...but I still kept asking myself the same question all week.... I tried to tell myself you were pretending when you were with me...that you hadn't really felt the same way I did when you were in my arms. I figured I was well off, having you walk away. I just about had myself convinced until I saw you again today. It ate me up seeing you with the others, knowing you were keeping me on the outside. Then you pulled that stunt when you were racing on the track tonight. Do you realize the chance you took? Anyway...it suddenly occurred to me that I was just being stubborn—more pigheaded than I had accused you of being—just to avoid swallowing my pride and asking you why you left. So, I'm asking you again, Trina. Why did you leave? You can't tell me you don't feel anything when you're in my arms."

"I never said I didn't feel anything, Slate. You're just making more of it than it is."

"Am I?" Slate was holding her close against him. The distinctive, heady scent of his skin was in her nostrils, taunting her as the palm of his hand moved sensuously on her back. Slate cupped her chin with his other hand, forcing her to maintain contact with his eyes. His breath was warm against her lips as he whispered softly, "We have something we can build on, Trina. Something we can make even more beautiful...."

Trina was desperate to regain her perspective. Had it only been this afternoon that she had been so sure she wouldn't succumb to his magic again? "Building is a slow process, Slate. My mind is on speed right now, and you're still collecting red barrettes."

"Red barrettes?" Momentarily puzzled, Slate hesitated before realization dawned in his eyes. "You mean Sally's barrette...the one I picked up off the seat of my car after I took her home? I don't even remember what I did with it, and I couldn't care less. You're the only one I care about, Trina, the only one."

This time he wasn't waiting for her response. He was lowering his head toward hers, trailing his lips against her cheek. Trina steeled herself against the light, teasing contact but it was no good. His mouth closed on hers, pressing deeper. His tongue separated her lips. He was tasting her...drawing from the sweetness of her mouth, his tongue fondling and caressing. Reality was slipping away. His hand slipped under the edge of her thin T-shirt and moved sensuously upward to cup a small breast, and a glowing sense of elation spread through her. She was swirling in a mist of heady sensation, beginning to lose herself in the wonder of the moment, when cold consciousness again began to invade her mind.

"No...no, Slate, please."

The warm caress of his hand stilled momentarily, giving her the strength to go on.

"Slate, please, I don't want this...."

"You don't want..." Slate drew back, directing a disbelieving gaze into her disturbed expression. "You know how good it can be, Trina. Don't throw it away."

Trina shook her head. "No, this is all happening too fast. I don't want to wake up tomorrow as full of regrets as I was last week."

"Full of regrets?"

"I told you, easy access isn't my bag, Slate."

"Trina, why won't you believe me? I'm not just looking for someone to fill my weekend...."

Trina shook her head. "No."

"Trina, we..."

Thankful for the returning gift of sanity, Trina pushed firmly at Slate's chest. Her hands were still trembling, but the dark eyes she raised to his were becoming resolute.

"There is no 'we'. I want you to go, Slate."

"You don't really want that..."

"You're right. I don't really *want* you to go. But what I need right now is some time to think."

"Thinking might be the worst thing for us both..."

"Don't push me, Slate." There was a ring of desperation in her tone that drew his light brows together. "If you really think we have something special, you'll do what I ask. You'll go."

"Are you testing me? Is that it, Trina? Do you want to see if I'll really leave? If that's it, just be sure before you ask me to go...."

"The only thing I'm sure of now is that I need some space...I need to keep control of my life and..."

"I don't want to control you. I only want to make love to you."

"Slate..."

Slate's expression was stiffening. "You mean it, don't you...?"

She nodded.

Myriad emotions moving across his face, Slate hesitated briefly. Abruptly, his hands fell to his sides. Stepping back, he shook his head. "I must be crazy...but all right. If you really want me to leave, I'll leave...this time."

She had not had the time to digest his words when he moved suddenly toward the front door. His face clearly reflected the anguish of his words.

"I don't believe I'm doing this...I don't want to leave, but neither do I want to make love to you tonight and find you gone again in the morning. The next time we make love, Trina, it'll be because you want it as much as I do...no holding back."

She had come to stand within a few feet of him, and he frowned. Suddenly reaching out, he snatched her tight against him. His voice was ragged. "I'll wait, Trina, until you're ready. I'll give you my word on that right now. But don't wait too long because..."

His voice trailing off as words failed him, Slate crushed her closer against him, his arms imprisoning her as his mouth closed over hers.

She was still shaken and breathless as the door closed behind him. Her breathing had not yet returned to normal by the time the car door slammed, the engine started and he pulled away from the curb.

Slate had left...given her the time she needed to get her emotions back on an even keel. It was what she wanted. So...why did she feel so bad...?

CHAPTER FIVE

TRINA HAD HAD a terrible night. Supremely annoyed with the conflicting emotions that had kept her awake all night long, she flung back the covers and drew herself slowly to her feet. She glanced at the clock on the small maple night table beside her bed as she staggered toward the bathroom. Seven o'clock... Refusing to acknowledge the cause of her sleepless night, except to frown unconsciously as a familiar pair of blue eyes returned to haunt her thoughts, Trina marched to the sink and splashed her face with water. Damn! She would get rid of that haunting image if it was the last thing she did....

A few minutes later she was moving through the front doorway and down the front steps. Well-worn jogging shoes on her feet and a faded sweat suit covering her slender proportions, she started down the all-but-deserted street. She had only turned the corner when she felt her silent anxieties beginning to slip away. Smiling up into the cloudless blue morning sky, she took a deep breath and lengthened her stride.

An hour later, a glistening veil of perspiration covering her face, Trina made a conscious effort to slow down her pace as she approached her house. She was now merely walking briskly in an attempt to cool down. She checked her watch again. Eight o'clock. She felt great! Her physical elation was a far cry from the exhaustion she had felt upon arising. That was one of the main reasons she had begun to run, over two years ago. Nothing else had seemed to overcome the mental malaise that had afflicted her after Spence. Trina felt a sense of discomfort return momentarily. She had not really used her jogging as therapy for a long time, and was disturbed at the need to resort to it again.

She was frowning as she pushed open the front door and stepped inside, but her frown did not last long. It was a beautiful Sunday morning and she now felt healthy and invigorated. If she didn't miss her guess, Buck would be arriving by nine o'clock to look over his car. Trina knew her brother well; his discouragement last night had been temporary. Karen liked to sleep late on Sunday, but Buck could never stay in bed past eight. So he should be arriving soon, and would probably end up working on his car until noon.

Trina was moving through the kitchen toward the bathroom when she changed her direction and flicked on the oven. Walking to the pantry, she opened the door and scanned the top shelf. There it was...blueberry muffin mix...Buck's favorite. After yesterday, they both deserved a little pampering, and she was in a mood to do it. Within a few minutes the muffins were in the oven, the coffee was in the automatic brewer, and she was again on her way to the bathtub. She'd get that Slate Montgomery out of her mind today if it was the last thing she did!

Oh, heavenly! Sinking down a little farther into the luxuriously scented water, Trina smiled as the dull aches in her calf muscles began to dissipate. She hadn't been jogging for a few weeks, and her muscles were protesting their nonuse. With a low sigh, she poured a small circle of shampoo into her hand and began rubbing it into her hair. She had rinsed her hair free of shampoo with the small spray attached to the tap when she decided to allow herself a few minutes longer in the tub. It was Sunday. She had time to indulge herself.

Trina lazily opened her eyes... She must have dozed. The water was beginning to cool, and it was time to get out of the tub. The room smelled almost sweet...like spring...with the scent of fresh berries or...

Blueberries! She had forgotten the muffins in the oven!

Scrambling wildly to her feet, Trina jumped out of the tub. Grabbing at the bath towel hanging nearby, she wound it around her in a makeshift sarong. Taking just a second longer to wrap her dripping hair in another towel, she jerked open the door to the bathroom and ran toward the kitchen. The aroma was getting stronger, but it didn't smell like the muffins were burning...yet.

She entered the kitchen at a full run, only to come to a jerking halt at the sight of a tall masculine figure bent over the oven door.

"What the...!"

The sound of her startled gasp turned the unexpected visitor in her direction as she stammered, "What...what are *you* doing here?"

The brilliant blue eyes that had haunted her all night were now staring accusingly at her.

"I'd say it's pretty lucky that I happened to stop by. Look at these muffins! A few more minutes and they'd be burned!"

Having had time to overcome her surprise, Trina's expression was more than slightly disbelieving. "You 'just happened to stop by'? Somehow I didn't think that Fort Lee was just around the corner from Ridgewood."

Slate placed the hot pan on the rack she had left on the counter prior to going into the bath, effectively ignoring her remark. Turning back in her direction, he allowed his eyes to flicker over her terry-clad figure. His thoughts were transparent, and Trina felt a slow flush of embarrassment suffuse her face. Clutching her damp sarong more tightly around her, she said defensively, "By the way, who let you in here?"

"Let me in? This house is a standing invitation. The door was unlocked. As a matter of fact, it swung open when I knocked. Don't you have the good sense to lock your doors, lady?"

"Who are you, my keeper? I never lock my doors during the day. I don't believe—"

"You're kidding, aren't you?" Slate had taken a few long steps that brought him directly in front of her. An incredulous expression spreading across his face, he shook his head. "You don't lock your doors? Are you crazy? What if it had been someone other than me who had knocked on your door this morning...been standing here when you ran out in that...that..." His eyes, sweeping her bare dripping limbs, adequately finished his statement.

Getting a tighter grip on her damp sarong, Trina felt a surge of impatience. "Look, if you don't mind, I'm in no mood for a sermon. I was expecting someone, and I didn't want to lock the door in case he had forgotten his key..."

"You were expecting..." Slate's expression doing an abrupt change from incredulity to jealous anger, he continued in a low voice, "I should have realized...blueberry muffins in the oven...coffee ready...you all fresh and sweet smelling...The guy has it made, hasn't he? Who's the lucky man, Trina?"

"It's really none of your business, is it?"

Conscious of the rigid set of her shoulders, which only too clearly displayed her growing anger, Slate forced himself to control his own flaring temper. "I'm sorry, Trina. I suppose you have a right to your...friends. I don't have to like it, though, do I?"

Trina responded tightly, "No, you're entitled to your own reactions, however presumptuous they may be...just as long as you don't impose them on me. So, if you don't mind, I'd like to finish dressing..."

"Oh, don't let me hold you back. Go ahead and get dressed...dry your hair...whatever. I'll wait here as quiet as a lamb until you come back. And this way you won't have to run for the door when your friend arrives. I haven't eaten yet. We can have breakfast together...the three of us...."

"I don't think that's a good idea, Slate. I think it would be better if you left now so that I..."

His smile stiff, Slate took a step closer. "I don't want to leave yet, Trina. Now, are you going to get dressed, or do you want me to come in and help you? You can believe me when I say I'd enjoy that...very much..."

The sound of the front door opening distracted Trina from Slate's words. She turned around in time to see Buck come to an abrupt halt as he came into the doorway of the kitchen. His eyes moved from Trina in her unexpected state of undress, to Slate and back, narrowing as he addressed Trina quietly.

"Am I interrupting anything, Trina?"

"No, Buck. As a matter of fact, I've been expecting you." Her smile flashed appealingly as she pointed to the freshly baked muffins, without showing any of the discomfort that all but curled her toes. "The muffins are still warm and the coffee's ready. Why don't you just pour yourself a cup while I slip on some clothes? I'll be back in a minute."

Not waiting for Buck's response, Trina turned and fled from the room. Only taking the time to pull on a pair of bikini briefs, she stepped into the dungarees that lay on the chair and slipped a fresh blue T-shirt over her head. Thankfully, her hair was no longer dripping, and giving the damp spirals a fast brush, she slipped her feet into the scuffs at the side of her bed before rushing back into the kitchen.

She approached the kitchen almost at a dead run before she stopped to pull herself under control. What was she doing? Buck and Slate were two reasonable men. Surely they could entertain themselves for a few minutes until she returned.

The sound of two low voices in stilted, polite conversation gave her the edge of confidence she needed. Trina stepped into the kitchen and walked toward the cabinet. She was taking out dishes and cups when Buck stopped her.

"No, don't take out anything for me, Trina. I'm not staying. I just came by to pick up some tools. Karen's Chevelle needs some work, so I won't be able to spend time on my car today. I'll go through the garage and pick them up on the way out. See you tomorrow."

Giving Slate a brief nod, Buck left the room through the garage entrance. At the click of the door Trina turned to Slate's apologetic grimace.

"I'm sorry, Trina. I should've realized..."

Angry to see Buck leave so early...angry at the surge of emotion that accompanied the realization that she and Slate were alone again, Trina snapped, "What you should've realized is that you have no right walking into my house as if you own it...no right to expect an explanation of any sort from me...no right to..."

"I know, I know. You're right, Trina."

A bit startled at Slate's repentant expression and his immediate concession to her point, Trina was momentarily at a loss for a response. Unable to proceed with her angry harangue, she finally lifted her shoulders in a futile gesture.

"Why did you really come here this morning, Slate? I thought I made myself pretty clear last night. I told you I needed time."

Taking a step closer, Slate raised his hand to Trina's cheek, his fingertips trailing a gentle, tantalizing trail down her cheek as he responded softly, "Well, other than the fact that I wanted to see you, I came to ask you how you slept last night. I had a hell of a night."

Carefully steeling herself against the immediate tug of response she felt to his touch, Trina lied blatantly, "I had a very good night's sleep, as a matter of fact."

"Liar."

Her face flushing at his knowing response, Trina retorted hotly, "Well, if you're not going to believe a word I say, why did you ask?"

"Because I wanted to see if you'd try to protect yourself."

"Protect myself? Against what?"

"Against what we both know is happening to us."

"Nothing is happening to us!" A light tremor ran up her spine as Slate's finger traced the line of her lip. And infuriated at herself for her sensitivity to his touch, Trina snapped as she slapped away his hand, "Stop that!"

His grin broadening, Slate stepped back. "Okay, I can take a hint. 'Don't touch...I'm vulnerable....'"

"Slate...!"

"'And don't press, I'm touchy in the morning before I have my breakfast.'"

"Slate, you're impossible!" Unable to hold her anger, Trina felt her lips moving into a smile. "And if you want to add a third point to your list, it should be, 'And don't waste my time talking when I'm hungry.'"

"I thought love was supposed to make you lose your appetite."

"Well, then I guess that statement should tell you something."

"I should've quit while I was ahead." Slipping his arm around her shoulders with a small laugh, Slate urged her toward the table. "All right, let's eat. And then you can tell me how you want us to spend the rest of the day."

Stopping suddenly in her tracks, Trina frowned at him. "I don't know how *you* intend to spend the day, Slate, but I'm going to work on my car."

"All right, *we'll* work on your car."

"No, thanks...private property. Only *these* hands touch that engine."

"So, I'll work on the rear end. I want to check your coil springs. Your car seemed a little loose in the corners."

Trina's frown slipped into a look of incredulity. "You notice everything, don't you?"

"Trina, when it comes to you, nothing escapes my attention." Lowering his head, Slate pressed a light kiss against her slightly parted lips, a flicker of a warmer emotion moving across his face as he continued quietly, "But I warn you, I'll only give you the benefit of my expertise this morning if you agree to do what I want to do in the afternoon."

Her eyes moved warily on his. Trina asked cautiously, "And may I ask you what it is that you want to do?"

"What I want to do, or what I'll settle for?"

A flicker of a smile moved across Trina's lips. "What you'll settle for."

"I want to go to the computer show at the Coliseum."

"The computer show!"

"Right. I have to buy a few computerized machines and I thought I'd get a look at what's new in the field. Why, what did you think I'd suggest?"

Not willing to touch that leading question with a ten-foot pole, Trina shook her head. "Oh, nothing...nothing...really! That sounds like fun. Maybe I can learn something. It's a deal."

"Want to seal our deal with a kiss?"

"Slate..."

"All right, all right..."

"WELL, ONE MYSTERY is solved, anyway."

They had spent the morning working on Trina's car, and a long afternoon at a very educational computer show. Presently they were seated in a large, round booth in a dimly lit Chinese restaurant. They had already eaten a delicious meal, and Trina had consumed most of her Mai Tai. She was feeling quite mellow. She lifted her eyes to his amused expression and gave the inevitable response.

"What mystery is solved?"

"The reason Tom Harper called you 'Doc' at the track that first day..." He shook his head with a small laugh. "Surgical gloves when you work on your car. I wondered why you don't have grease under your fingernails like the rest of the drivers."

"Yes, some of the guys still find my gloves pretty funny, but I'm so accustomed to wearing them..."

"I don't blame you, sweetheart. Your hands are too beautiful to spoil..."

Somehow, Slate's remark struck a nerve and Trina retorted sharply, "I'm not ashamed of a little grease, Slate. The only problem is that I have to earn a living, and Ingrid would frown on an employee with less than presentable hands. Besides, the habit of years is hard to break. My dad wouldn't allow me to work in the garage unless I wore gloves. He said my mother always had well-tended hands...that she wouldn't have approved of a daughter who had a grease monkey's hands."

Slate's smile softened as the picture of the young Trina working beside her father and brother in the garage flashed across his mind. A new tenderness flushed his senses. They had spent the whole day together, and this was the first thing Trina had told him about her personal life. She was so cagey, unwilling to open up to him. He was going to have to take it slow if he expected to get past a few smiles and lightly traded quips to the real Trina Mallory. And he was determined he would.

"It must be pretty difficult supporting a sportsman car on the salary you make as a salesperson."

"Salesperson and manager, remember? I also do her books and...other things..."

"Other things?"

"Yes...well, I occasionally model in her shows."

Trina could not help but laugh at the spontaneous raising of Slate's brow. "Okay...I concede the point.

I'm the last person in the world you'd expect to see as a model."

"Not because you don't have the right equipment, Trina, believe me. It's just that I can't quite imagine you flouncing around a runway..."

"I don't exactly flounce...but I get the picture. Anyway, I don't enjoy it much, but it's extra money and it's convenient. We have another show this week, and I'm..." What was she doing? The drink must have been more potent than she had thought. She was talking too much.

"What do you model, Trina?"

"Whatever Ingrid asks me to model." Beginning to feel an edge of impatience, Trina snapped, "What is this, twenty questions?"

His smile stiffening, Slate shook his head. "What's the matter, getting too close?"

"I don't know what you're talking about." Registering that he was sharp...much too sharp, Trina smiled unexpectedly. "Well, in any case, now it's your turn. What exactly is Wright-Montgomery Precision Tooling?"

His eyes showed that he was fully conscious of her ploy. He responded agreeably, "Don't tell me there are still some things you haven't heard in the scuttlebutt around the track?"

"A few."

"Well then, listen closely and I'll tell you my life story."

Raising her eyes heavenward with mock horror, she shook her head, "Please...you don't have to go that far."

"You asked for it, so here it is. I was born of poor but loving parents in Englishtown, New Jersey. I was an only child. Now doesn't that make you feel sorry for me right away?"

"Not really."

"It figures. Anyway, my parents managed to send me to college on the meager earnings from their farm...."

"Oh, come on, Slate, be serious."

"I am being serious. What's so surprising about my being raised on a farm?"

Unwilling to respond that his rather sophisticated charm and his obvious success at such an early age did not go with the farm-boy image he was projecting, Trina just shook her head. "Nothing I guess. Go on."

Slate continued determinedly, "As a matter of fact, the farm is where I got my first experience with engines and machinery. In any case, I worked my way through college in my uncle's machine shop. I had a real talent, or so my uncle said, and if it hadn't been for my parents, I'm sure I would've quit college and gone to work full-time for my uncle. I liked that work very much. In any case, I got my degree instead...Business Administration...only to find out when I graduated that I wasn't the type who wanted to join the quest for the top rung on the corporate ladder. I went back to work for my uncle...sort of took over for him when he began to think of retiring.

"I ran into Dave Wright, my present partner, about that time, and when my uncle decided to retire, we managed to scrape up enough to buy out his business. So, here I am, at age thirty-four, part owner of Wright-Montgomery Precision Tooling, and for some reason the prime subject of the scuttlebutt at Middlevale Raceway."

Trina shook her head. Everything he had told her confirmed her earlier assessment of him. His interest in racing was obviously only temporary...a hobby. He probably used it as a write-off for his income tax. His interest would doubtless fade in a few years, while in a few years, she would just be working her way to the top....

"Why do I get the impression that you're less than impressed with my financial success?"

"I don't know...why do you? Where are your parents now, Slate?"

"Oh, they sold out the farm a few years ago. Dad was getting a little too old to work it, and the developers were hot on his trail for the property. At present my parents are living in a new condominium in Florida and, the last I heard, are just loving it."

"And it's a happy ending for all..."

Shaking his head to negate her statement, Slate responded soberly, "Well, I wouldn't say I was very happy last night. And I can tell you truthfully, Trina, it would've been very easy for you to make me happy...."

Momentarily mesmerized by the softness that had pervaded his gaze, Trina took a firm hold on her self-control. Pulling herself into a stiff sitting position, she responded with a soberness of her own, "Look, Slate, I have the feeling...have had it from the beginning, that we're approaching life from different angles right now. I have only one goal in mind...racing. You can laugh if you want, but I'm going on to the Grand National. Buck and I are going to make it together. I was sidetracked once, and I don't intend to allow it to happen again."

"'Sidetracked once'?"

Ignoring his inquiry, Trina continued, "And I don't think you'd like playing second fiddle to racing."

"Trina, honey, I don't know what you think I want, but I *don't* want to take over your life. I just want to be with you. I like being with you...touching you. I like the way you feel in my arms, and when I make love to you..."

The arrival of the waiter gave her the opportunity to break free of the spell Slate was creating with his words and Trina directed her eyes to the new drinks he placed on the table. But her respite was only temporary as Slate's hand closed warmly over hers, drawing her eyes back to his. Noting her reluctance, he shook his head.

"All right, Trina. I can see you're getting uncomfortable. We won't talk about it anymore right now. Tell me more about your modeling."

"I don't really care to discuss it."

"Do you do calendars...?"

"Slate, are you trying to get me mad?"

"Yes..."

Bursting into a laugh at his unexpected response, Trina felt the weight of the moment slipping away. "Well, you almost succeeded!"

Slate's eyes moved appreciatively over her broad smile. He prompted, "Almost?"

"Temporarily, only. I'm not mad anymore."

His arm moved to slip around her waist as he whispered in a soft voice, "I'm glad, Trina...I'm very glad of that...."

IT WAS LATE. They had finished their dinner at the Chinese restaurant and had spent a few more hours at the bar before returning home. Trina walked up the front walk, aware that Slate was close behind her. She was on the front step withdrawing the keys from her pocketbook when Slate took them from her hand. He unlocked the door without a word and turned toward her.

"Well, good night, Slate. It was nice."

Taking her into his arms, Slate fit her comfortably against his long body. "Too nice to end the night here, Trina. Aren't you going to ask me in?"

"No."

Suddenly frowning, he lowered his head to press a light kiss against her mouth. His voice was low, insistent. "Yes, Trina." He kissed her again, this time lingeringly. His mouth separated her lips, his tongue darting inside to caress hers.

Her reaction was immediate, acute. Trina could feel her thoughts beginning to blur as desire began to threaten her control. She would not submit to the heady languor that began to assail her. Somehow she could not...could not...

"No, Slate, please..."

Managing to pull free of his kiss, intimately aware of the swell of his passion as his body remained pressed tightly to hers, she continued quietly, "I'm sorry, Slate. I...I told you how I feel. I don't want to slip into something I'm not ready for."

"Trina, why can't you believe me when I tell you I don't want to control you. I just want to hold you in my arms...make love to you..."

"I'm sorry, Slate. Please let me go."

Slate's face was in the shadow of the streetlight at his back. She was unable to see the expression her unyielding tone had summoned and was aware only of a spontaneous stiffening of his frame.

"You're sure you want me to go, Trina? I promised you I wouldn't push you...I'd wait until you were ready...damned stupid promise it was...but I'll stand by it if you're sure."

"Slate, please go. I don't want to wake up tomorrow morning full of regrets."

"I wouldn't give you cause for regrets...only cause for remembering."

"Slate, please..."

"Okay. It'll be your way, Trina. I'll pick you up tomorrow—"

"No, I'm busy tomorrow."

"Tuesday..."

"I have a lot of things to do this week, Slate. I'm going to be busy every night until the show on Thursday."

"Friday, then. All the hassle will be over and we can..."

"I have another appointment Friday."

"Another appointment? You mean a date?"

Beginning to feel annoyed at the tone that was creeping into his voice, and his unrelenting persistence, Trina responded tartly, "Anything you want to call it. But I have to go in now."

Slate pulled her more tightly against him. It was obvious he wasn't ready to release her yet. His one arm formed a tight band around her waist. He raised his other hand to her cheek, cupping it as his thumb caressed her chin...her lips. His mouth was pressed into a straight, hard line.

"I'll call you tomorrow. Or should I request an appointment to do that?"

"You needn't bother calling..."

Reacting sharply to her casual dismissal, Slate snapped, "All right, damn it, I won't call. Forget what I said. Forget everything but this."

There was a deep hunger in Slate's kiss as his lips seared into hers. All but consuming her, he ravaged her mouth with his kiss, his tongue fondling and caressing, relentless in its quest as it delved into the intimate sweetness of her mouth. His hand slipped into the black silk of her hair, his fingers wrapping tightly around the fragrant ringlets. His other hand slipped down to cup her rounded buttocks, crushing her against the full rise of his passion.

Drowning in the flood of emotions his kiss elicited, Trina was startled as Slate suddenly pulled his mouth from hers, forcefully separating himself from the clinging warmth of her body.

There was a tinge of anger in his voice as he whispered hoarsely, "Remember that, when you're too busy to see me this week, Trina. I know I will...."

Turning away without another word, Slate strode down the walk toward his car. Watching him for only a few seconds, Trina turned and pushed open the front door. Closing it behind her, she hesitated, her eyes going to the small window to peer out as his headlights snapped on and he pulled away from the curb.

HER CAR'S POWERFUL ENGINE roared in the limited space of the garage, but Trina was immune to the sound. Her head tucked down into the engine, she carefully adjusted the distributor as she held the timing light steady in her other hand. She had been reassessing the engine's efficiency for two days, realizing she could not afford even one weekend of poor performance.

Trina was a bit disgusted with herself. Her concentration was off, affecting her work, and this was the second time she was attempting to adjust the timing without success. The telephone had been amazingly silent for the past two days, and she was annoyed with the fact that her ears strained for the sound even as she worked.

It was just as well Slate hadn't called. As a matter of fact she was glad he apparently had given the matter some thought and was following her suggestion. She had put the check for the tires into an envelope that afternoon and mailed it to him at Wright-Montgomery Precision Tooling. He would probably get more angry with her than he had been on Sunday night. But she was not about to let him pay for her tires and that was all there was to it!

Pushing Slate firmly from her mind, Trina attempted to concentrate on the engine. The time available to devote to her car this week was limited. Ingrid needed her at the boutique on Wednesday to prepare for the show the following night, and she had a long-standing date with Monica this Friday, which she could not cancel in all good conscience.

She had not been able to turn down Ingrid's invitation to model this week. The selection of summer clothes that had arrived in the store was glorious. Pierre's Restaurant had arranged to celebrate the boutique's fifth anniversary with a showing of Ingrid's new line of French swimwear along with a complete range of summer clothing. Ingrid needed her help and she definitely could use the money.

Trina squinted at the flickering light for a moment longer and shut it off.

"What's the matter? Losing your touch?"

Trina's head jerked up at the unexpected sound of Buck's voice. Still dressed in the khaki uniform he wore while driving his truck for Parker Shipping, he stood hesitantly at the door of the garage. A spontaneous smile flashed to her lips. Without hesitation she put down the timing light and, walking to his side, pressed a light kiss against his bearded cheek.

"Well, what's with you? I wasn't expecting to get a kiss out of that remark."

"I was wondering when you'd show up here again. I knew you wouldn't be able to stay away from your car much longer."

Buck's face suddenly turned serious. "I want to apologize for Sunday morning, Trina. I have to admit I wasn't too happy to see Slater Montgomery in your kitchen, looking like he had a long-term lease on the place. I have no right to tell you what to do, I know that. If you're determined to see Slater Montgomery—"

"It's not a problem, Buck. I don't expect you'll be seeing that much of him around here...."

Buck was instantly alert, his eyes intent on her face. "Why? What happened? If that guy gave you a problem—"

"No, no, no..." Shaking her head, Trina made an attempt at lightness. "It was nothing like that. I just told him I'm not interested in anything heavy. I think he got the message."

Surprisingly, there was no satisfaction in Buck's gaze as he looked down into his sister's level black eyes. "You're sure everything is all right...you're not unhappy...?"

"The only thing that's making me unhappy is my butterfingers tonight. I can't seem to get the timing straight. The engine just doesn't sound right."

Walking the few steps to the car, Buck looked down into the engine. He picked up the timing light and bent over the side. Throwing a quick glance over his shoulder he winked. "The old master will take care of it."

"The old master?" Trina mumbled loudly enough for Buck's benefit as she bent over the side of the car beside him, "Now I've heard it all..."

But Trina was immensely relieved to see her brother again. Now if she could only make herself stop straining to hear the phone....

SLATE STRODE into his modern office in Wright-Montgomery and closed the door behind him with a firmness that was close to a slam. He walked over to the bathroom door and jerked it open, stalking immediately to the sink in the modest gray-and-white tiled room. His custom-tailored white shirt was rolled up to his elbows, and his raw silk tie had a motor oil spot on it. He had spent the entire morning going over the parts that were needed for the Space Agency contract they were presently working on. The new computerized machine that had been delivered the day before would certainly make the job easier if he could ever get it set up right!

The slamming of his office door interrupted his train of thought, and he snapped his head up to Dave Wright's agitated face as he appeared in the doorway to the room.

"What the hell is the matter with you today?" Dave asked, glaring at Slate. Dave's dark face was flushed with agitation, horn-rimmed glasses sitting uneasily on the bridge of his well-defined nose.

"What do you mean, what the hell's the matter with me? That damned machine—"

"That damned machine is a beauty, and you know it! What happened to your patience? I've seen you work with a new machine for hours until you had mastered an intricate process. But today, after a half hour's work, you blow your top and stalk away like an outraged prima donna!"

"Damn it, Dave, the specifications were all messed up and the drawings were—"

"And you haven't had your mind on your work since the weekend. You've been walking around here like a bear with a sore paw, snapping at everyone, including me."

"Oh, come on, Dave, I haven't been that bad!"

"You haven't, have you? For your information, I had to talk Willa out of quitting yesterday."

"Willa? The only thing I did was point out her mistake in the promotional letter she had ready to send out."

"Slate, for God's sake, you embarrassed the poor girl, and then didn't even have the sense to realize you did it!"

"Oh!" Turning to wipe his hands, Slate shook his head. He certainly hadn't meant to hurt Willa's feelings. She was a nice person, even if she was a little slow. "I'll apologize to her today. I guess you're right, Dave. I've been a little preoccupied...."

"You're a little more than preoccupied. More like obsessed, I'd say! What's wrong? What happened this weekend? You did very well at the track...your car's in good shape, or so you told me. You're not sick. Wright-Montgomery isn't in financial danger. As a matter of fact, prospects are pretty good, so that leaves only one other thing. *Cherchez la femme.*"

"Dave, please, spare me your high-school French!"

"I'm right, though, aren't I? Charlie Spinnel saw you with a tall, good-looking brunette at the computer show."

"A tall, *beautiful* brunette."

"And he said you looked like it was all you could do to keep your hands off her."

"Hell, was I that obvious?"

"Well, maybe not to everybody, but to Charlie, yes. You know how he envies you your women."

"Dave, you make me sound like a real Don Juan. I'm not. I'm just—"

"A healthy American boy? Come off it, will you, Slate!" Not waiting for Slate's response, Dave continued with a broadening grin. "So you finally met someone who has you stymied...."

"Dave, if you don't mind, this is my own, personal business. I really don't care to discuss it."

"Slate, it's only your personal business if you leave it at home when you come here. When it interferes with our work..."

"All right, you don't have to elaborate. I get the message."

"So, what's up?"

Raising his brow, Slate directed a meaningful look into his friend's eyes, eliciting a loud, spontaneous guffaw.

"I mean, besides that."

"I told you, you're not going to get anything out of me, Dave. I agree with what you've said. I shouldn't bring my rotten disposition into the office. I won't inflict it on anyone here any longer, but that doesn't mean you're going to get an earful. You married guys are all alike...living vicariously on a bachelor's imagined lovelife."

"Imagined?"

"Believe me, it's not all that great being single. You don't know how good you have it with Linda and the kids. As a matter of fact, there are times when I envy you myself."

"Oh, this has to be one for the books. Tell me something, Slate. Are you the same guy who was telling me a couple of weeks ago that marriage just wasn't your speed...that you had too many good years ahead of you to tie yourself down to one woman?"

"Did I say that?"

"Don't get cute, Slate."

"Don't get nosy, Dave."

Stopped by Slate's quick response, Dave finally smiled and shrugged his rounded shoulders. "So I guess it's time for me to say, 'I get the message.' But hell, Slate, you spoil all a guy's fun!"

Unable to resist a smile, Slate shook his head. "Dave, don't you have something to do this morning?"

"I told you, I get the message! I'm going back to that machine to try to figure it out. When you've regained your patience, I expect you'll join me." Waiting a few minutes for a response that didn't come, Dave gave a small smile. "Oh, Slate, I forgot to tell you. You have a spot on your tie."

Turning, Dave walked away without another word. Watching as the door closed behind him, Slate suppressed a rueful laugh. The curiosity was killing Dave. Everybody in the place thought he was a real threat with the ladies. Come to think of it, he usually was. This time he really laughed, but it was at himself. A real killer with the ladies, and when he finally found the one who knocked him for a loop, she didn't want anything to do with him. Damn it!

He stalked back to the old mahogany desk in the center of the otherwise modern office. It was the only personal office furniture he had taken from his uncle's old building when Dave and he had decided to relocate the company. Somehow the old desk at which Uncle Mike had sat for so many years had assumed an importance in his mind that was an exaggeration of its actual value. But to him it represented the best of what the company had been, and was significant of the growth it would see. He had long ago decided that he would never part with it.

His mind wandered to a familiar dark-eyed image. He had deliberately refrained from calling Trina. She had made it clear that she hadn't wanted to hear from him. He didn't *want* to call. It only took him a few seconds to shake his head in silent refutation of the thought. Who was he kidding? He hadn't been able to shake Trina Mallory from his mind for more than the space of a second since he had first met her. Dave was right. He *was* obsessed.

Slate absentmindedly flipped back the cover of the mail folder that sat in the middle of his desk. His attention was caught by the vaguely familiar writing on the letter lying on top. There was a check attached to the front of it. He picked it up, his eyes darting to the signature and then to the amount. What the hell! Five hundred dollars from Trina! Damn! He had told her he didn't want that money!

Well, that did it! He'd call her right now. He felt a momentary flush of frustration. Why hadn't he asked her the exact location of the boutique where she worked...and the phone number? Now he had to wait until she came home tonight to talk to her. If she came home. It was Thursday. The "show" was tonight, and he had no idea what her usual routine was. He looked at his watch. It was only eleven o'clock. It was going to be a long day.

Running a hand through his heavy blond hair in frustration, Slate shrugged his shoulders. Well, he might as well go out and give that machine another try. Maybe he'd be able to get his mind off...oh, hell!

Striding angrily toward his office door, Slate paused momentarily with his hand on the knob. Affixing a stiff smile on his face, strictly for Dave's benefit, he opened the door and stepped out into the hall.

IT WAS THURSDAY and Trina was late. Where she had lost the time, she had no idea, but she had promised to meet Ingrid at the restaurant at seven. The show didn't start until seven-thirty, but there were so many things to do... It was six-thirty already and she was a half hour's drive from Pierre's.

Snatching up her bag, Trina made a quick dash for the front door and jerked it open, only to gasp at the unexpected figure standing in the doorway.

"Slate! What are you doing here?"

"I've been asking myself the same question since I pulled up in front of your house." Slate's reply was automatic as his eyes moved critically over her appearance. He frowned. "You're ready to leave?"

"Yes, I am. As a matter of fact I'm late...."

Pulling the door shut behind her, Trina attempted to brush past Slate when his broad hand reached out to stay her in her flight. She darted a quick glance up toward his face. He was frowning.

"I got your check."

"Good."

"I think I told you I didn't want that money."

"And I think I told you I don't pay for my equipment with my body."

Wincing at her reminder of their conversation that had inspired her response, Slate shook his head. "You didn't need to remind me of that...and you know I didn't really mean it the way it sounded."

"Slate, I really am late."

"I'll drive you to wherever you're going."

"No, Slate. I'll be late in coming home and I'll need transportation. The show usually takes a couple of hours."

A smile flashed across his lips. "I don't mind waiting. Besides, I've never seen you 'work' a show before."

Trina hesitated, her eyes flashing to the light shirt and slacks he wore. "You're not wearing a jacket, Slate. You can't get into the restaurant without one."

"I have a jacket in the back of my car."

"Talk about being prepared." Considering him for a moment longer, Trina added, "Well, if you don't mind waiting..."

Taking her arm without another word, Slate began moving her down the steps. At her startled expression, he offered lightly, "Well, you did say you're late."

SEATED ON A STOOL, his back to the bar, Slate raised his glass to his lips. His eyes were glued to the small platform in the middle of the large, well-lit main room of Pierre's restaurant. Ingrid was in place at the microphone on one side of the platform. The first models had already entered and had taken a basic turn on the platform before circulating among the tables and exiting on the other side of the room. The show seemed to be well received by the diners, especially a few women among them who made a point of calling some of the models over to their tables for closer inspection of the garments.

But he was growing impatient. He had no interest in fashion or the tall, shapeless women who modeled the stylish clothes. In truth, he could not understand what Trina was doing among them. She was too vibrant, too alive. She would stand out among them like a...

Suddenly she was there, on the platform, and Slate took a deep breath. Unconsciously leaving his stool, he walked to the edge of the dining area. Ingrid's softly accented voice bubbled lightly as Trina stood motionless for a few long moments in the center of the platform. Slate swallowed hard, his eyes moving over her slender, willowy proportions in a brilliant gold gauze pants dress that set off her dramatic coloring to perfection. The neckline was off the shoulder, exposing the gentle curves of her shoulders and the slender column of her neck; the puffed and gathered sleeves ended just above the elbow. The bodice of the overblouse was loose, caught in at the waist with a wide orange belt that emphasized her slimness. The pants were full, in almost a harem style, gathered tightly at the ankle and allowing just a faint outline of the long slender legs beneath. On her feet she wore straw wedged shoes, and on her head a large straw hat, which she swept off theatrically as she tossed her long, gleaming black ringlets and stepped off the platform to move between the tables. She was beautiful, sensually appealing while appearing warm and innocent at the same time. Irresistible...

Unable to take his eyes from Trina as she made her winding way toward the exit, Slate raised his glass to his lips again. Trina was having a difficult time escaping the many requests for a closer inspection, and he felt a small smile move across his lips. She was smiling pleasantly, answering the questions in a perfectly professional way, but he knew she was smarting inside. There was a light in her eye, a particular twist to her lips as she talked, which revealed to him her distaste, although he was certain that no one else in the room would suspect her true feelings.

He was beginning to be amused by the manner in which her departure from the floor was delayed, until Trina was called to the table of a large group. All five couples were well dressed and obviously accustomed to being catered to. It was not the elegantly coiffed woman asking Trina the questions who caught Slate's eye, but the dark-haired, well built man seated beside her. He felt himself stiffening at the intimate manner in which the man's eyes moved over Trina and his comment that caused Trina to turn in his direction and flash him a quick, surprisingly warm smile.

An emotion Slate did not care to name flared within him, and he took another sip of his drink. The dark-haired man made a few other comments, straining Slate's patience to the extreme before he allowed her to leave the table. Slate followed Trina's figure until she left the floor, experiencing a sense of relief as she disappeared behind the partition. He was going to have to learn to deal with this a little better in the future.

A few minutes later, Slate was beginning to perspire. Swimsuits...the models who had preceded Trina had paraded one after another in exotically styled swimsuits. If he wasn't mistaken, Trina would be next. As if summoned by his thoughts, Trina appeared on the platform in a long leisure gown in a startling red jungle print. Strapless, it was draped casually to the side, the skirt of the gown straight and slit high in the leg when she walked. She wore a wide gold bracelet high on her upper arm and a matching band around her narrow ankle. But in one swoop the long skirt was gone, revealing the one-piece bathing suit, which had served as the bodice of the gown. Gasps echoed through the room as Trina moved across the stage. The leg openings of the suit were cut in the French style, high on the hip, extending the length of already long, exceedingly beautiful legs, so that half the audience was left breathless and the other half was green with envy.

Trina stepped down onto the floor of the room and began making her way among the tables. As she walked she gracefully fastened the skirt back over the suit, and Slate unconsciously let out his breath. Once again she found it extremely difficult to leave the floor, and Slate found himself getting annoyed by the same people who had amused him only a few moments before.

Trina was nearing the side of the room, and Slate tensed as she was called over to that same large party who had called her the previous time. This time it was the dark-haired man who motioned her toward them and spoke to her for a few moments. With an obliging smile, Trina removed the skirt of the ensemble once again and turned for their inspection. Slate felt a slow flush suffuse his face. But Trina was smiling...really smiling as the fellow spoke again, and Slate felt a stab of anger. Turning away, Slate walked back to the bar.

Slate had ordered another drink and had taken a large swallow, when the ridiculousness of his surly reaction hit him for the first time. For a moment he was incredulous. He was jealous! He had never had a jealous moment in his life before this...but he had never felt this way about a woman before...and had his feelings unreciprocated. Damned if he wasn't going to have to learn to handle this new, startling facet of his personality. If he knew anything at all, he knew Trina would never stand for it.

The remainder of the show dragged on as Slate mentally groaned his way through Trina's afternoon wear, active wear and evening wear. He thought he had borne it all when the first model arrived on the platform in a negligee. He had begun to realize that Ingrid was well aware of Trina's effect on the spectators and capitalized on her most impressive styles by having Trina model them. But he was anything but prepared for the effect Trina achieved in the black filmy creation in which she now arrived on stage. Unfastened in the front, a sheer, voluminous black peignoir streamed back behind her as she walked, her slender, graceful arms outlined vaguely through the diaphanous, billowing sheeves. The black satin gown beneath was simply cut, and molded itself in a slim sheath against her body. Narrow straps held the bodice on her slender shoulders as it dipped deeply into the bosom to reveal the swell of small, rounded breasts. The soft flair of the skirt clung to the smooth line of her hips, thighs and firm buttocks. On her feet she wore high-heeled black satin slippers, and in her hand she carried a single, long-stemmed red rose.

Overwhelmed by the sight of her, Slate was unable to turn his head as Trina again moved between the tables. Tensing as Trina was again called to the large table at the side of the room, Slate watched as the dark-haired man stood up and taking her hand, kissed it gallantly. Trina remained to talk to the man for a few seconds longer. She seemed to have no inclination to move away, and unable to stand any more of his fawning, Slate again turned back to the bar. Damn...she was driving him crazy....

ALLOWING HER HEAD to fall back against the headrest, Trina closed her eyes. She was exhausted. It had been a long day, and an even longer evening. The show had gone well, and she was extremely happy for Ingrid. It also looked as if the outfits she had worn had received a lot of notice. All the better. She could use every cent she got right now. She did not intend to let this year pass without winning the sportsman championship, and if it meant sinking every penny she could spare into her car, she would do it.

A warm hand moved to cover hers, and Trina opened her eyes to Slate's quick glance as he moved his car cautiously through the darkened streets.

"Tired, Trina?"

"Very."

"Too tired to stop for a drink?"

Trina glanced at her watch, hoping to stall for time. She was really too tired, but after making him wait three hours, she certainly could not have Slate drive her directly home and say good-night. And she definitely did not want to invite him in. No... She had found out the hard way that once she was in his arms, all her resolutions seemed to slip by the board.

"It's only ten o'clock. All right, Slate."

Giving her hand a tight squeeze before releasing it, Slate nodded.

"These shows take a lot out of you, don't they, Trina?"

"I suppose... But the truth is, Ingrid's shows have pulled me out of the financial barrel too many times for me not to be grateful for them. And there are times when I actually enjoy some of the people I meet at these affairs."

"You mean like that dark-haired guy with that party at the side table...?"

Shooting a quick look in his direction, she nodded. "Yes, him and others..."

Unable to prevent the appearance of the green-eyed monster, Slate offered lightly, "What did he say to you, by the way? Whatever it was, he had you grinning from ear to ear."

"I think you're overstating that a bit."

"Maybe, but the guy seemed to have a real efficient line."

"Possibly..."

Inexplicably annoyed by Slate's line of conversation, Trina pulled herself up straight in the seat as Slate glanced toward her once again.

The stiffness of her movement did not go unnoticed by Slate. Giving himself a hard mental kick, he took a deep breath.

"Annoyed?"

"That's a stupid question! Do I look annoyed?"

"Yes."

"Well?"

A small smile began to move across Slate's lips. "Well, you won't be annoyed for long."

Turning toward him with a raised brow, Trina questioned warily, "And why won't I be annoyed with you for long?"

"Because I'm going to charm you out of it."

A smile began to move across her lips despite herself. Her stiffness was receding. "You're so sure...?"

"Of course."

Flashing her a quick smile, Slate made an abrupt turn of the wheel and urged his Porsche into the parking lot of a brightly lit bar. He pulled to a stop and turned toward her. The direct look he sent into her eyes succeeded in sending little chills down Trina's spine even in the dim light of the car.

"Going to give me a fair chance to succeed, honey?"

Trina mentally shook her head. She could feel the warmth of his smile down to her toes. He was already succeeding....

"Maybe..."

"All I ask is a fair chance."

Not waiting for her reply, Slate got out of the car and walked around to Trina's side. He opened the door and pulled Trina gently to her feet beside him. Hesitating, he looked down into her face while a thousand emotions chased across Trina's mind. Curving his arm around her waist, he guided her toward the entrance to the bar.

Slate spotted a table in the corner, and urged her toward it. The dim lights and soft music were soothing...too soothing, almost akin to a lullaby. They were seated and their drinks had been ordered when Trina realized Slate's eyes were trained on her face.

"You're ready to fall asleep, aren't you?"

Trina gave a small laugh and nodded her head. "Does it show that much? I must be slipping."

"No, I'm the one who must be slipping..."

A small laugh escaped Trina's lips. "Could it be that the great Slater Montgomery is capable of a few self-doubts?"

Contrary to her expectations, Slate didn't laugh. Instead, he took her hands in his across the small table, his expression serious. "Is that really the way you see me, Trina?"

Startled by his question, Trina responded as honestly as she dared. "I think you have a high opinion of yourself, Slate, and I'd be the last to say it's undeserved."

"Would you? If that's true, why do I get the feeling that the more I try to get close to you, the more you try to slip away?" Raising his hand to touch her face with a disturbing tenderness, he continued softly, "And I don't intend to let you slip away." Leaning forward, Slate pressed a light kiss against her parted lips.

The brief contact affected her more deeply than she dared admit even to herself, and Trina felt a nudge of panic. "Don't try to take advantage of my less than fully conscious state, Slate."

"How many times do I have to tell you that I'm not trying to take advantage of you, Trina? I have a far different purpose in mind."

"Maybe that's what worries me."

"Damn it, Trina, you..."

The arrival of the drinks cut short Slate's response. Reaching for his glass, Slate took a deep swallow. Putting the glass back down, Slate reached across the table and cupped her face in his hands, the peculiar light in his brilliant eyes making her heart do a little flip-flop in her chest.

"You don't trust me, do you, Trina?"

Returning his gaze, Trina whispered, "Maybe it's just that I don't quite trust myself..."

The silence that followed her remark was broken by Slate's gruff "Let's get out of here."

Paying no attention to the fact that Trina's drink stood before her untouched, Slate pulled her out from behind the small table and to her feet. His arm was firm around her waist as he guided her back toward the door they had entered only a short time before. They had not gotten more than a few steps into the parking lot when Slate pulled Trina into a shadow and into his arms. Within moments, his mouth was on hers.

The sweet warmth that had haunted her all week long again pervaded her senses. His heady maleness pressed tight against her, his obvious arousal answering her unspoken need, Trina separated her lips under Slate's kiss. The sweet plunder that followed eliminated the last of her reserve. Raising her arms around his neck she returned the warmth of his embrace. When finally Slate tore his mouth from hers, they were both trembling.

Reluctant to release her, Slate whispered against the soft lips that moved warmly against his, "I've wanted to do that from the first minute I saw you this evening, but I thought it would be best to take it slow..."

His hand was moving sensuously in her hair when Slate pulled himself away from her abruptly. "Come on, I'm going to take you home."

Pressing a light kiss on her mouth, Slate drew her with him toward the car.

Within all too short a time, to Trina, they were in front of her house. Experiencing a familiar quaking inside as they approached the front door, Trina took a deep breath. Withdrawing her key from her bag, she resisted as Slate attempted to take it from her hand.

"No, Slate. I...I think it would be better if you leave now."

"Leave...?"

"Slate, you wanted to take me to the show. You did, and I appreciate it. But I didn't make any other commitment with you. Nothing has changed as far as I'm concerned, Slate." At his disbelieving expression, she admitted openly, "I don't deny the fact that you affect me, Slate. I'd have to be a fool to deny it. And it would be easy...only too easy to let you come in with me tonight. But I don't want this now, do you understand?"

"No, I can't honestly say I do. I only know that I want you, and you want me. That should eliminate any other problem between us."

"But it doesn't. I'm sorry, Slate."

Slate's face stiffened as he began to speak. "So, it's a replay of last weekend." His need for Trina ached inside him. Slate swallowed visibly. Finally, with a small shrug of his shoulders, he continued soberly, "Well, if that's the way you want it, Trina, I suppose that's the way it's going to be. I told you before that I wasn't going to push you. But let me give you fair warning. Don't expect me to give up. If that's your tactic, it's doomed to failure." His voice dropped to a softer, richer tone as he whispered, "Damn it, Trina, I couldn't give you up now, even if I tried."

Looking up into Slate's shadowed face, seeing the faint gleam of hope that still shone in his eyes, knowing at that moment she wanted more than anything else in the world for Slate to take her into his arms, Trina was tempted...oh, so very tempted.... Drawing on the last reserve left in her body, she took a deep breath and stepped back. With her voice hoarse, she managed a soft, adequate reply. "Good night, Slate."

Slate whispered, his hands slowly dropping to his sides, "I don't want to leave you tonight, Trina." After lowering his head to touch her lips lightly with his, he drew away quickly. "Good night. Now get inside so I know you're safe before I leave."

Following his instructions without response, Trina stepped inside and closed the door, her ears intent on the sound of Slate's footsteps as they headed down the front walk toward his car. It was not until she heard his car leave that Trina released her breath and went silently to her room.

CHAPTER SIX

TRINA WALKED UP the slate walkway toward her front door, her step heavy. Friday.... Friday was no night to have gone out on the town with Monica, especially when "out on the town" had meant going out to dinner straight from work, a long night of shopping and gabbing and a final quiet hour over a few cups of coffee. The last hour had been relaxing, proving more effective than a sedative. All of her concentration had been needed to drive home without falling asleep at the wheel. The whole week had been long and exasperating, and as much as she enjoyed Monica's company, she was glad to see the night come to an end.

Trina adamantly refused to admit to herself that a good part of her restlessness had been due to the long, sleepless night she had spent after Slate's departure the night before and the fact that his face kept reappearing in her mind throughout her conversations with Monica. She slid her key into the front door lock with a deep sigh of relief. She hadn't been very successful convincing Monica that nothing was on her mind. As a matter of fact, she was certain that soon she would be getting a call from her very dear but nosy friend, who would again try to pump her for information.

Dumping her purse on the table near the door with a small frown, Trina shook her head. She simply would not allow herself to call Slate's image to mind. She was all too embarrassingly aware that last night her hold on her emotions had been tenuous at best...that it had been he, not she, who had taken the final parting step.

Trina had just started for the bedroom when the sudden shrill ring of the telephone stopped her in her tracks. It was eleven-thirty. Who could be calling at this time of night?

A niggle of apprehension slipped down her spine as Trina picked up the receiver. Her "hello" was answered by a deep familiar tone.

"Trina?" The strained impatience in Slate's voice was evident as he paused briefly. "I've been calling you since ten o'clock..."

"Oh, have you?"

There was another short pause. "Did you have a good time tonight?"

"Moderately good. I was really too tired to expend the energy needed to really enjoy myself."

The pause this time was shorter. "What's that supposed to mean?"

Startled at his sharpness, Trina responded tightly, "Take it whatever way you want, Slate, but I'm tired. What did you call me for?"

"Does there have to be a reason?"

"There usually is."

"I called you because I wanted to be with you tonight, and this was the next best thing."

Steeling herself against the purring need in his voice, Trina fought for her composure. "Well, it was impossible, I'm afraid. Slate, I'm tired. I'm going to bed."

The silence at the other end of the line was profound. Trina muttered impatiently, "Good night, Slate."

"Trina..."

"Yes, what is it?"

"Try to get to the track a little early tomorrow. I'd like to have a few moments with you before we get busy on our cars."

"As a matter of fact I'm going to be a little late getting to the track tomorrow. I have to stop to pick up some parts I ordered at the speed shop on the way."

There was another pregnant silence, then Slate's low, tight response. "That's right. First things first, Trina. We wouldn't want you to forget your priorities."

Refusing to acknowledge the sarcasm in his voice, Trina concurred, her voice stiff, "No. I don't intend to make that mistake.... Good night, Slate."

"Good night, Trina."

Trina replaced the phone on the cradle with a shaking hand and walked slowly toward her room. Damn, it was going to be another long night....

THE HEAT OF MIDAFTERNOON had turned the cab of her truck into a pressure cooker. She had been driving straight into the sun on her way to the track for almost two hours and she had just about had it. Oh, for the luxury of an air conditioner.

Well, she had been right. It *had* been a long night after Slate's call, and it promised to be a long day as a result. Trina was extremely irritated with herself. She had slept poorly and had needed sleep badly. The temperature and humidity were both high, adding to her physical distress. At her present rate of steam, she would be less than sharp on the track in a few hours when warm-ups began. Damn...damn that Slater Montgomery and his late-night calls!

Turning automatically into the pits behind her brother's trailer, Trina slowly followed his lead, finally coming to a halt at the far side of the pits. While refusing to allow herself to search the area for a familiar rig, Trina had still caught a glimpse of the blue and white 008 out of the corner of her eye as she had passed. So, Slate was here already. The races wouldn't start for another two hours.

Trina opened the door and stepped down from the cab of her truck, squinting against the glare. She was starting to get a headache already...a real throbber. She was reaching for her purse when Doug Frawley's voice sounded close beside her.

"I was hoping you'd get here early today, Trina. Did you see this?"

Doug held up a section of a local newspaper, from which her picture glared boldly. "You really hit the news with that wild drive of yours last week."

"It wasn't a wild drive, Doug, but let me see that."

Taking the paper with a smile, Trina raised her eyebrows at the sizable picture of herself and the caption underneath that read, Wild Ride Gets Trina Mallory Her First Win of the Season. The short article underneath contained the usual background information, and Trina smiled with a small shake of her head. "Trina Mallory, of the Mallory racing family...." *Dad would have been proud to know he had founded a racing dynasty....* The thought brought the heat of tears to her eyes for the briefest moment as she raised her gaze to Doug's smiling face.

"Thanks for letting me see this, Doug. You're a doll...." Taking a step closer toward him to press a friendly kiss on his cheek, Trina was startled when Doug turned his face to catch her kiss firmly on his mouth. The broad hand he slipped up to cup her head held her mouth against his far longer than she had intended.

Reluctantly releasing her, Doug flashed a quick smile toward the gaping pit crew.

"Don't you guys know when to make yourselves invisible?"

"Hell, no, Doug! It looked like you were having so much fun that we decided to watch!"

Unable to suppress the laugh that bubbled up to the surface at Bix's crack, Trina waved the paper she still held in her hand. "Well, I had to express my appreciaton for receiving a copy of my first bid for immortality...."

"What's that?"

Buck's deep inquiry interrupted the joking group as he walked toward them and took the paper from her hand. When his dark eyes moved back to hers a few minutes later, they were bright with amusement.

"So, little sister knocked them all for a loop with her fancy driving last weekend." The pride on his rough features sending a special warmth surging through her veins, Trina felt her smile broaden as Buck's arm reached around to squeeze her shoulders. "Well, they ain't seen nothin' yet, have they, honey?"

"That's right, Buck, because next week the headlines are going to read, Mallory and Mallory Take Both Feature Races!"

"Damned right!"

Buck's positive exclamation brought a round of laughter from the small group that surrounded them, and feeling warmed to the heart, Trina turned back to her car.

SLATE CONTINUED TO SQUINT in the direction of Trina's car, his teeth clamped together in irritation. Trina had already backed her car off the trailer and removed the hood. She was obviously preparing to work on the engine, and she hadn't done more than raise her head to send him a nod. But she had done more than nod to Doug Frawley. Slate was still seething inside. He had made a mistake last Thursday. It hadn't done him one damned bit of good when he had walked away from Trina at her front door, for all his noble intentions.

Slate became aware of Bob Mitchell's intense scrutiny, and he turned his head in his crew chief's direction.

"Do you want something, Bob?"

"No, but it's obvious *you* do!"

Bob's candor deepened Slate's frown. "If you don't mind, Bob, I'm not much in the mood for wisecracks right now."

"Well, if you don't want to hear a lot more comments like the one I just made, you're going to have to do something about the way you look at that babe. My advice would be to try to keep her guessing a little."

"The last thing I need right now is to make Trina Mallory suspect my motives."

"Well, you always kept them guessing before and seemed to do pretty well."

"Trina's not just any 'babe' to me. She's special."

"Oh, is she?"

Slate took a firm hold on his patience. "Are you trying to get under my skin, Bob? Because if you are, I want to tell you, you're succeeding."

"Touchy, aren't you?"

"Can't you do anything but ask questions this afternoon?"

Instead of responding, Bob merely shook his head, the glimmer of amusement in his eyes sending Slate's irritation up a few notches. "I never thought I'd see the day I'd have to offer *you* advice about women, Slate, but let me tell you something. It's obvious that that babe over there is giving you a hard time, and you're all tied up inside about her."

Slate's brow rose impatiently. "Oh, is it?"

"You're as transparent as glass."

"Bob..." Slate's low warning tone brought a quick addendum to Bob's statement.

"And as touchy as..."

"All right, you've made your point!"

"My advice would be to—"

Unable to get over the feeling that Bob was enjoying himself just a little too much, Slate responded tightly, "I think I've had enough of your advice, too." Shooting a quick glance toward the two men who were just rounding the side of his truck, beers in their hands, Slate bobbed his head in their direction. "I'll be back in a few minutes. Tell Chick and Henry not to disappear again. We'll start going over the car as soon as I get back."

"Don't be too long, Slate. We only have an hour and a half until warm-ups."

Pausing in midstride, Slate sent his poker-faced crew chief a quick grimace. "Smart ass."

Within seconds Slate was striding his way directly toward the pink and purple sportsman and the tall slender woman who was bent over its engine. He could not hear Bob's comment as Chick and Henry sauntered over to stand at his side.

"Well, boys, I think you're witnessing the end of a legend."

Exchanging looks as Bob continued to stare after Slate's rapidly moving figure, Henry and Chick came up blank.

"What are you talking about, Bob?"

"Nothin', Chick, nothin'."

Across the pits, Trina nodded appreciatively. Yes, the engine looked beautiful. She wouldn't have any problem there. Trina took a step backward, only to come up unexpectedly against a firm, unmoving body. She jerked around.

"Do you have to stand so close that I trip over..."

The words died in her throat as Trina's eyes touched on Slate's unsmiling expression. Doing her best to ignore the rapid acceleration of her heartbeat, Trina remarked casually, "Hello, Slate. I didn't expect to be tripping over you so early today."

"I don't know why you should be surprised. I told you I wanted to see you before the races."

"I have to do some work on my car, Slate."

"You had plenty of time to talk to Doug Frawley and a few of the others."

Trina chose to ignore his tone. "Did you see the local paper? I don't know where they got the picture, but I'm in a very prominent spot in living black and white...a real ego boost."

Slate nodded. "I'd like to see it."

"I'll ask Doug to show it to you." Trina made a move to turn away, only to be stayed by Slate's hand on her arm.

"Not now, Trina." Abruptly his expression softened. "You've been working on that car all week. You can spare a few minutes away from it for a while. Come on, walk with me."

"Walk where?"

"Let's go for coffee...that little coffee shop around the corner."

Appearing to consider it for a moment, Trina shook her head. "No, Slate. I don't want to take that much time."

"You have an hour and a half until warm-ups, Trina! Twenty minutes isn't going to make that much of a difference."

Slate's hand was firm on her arm when Buck appeared around the side of the car to shoot a quick glance between them. "Anything wrong, Trina?"

Immediately responding to the sharpness in Buck's tone, Trina smiled. "No, nothing's wrong. Slate was just suggesting that we go for coffee. I told him I didn't have time."

His eyes moving to Slate's hand where it still gripped Trina's arm, Buck raised his gaze slowly to Slate's face. "That answer sounds clear enough to me."

Making a quick assessment of a potentially dangerous situation, Trina added hastily, "Well, I don't know, Buck, maybe Slate's right. I could use a break and a bit of air conditioning right now. I've already checked out the engine and it looks great."

His eyes narrowing, Buck glanced back at Trina. "I thought you said you wanted to check the stagger and the tire pressure."

"Yes...well, I can do that when I come back."

Shrugging, Buck turned away.

Watching only until Buck had started back toward his car, Trina turned to Slate. "Okay, let's go."

A small smile flashed across Slate's lips as he urged her toward the pit gate. "Looks like I have something to thank Buck for."

Trina glanced up, her heart doing its usual dance as Slate's eyes moved warmly over her face. For a moment she was at a loss as to how she hadn't considered

Slate handsome the first time she had seen him. A golden boy...heavy golden hair, golden brown tan....virility and sex appeal almost irresistibly packaged in a six-foot-three-inch frame. Female heads turned predictably even when he was grease-covered. She was intensely uncomfortable with his effect on her senses.

Slate laughed. Slipping his arm around her shoulders, he hugged her to his side. "Come on, Trina. I'm buying you a cup of coffee, not hemlock."

Begrudgingly, Trina leaned into his casual embrace. "I really don't have time to—"

"But your brother stuck his two cents in and here you are."

"Sometimes it doesn't pay to have a big brother..."

Trina's low mumble broadened Slate's smile. "And sometimes it does."

A few minutes later, their gasps of relief were simultaneous as Trina and Slate stepped into the small coffee shop.

"Air conditioning...mmm..." Her eyes half closed with pleasure, Trina savored the sensation of the cool air against her skin.

"Now that's the kind of expression I'd like to see on your face when you see *me*."

At Slate's low-whispered comment Trina turned her head toward him with amusement. "You don't want much, do you?"

"No, just some plain down to earth devotion."

Choosing to ignore his remark, Trina turned in the direction Slate urged, realizing his intentions too late as he steered her toward a large round booth. He motioned for the coffee and slid in close beside her. His hand moved to her back to tangle in the hair at the base of her neck.

"You're perspiring. Your hair's damp."

Slate's eyes moved to the black, shiny curls in his hand. The humidity had tightened the ringlets into gleaming coils. The effect was glorious when Trina turned her great black eyes up to his, the long fringe of lashes touching her dark eyebrows.

Slate offered softly, "You haven't given me a proper 'hello' today, Trina. It's time to correct the oversight."

Before she had the chance to react to his statement, Slate had lowered his mouth to hers. With a subtle hunger, his lips moved gently against hers before Trina pulled herself free. She shot a quick glance around the almost deserted shop.

"There's a time and a place, Slate..."

"You're right, and it's here and now. We have some things to discuss..."

"Like what?"

"Like when we're going to—"

But Slate got no further before a booming voice interrupted.

"Well, what do you know! Look who's here!"

Recognizing Bill Watson's voice, Trina turned in its direction, grateful for the interruption. Bill, Tom Harper, Biff Martin and Doug Frawley were walking directly toward them. Trina was intensely aware of Doug's gaze as it shot between Slate and herself. Sensing Slate's annoyance, she responded warmly, "Hi, Bill! Just get to the track?"

"That's right, honey, and it was one hell of a ride up here today. My old truck doesn't have air conditioning. We looked for you in the pits. We wanted to rescue both you and Buck for a few minutes, but Buck said he was too busy with his car. You know what a hard-nose he is. He said he didn't know where you'd gone."

Sliding into the booth next to her with hesitation, Bill motioned for the rest of the boys to follow, not batting an eye as Slate mumbled irritably, "Oh, join us, by all means."

"Saw the spread on you in the paper, Trina. It was great! I bet now that our racing beauty queen has been discovered, you'll be all over the papers up here."

"Bill, you're an old flatterer! No wonder my dad always told me to 'watch out for that old boy.'"

Bill let out a hoot of laughter that was echoed by the others in the booth. "I don't know if he really said that, honey, but I know I'm watching out for you! If you win again today, you're going to bring the stands down! I wouldn't be surprised if they start selling pinup pictures of you pretty soon!"

"Yea...sure. I'm another Raquel Welch."

"Hell, Trina, you got her beat by far!"

"Whoa, there, Bill!" Trina could hardly contain her laughter. "Give me time to get my boots on! It's getting pretty deep!"

"Bill's right, Trina." Doug's voice brought her attention toward his smiling gaze. "Raquel's got you beat only in one spot. And who gives a damn about that extra padding? I'd rather have a tall, 'slender' woman like you pinned up against me any time..."

"Doug!"

A twinkle appeared in Doug's warm brown eyes. "That is, theoretically speaking, of course...."

The chorus that followed his remark came in unison. "Of course, of course...."

Slate was unnaturally quiet, and turning toward him, Bill said unexpectedly, "Who do you think's going to win the modified feature today, Slate?"

Slate was cagey. "Who do you think?"

Bill shook his head. "Funny, I asked Buck the same question and got the same answer!"

"Guess we'll all have to wait and see, won't we?"

A few laughing comments followed Slate's last remark, and he was drawn into earnest conversation with Tom as Trina turned toward Doug. "How are Stitch's chances of winning today, Doug?"

"Stitch is still feeling out his car. He doesn't expect to do much this season. He's really racing just for the hell of it. He may take a few wins if he's lucky, but today he's a longshot."

Trina nodded. There was a lot of talent there if Stitch could manage to get his act together. The crazy kid had the best in the way of mechanic and pit boss. Trina smiled warmly at Doug. She always felt comfortable with him.

"Don't look at me like that, honey," he said, glancing toward Slate, who was still engrossed in conversation with Tom, "I don't think that guy beside you would like it much."

Trina frowned. "How was I looking at you, Doug?"

"Like I was somebody special to you."

"You *are* somebody special to me."

Doug gave a low, disbelieving laugh. "Not as special as I'd like to be."

"Hey, what's going on here behind my back?"

Slate's question was posed in a joking tone, but the gaze he turned down into Trina's eyes held little humor.

A bit irritated by his manner, Trina repeated testily, "Behind your back?"

"Uh-oh!"

"Looks like trouble, Slate!"

"Get him, Trina."

The short, teasing remarks of the group around them drew a smile to Trina's face.

"Troublemakers! I think I've had about enough of the bunch of you this afternoon."

Finishing up the last of her coffee, which had been delivered during the boisterous exchange, Trina turned back toward Slate.

"I still have some work to do on my car, Slate. Don't feel you have to leave with me if you want to stay here a little longer."

Giving her a short look that signified exactly what he thought of that idea, Slate shook his head. "No, I have some things to do, too." Turning to the men who pinned them in the center of the booth, he said lightly, "Raquel, here, has to work on her car, so move over, boys."

"Hey, Doc, do a good job, will you? And when you're done, if you want to operate on my car..."

"Funny...very funny." Trina's grimace for Tom's belaboring of the old joke was met with a few low snickers.

"Wait a minute, Trina. I'll walk back with you and Slate." Doug's interjection was unexpected. She turned in his direction as he got to his feet. "You were telling me last week that your steering seemed to be a little off. You told me you had just put in a new steering box, and I gave it a lot of thought during the week. I'll tell you about it on the way back."

The question of the steering box remained unresolved, but Trina was endlessly thankful to Doug's domination of the conversation on the way back. She could feel Slate's tension as he walked at her side, and was about to attempt a hasty withdrawal when Buck's voice came over the roar of the car being tested beside them.

"Trina, it's now or never. I've got something to do on my car that can't wait much longer."

"Okay, Buck."

Slate's expression had already hardened by the time she looked up into his face. "I have to go, Slate. Thanks for the coffee."

"Are you going to be at The Last Pit Stop later?"

"Probably."

"Wait for me. I'll take you."

"No, I'm going with Buck and Karen."

Slate's expression tightened. "You don't give an inch, do you, Trina?"

Without waiting for her response, Slate turned away and strode toward his car.

"Trina..."

"All right, Buck."

Scrambling for her gloves, Trina walked over to her brother's side, her effort to forget the look in Slate's eyes as he turned away decidedly unsuccessful.

THE CROWD ROARED as Trina braked her car to a stop in front of the main grandstand, jumped out, and pulled off her helmet. The shrieking wolf whistles that persisted long after the roar had died down brought a smile to her lips. She was exultant! She had won! Two feature races in a row! Her spirits were soaring! Trophy and check in hand, she walked rapidly to the spot where the microphone awaited her comment to the crowd. She was speaking, her elation bubbling spontaneously out of her lips. She was not truly aware of anything she said. It was all beginning to happen...it was coming true! Another win next week, and she would be at the top of the points standing! She laughed at a crack made by the commentator. A flash went off...and then another.

Her eyes shot to the modified cars lined up for their feature race. The pace car was drawing them out onto the track even as she walked back across the track toward her car. Her eyes automatically sought out the red and white number 82. Buck raised his hand in a broad salute, and Trina's elation increased. It's happening, Buck! And it's going to happen for both of us....

The line of cars moved out farther onto the track as Trina began to get back into her car. The blue and white number 008 caught her eye. Slate's congratulations were more personal. He blew her a kiss. Trina slid into her car and started the engine, pulling rapidly into the pits. She suddenly had a knot in her stomach, and refused to ask herself why.

THE PARKING LOT of The Last Pit Stop gave credence to its name. Despite her determination to the contrary, Trina's eyes scanned the parked rigs as she drew her own to a stop. Slate's was not among them. Uncertain whether the pang she experienced was happiness or disappointment, she shut off her engine and hopped out of the cab of her truck.

She had barely had time to sponge herself off in the ladies' room at the track and change from her sweaty yellow T-shirt to the deep red she now wore before Karen had come with the message that Buck was threatening to leave without her. Her reaction had been immediate annoyance. For as long as she could remember, Buck had been chasing her out of the bathroom, and she supposed he would never get out of the habit.

The modified feature race had been an anticlimax to the excitement that had prevailed after her win. Buck's car had broken down in the tenth lap, and Slate had had a minor mishap with another car, which had rendered his car unable to finish. Down one, both of them. Buck had been silent about his breakdown, and Trina's worries about his intensity had increased. She had noticed a slight tension between Karen and Buck and made a mental note to talk to Karen when Buck was otherwise occupied this evening.

But if Buck had been unnaturally silent earlier, he was a changed man as he walked beside her through the lot, his arms thrown casually around hers and Karen's shoulders.

"In the mood for a big celebration, Trina? Something tells me you're going to make the racing papers big again this week."

"You're prejudiced, Buck."

"No prejudice involved, honey. You're the best looking woman up here...except for this little blonde at my side, of course."

Karen laughed. "If you hadn't added that you'd have been in big trouble."

"And if there's one thing I don't want, it's trouble with you, mighty mite."

A short intimate glance was exchanged between Buck and Karen, and Trina felt a warm reassurance flood her senses. They were all right, these two. Really made for each other...if racing didn't manage to get between them. All Buck really needed was a little good luck for a change....

Buck was drawing her along with Karen toward an empty spot at the bar when Trina's eyes touched on a table in the darkened corner of the bar. Obviously unaware that she had entered the room, Slate was busily engrossed in speaking to Sally Griffin who was perched intimately on his knee. Sally's arm was resting comfortably on his shoulder as she moved her hand familiarly in the hair at the back of his neck.

One glance up into Buck's face revealed he had seen Slate as well.

Trina's comment was light, belying her true reaction to the scene. "Interesting...looks like he's looking for greener pastures..."

"Greener pastures? The man can't be that big a fool."

"Whatever..."

Shrugging off Buck's remark, Trina attempted to ignore the dull ache that had begun inside her, and walked toward the group smilingly awaiting them.

An arm slid warmly around her waist as Trina reached the bar, and she smiled up into Doug's face.

"We've been waiting for you, Trina. This place was dead without you last week."

"Sure. I bet everyone just sat around and said, 'I wish Trina Mallory was here.'"

"I don't know if anybody said it, but I sure was thinking it."

Trina returned Doug's direct gaze. She believed him. How could a person not believe a guy like Doug Frawley?

The question had not yet left her mind when she heard Doug's voice ask, "Dance with me, Trina?"

"I haven't even had a drink yet, Doug."

He called to the bartender, "Hey, Phil. A gin and tonic for Trina." Turning back to her, Doug smiled. "All right, your drink is ordered. It'll be waiting for you when you get back. *Now* will you dance with me?"

"How can I refuse such an efficient man?"

Smiling as Trina walked toward the dance floor, Doug shook his head. "I don't know, you've been doing a pretty good job so far."

"Fool that I am," Trina joked as Doug's arms closed around her.

"Well, maybe tonight will be my lucky night."

Trina was beginning to become uneasy with the joking conversation that was hitting too close to sensitive subjects for comfort. Her eyes shot around the immediate area. "Yes, maybe it will. I see Helen's here tonight. I tell you, Doug, you're missing out on a good bet there."

Trina was aware of Doug's spontaneous stiffening before he finally let out a small laugh. "Still trying to steer me in another direction, aren't you, Trina? I thought you'd have given up on that by now. Just for the record, I don't even *see* Helen when you're around."

"And when I'm not around?"

"I make do. But my heart isn't in it."

Looking seriously into Doug's eyes, Trina offered quietly, "Doug, I'm not right for anybody just now. I have one thought on my mind, and everything takes second place to it."

"Racing?"

"That's right."

"Well...just as long as it isn't *someone* else on your mind, I guess I can handle it."

"Doug—"

"Look, that's enough talking for now. Let's just dance. This is the only chance I ever get to hold you, and I intend to take full advantage of it."

Doug pulled her tight against him and Trina slid her arms around his neck. She reinstated a smile on her lips, and said quietly, "Okay. Any man who can compare me favorably to Raquel Welch certainly deserves at least a dance."

The dance was over and Trina extricated herself carefully from Doug's arms. The expression in his eyes was more revealing than words. Doing her best to ignore the obvious, she said softly, "That was fun, Doug. I always enjoy dancing with you."

"You're right. That was fun...so much fun that I think we should do it again."

Trina shook her head, forcing a smile to her lips. "Oh, no you don't. Helen's at the bar, and from the look on her face, you did more than 'make do' last week. She's a great girl—"

"Trina..."

"And I'm going back to the bar...now."

"Well, it looks like I got here just in time."

Slate's unexpected voice in her ear drew her attention to his smile as his arm slid around her waist.

"No, I don't think so, Slate. I'm going back to my friends at the bar."

The music began again. Ignoring her response, Slate slid her into his arms. His eyes moving between them, Doug finally turned away and made his way back to the bar. Unwilling to make the scene required to free herself from Slate's tight embrace, Trina remained placidly in his arms, her expression bland.

"What's the matter, Trina?"

"Nothing's the matter."

"So you saw me with Sally."

"How could I miss it?"

"Jealous, Trina?"

Turning in his direction, Trina quoted quietly with a small smile, "'It's different between us, Trina...'"

"Look, Trina. I was sitting at the table and..."

"Don't bother."

Slate began again adamantly, "I was sitting at the table, waiting for you when Sally came over and made herself comfortable on my knee. I couldn't very well stand up and let her drop on the floor, could I?"

Not bothering to answer, Trina averted her face.

"Stubborn little... Look at me, Trina!"

Gripping her chin, Slate forced her face up to his. "Sally sat on my lap *without* an invitation. I got rid of her as diplomatically as I could under the circumstances and went to the bar to watch Doug paw you until the dance was over."

"I resent that statement. Doug did not paw me."

"I can't say I blame the guy for making a play, but I'll be damned if I'll stand around watching—"

"You don't have anything to say about it, Slate. What I do and whom I choose to dance with is *my* business."

Hesitating momentarily as his eyes roamed over Trina's flushed face, Slate nodded.

"All right. Stalemate. I can have Sally sit on my lap if I want, and you can have Doug paw you. We're both free to do what we want, but I'll be damned if I let you get more than two steps out of my sight for the rest of the night."

Releasing her unexpectedly, Slate drew her firmly behind him as he led her off the dance floor. They were moving toward the exit of the bar when Trina finally managed breathlessly, "Where do you think you're taking me?"

"To prove something to you."

"Prove what?"

They were moving through the parking lot exit. The doors had just closed behind them when Slate turned toward her and pulled her into his arms.

"I'm tired of talking, Trina."

She was in Slate's arms, tight against the hard, male length of him as his mouth moved roughly over hers. But the fierceness in Slate's kiss was short-lived, doomed to dissipation in the face of the hungry swell of longing that came to life between them. Unable to be denied, it grew to shuddering proportions as Slate's tongue penetrated the barrier of her lips. The rough hands became caressing, erotically stimulating as they held her closer against him, moving hungrily against her back, her ribs, the rounded swell of her buttocks. Finally drawing his mouth from hers, Slate looked down into her eyes, his chest heaving with emotion.

"I had a table in the corner...a nice private corner where we could talk, and I was waiting for you. Sally came over and you came in. I wanted us to straighten everything out between us tonight. I wanted to take it slow, convince you that you're not in any danger with me."

Trina's heart was hammering in her chest. The taste of Slate's kiss was still on her lips and she wanted more...much more. She could not deny that any more than she could deny her own name.

"Trina, I want you, honey. Stay with me tonight.... It'll be good between us, I promise you."

"No."

"Trina..." Forcing her to turn her eyes up to his face, Slate whispered softly against her lips, "Sweetheart...I made you a promise. I said there wouldn't be a next time unless *you* said you wanted it...unless you asked me to stay with you. I'm committed to it, Trina.... I won't just take you with me like before. You're going to have to say the words...."

"Slate, I..."

Slate's eyes were looking intensely into hers; his breath was against her lips, teasing, drawing her. The tensions of a few moments before, the doubts that had tortured her mind seemed to fade as the desire to be in his arms again blossomed inside her. She could not deny the way she felt. Nor could she deny the desire that flared in the eyes staring so intensely into hers. Slate's hand caressed her cheek, his lips moved lightly against hers.

"Trina, honey, please..."

She was only fooling herself saying she didn't want him. She did. She had to come to terms with her feelings. She was probably only making it worse...holding him off with one hand while she pulled him close with the other.

His lips were trailing down her neck. His tongue was dipping into the delicate hollows at its base, sending little chills of desire up her spine. He was spreading light, butterfly kisses on her shoulders as his mouth dipped to follow the scooped neckline of her shirt. Her heart was pounding, her breathing becoming short and labored.

"Slate...I don't want this.... I don't want to get involved with anyone now."

"It's too late, darling. Much too late."

His mouth was on hers again, drawing from her even as he gave. His hands were seeking, relentless in their quest as they smoothed, fondled, caressed her, clutched her close...closer still. She was breathless under his touch, her skin on fire. Her arms were around his neck, returning the strength of his embrace. Her fingers worked in the heavy gold hair at the base of his neck, and she stifled a groan at the wealth of feelings that began to infiltrate her mindlessness.

Slate was right. She wanted him as much as he wanted her. She could deny it no longer...no longer....

Slate's lips grazed hers once again. "Trina..."

"All right, Slate..."

"Say the words, darling."

"I...want to be with you tonight, Slate."

Almost disbelieving of the words she spoke, Slate remained motionless for long seconds before abruptly separating himself from her and taking her arm to move her back through the exit door. At her questioning glance, he said shakily, "Tell your brother not to wait for you. Tell him you'll be coming home sometime tomorrow. You can give him a call when you get back if he's worried. I don't want anything or anyone to interfere with us, Trina. I want to be alone with you...completely alone."

A few minutes later the hard part was done and they were in Slate's car. The picture of Buck's stiff face still in her mind, Trina sent a short glance at Slate's profile, etched against the darkness of the streets through which they passed. He was pulling up before a well-lit motel, and Trina closed her eyes momentarily. She hated this. It made her feel...

The door on her side of the car opened, and Slate pulled her to her feet, his arm slipping around her waist as they walked to the doorway directly ahead of them. There was a slight fumbling of keys before the door swung open and Trina stepped inside. Slate flicked on the light, simultaneously pushing the door closed behind them and pulling her into his arms.

"Oh, Trina...at last. I was beginning to get scared, honey. I was beginning to think your stubbornness was going to keep us apart. Don't ever do that to us, sweetheart. Not ever...."

His lips were on hers once again and there was a wildness between them that would not abate. His hands trembling, Slate pulled her light T-shirt off and threw it to the chair. His hands moved immediately to the button on her jeans. Within moments he had pulled them down and had lifted her free of them.

His eyes remained focused on hers as he undressed. Trina was trembling. Slate's effect on her senses, his threat to her control, was overwhelming.

Defending herself against the intensity of her true feelings, Trina whispered shakily, "Tell me the truth, Slate. I'm here, and I won't leave. How do you feel? Does it give you a sense of power knowing I couldn't hold out against you?"

His startling blue eyes jerked suddenly to hers. Slate hesitated before returning huskily, "What do *you* feel, Trina? Tell me, because I feel the same thing.... We're both in the same boat, darling. I'm as defenseless against my feelings for you as you are against yours. You don't feel this way with Doug, and I don't feel this way with Sally, or any other woman I've ever known. And sometimes the way I feel scares me, honey...just as much as it scares you."

Reaching out to cup her face with his hands, Slate kissed her deeply, his mouth moving endlessly in a lingering, erotic quest that sent her pulse pounding. When Slate tore his mouth from hers at last, his voice was a breathless rasp. "This is the truth...the only truth, darling. It's the only truth we'll ever need between us."

A great tenderness overwhelmed Slate as he lifted Trina into his arms, carried her the few steps to the bed and placed her there. A moment later he was lying beside her. The fragile wisp of her bikini pants was the only impediment between them. Trina closed her eyes as Slate's hand moved to stroke her cheek, then he was kissing her, his hand trailing into her hair to clutch at the curling spirals before moving in a downward path to trail fleeting caresses along her cheek, her throat, the curve of her shoulder, finally coming to rest at the small, rounded swells of her breasts.

His kiss was deepening, his tongue, no longer satisfied to ravage her mouth, moved with small, nibbling bites to the soft flesh he had caressed only moments before. Tortured by his unrelenting quest, Trina felt a new longing grow inside her. She wanted...she needed... A low gasp escaped her lips.

With a low, muttered epithet, Slate covered the aching, burgeoning crests of her breasts with his mouth, sending her soaring in a wild, kaleidoscoping path of mindless sensations as his hands moved lower, caressing, fondling.... His fingertips trailed at the elastic of her bikini pants, his hand finally slipping underneath to cup the warm mound of her passion. Even in her bemused state, Trina could feel the new strain the intimacy put on Slate's tenuous control. A moment later he raised his head from her breasts to slip the sheer wisp from her body and toss it to the chair.

His eyes gleamed in his flushed face as he slowly lowered his mouth to hers again. He was kissing her lingeringly, deeply, when she felt him cup the soft mound again, his hand caressing, searching. Gasping as he found the bud of her passion, Trina was rewarded with a fierce renewal of his insatiable quest as Slate ground his mouth hungrily into hers, drawing deeply from its sweetness. His sensuous caress deepened, broadened, transporting her to a plane of sublime madness from which she did not care to escape. She was writhing under his knowing touch, groaning her need. She was suddenly aware that she was trembling at the brink of fulfillment, poised there alone for the pitching descent.

Opening her eyes, she caught the glimmer of a similar need in Slate's gaze as she whispered softly, "Slate...what...what are you doing to me? I can't take much more of this..."

"Yes, Trina, I know." His voice low, Slate continued softly, "Look at me, darling. I want you to give to me.... I want to see the glory of that giving on your face, Trina. I want to seal it in my mind, remember your eyes when you climax...see them glow...set on fire by the joy I make you feel." Deepening his caress, lovingly torturing her body to the brink of its ultimate reward, he whispered against her ear, his tongue exploring the hollows, "Now, darling...give to me...show me how I make you feel, show me that you want me...me above all others...only me.... Give to me darling...give to me now...."

Her body was shuddering, heaving its response, giving to him in deep, undulating spasms, and Slate reveled in Trina's breathless tribute to his lovemaking. His eyes consumed her as passion transfused her face with color, her full lips separating with a soft gasp, the thick fan of her lashes fluttering against her flawless cheeks as she yielded to the ecstasy that overwhelmed her.

Then she was still under his touch, her slender, graceful body unmoving, her eyes closed in the warm temporary exhaustion of total release. Lowering his head, Slate pressed a light kiss against the warm sensuous nest between her thighs. He moved to cover her body with his as he cupped her face in his hands and whispered against her unmoving lips.

"Trina, darling, look at me. Open your eyes."

The heavy lids fluttered lightly, raising at last to allow a misted, black-eyed gaze to touch and hold his. Raising himself above her, he slid into the moist crease that awaited him, his own eyes dropping briefly closed as her body welcomed him with its warmth.

"Trina, darling, you know this is the way it was meant to be between us. My darling... Trina..."

His own passion at its summit, Slate moved deep and sure inside her, a few brief thrusts sufficient to push him over the edge of the passion he had sustained so long... so very long....

A short time later, the glory of his own fulfillment complete, Slate lifted his head. The perspiration of their mutual passion sealed them together with yet another bond of intimacy, and in a quick movement, still joined to the tender sheath of her body, he rolled over onto his back, taking Trina with him until she lay cradled atop him. Holding her against the firm length of his body, unwilling to separate from her, he reached down and pulled the sheet over them. When she attempted to move, his arms tightened around her.

"I just want to hold you, keep you a part of me a little while longer, Trina. For just a little while...."

AUTOMATICALLY PULLING the pleasing warmth against him, Slate smiled in his sleep. His hand closed around a small, rounded breast. His eyes began to drift open, focusing at last on the tousled black curls on the pillow beside him. Trina...she was turned with her back toward him, curled in the warm curve of his body. His arm was wrapped around her waist, his hand still enclosing her soft breast.

She was starting to stir, and Slate smiled. She raised her hand to her cheek and then rubbed her eye. A new wave of tenderness overwhelmed him. They had made love several times during the night, each exchange binding him closer to her, increasing his desire for more. There was an awareness growing inside him that nudged him, a budding realization that he had not sought, which would give him no peace. But his mental meanderings were brought to an abrupt halt as Trina turned toward him, her eyes moving over his face.

The first to break the silence between them, Slate pressed a light kiss against her lips. "You don't know how many times I've dreamed about this...lying with you in my arms...waking up with you beside me. Last Thursday...it was all I could do to make myself turn around and walk away from your doorstep. I didn't sleep much that night and the next day at the office was hell. I couldn't think straight. Your face was with me...in the corner of my mind...all day long, no matter what I did."

Slate's lips were beginning to move along her hairline, down her face to her ears. His words were becoming muted by the trail of kisses that grew increasingly warmer. His lips were moving against hers, touching, teasing. His tongue drew a tantalizing line across her lips, darting between the parted barrier of her teeth to taste the sweet moistness within. He was beginning to lose his train of thought as emotions assumed control, and he fought diligently for restraint.

But Trina was pulling away. The dark eyes that had looked into his with open passion the night before were now guarded, and Slate felt a stab of frustration. It was obvious Trina was preparing to run, and he wasn't going to allow that to happen. Not this time....

"Oh, no, you don't. Where do you think you're going?"

"I'm getting up."

He brushed her lips with his and shook his head. "No you're not. We're going to talk."

"Oh, was that what you had in mind? It didn't seem like you wanted to talk. Besides, Slate, I have to get up. I have a lot of things to do today."

"They're not as important as this. Stay with me awhile."

"And talk..."

"Yes, talk. Does that sound so strange? Just stop and think a minute, Trina. We've known each other about three weeks, is that right?"

"Approximately..."

"And I know next to nothing about you."

"You're exaggerating."

"Am I? Trina...you're not listening to me."

"Let me up, Slate."

Trina strained at the arm that held her down, almost succeeding in dislodging it before Slate flipped over to pin her against the bed with the full weight of his body. The intimacy of their position produced a small smile on his sensuous mouth.

"I didn't want to resort to holding you down like this, Trina. It's too dangerous...."

Recognizing the light that came into Slate's eyes, Trina abruptly stopped squirming. She wasn't immune to the feeling of Slate's body stretched out full atop her, and she avoided his gaze, mumbling almost inaudibly as he slid his hands up to cup her face.

He was pressing light kisses against her cheek when Trina offered reluctantly, "All right. What do you want to talk about?"

Slate's kisses were becoming warmer. "I don't know if I want to talk anymore...."

"Slate, it's now or never. I have to get home. What do you want to talk about?"

Stopping to renew his grip on his patience, Slate shook his head in silent exasperation. "Okay. We'll start with something easy. Tell me about yourself when you were growing up. You already told me you worked on engines since you were a kid. Where were you born?"

"I was born and spent the first five years of my life in Paterson, New Jersey."

"Paterson, New Jersey!"

"That's what I said. What's so strange about that? Paterson's a very old city, you know...real historic. Alexander Hamilton himself founded it. He saw the Passaic Falls and figured it would be a great site for a manufacturing city because of the water power. Of course, he didn't know at that time that the falls would be dry for several months each year because of summer droughts, but—"

Slate's expression was wry. "I'm not really interested in a history lesson, Trina...."

"And he founded the S.U.M., the Society of Useful Manufacturers. Later on, Paterson was known as the Silk City."

"Spare me, Trina. I'm more interested in *your* history than I am in the history of Paterson, New Jersey."

A small smile played at the corners of Trina's mouth. "Okay, but remember, you asked for this. Well, when my mother died, we moved out of the city."

"Moved where?"

"Not far. To Ridgewood...the house where I live now."

"That's when your father got interested in racing...."

"No, he was interested in it before that. He raced at Hinchcliffe Stadium...in Paterson, New Jersey."

Slate raised his eyes to the ceiling in exasperation. "We're back to Paterson, New Jersey, again."

"Do you want to hear this or not?"

"Go ahead."

"He raced midgets in Paterson long before I was born, and traveled around to tracks to race stock cars for a long time after that."

"Terrific...when do *you* come into this history of the Mallory family?"

"Maybe you should ask questions, Slate."

"I could also write up a questionnaire and have you fill in the blanks, Trina, but that isn't what I had in mind."

"Well, I could tell you more about Paterson, New Jersey...."

"Trina, please."

Trina was unable to suppress a small amused snort. "Well, I always liked that town."

"And I more than like you...and it's you I want to hear about." Slate's eyes were moving over Trina's face. He was grateful to Paterson, New Jersey, for one thing at least. Trina was relaxed in his arms, her temporary panic upon awakening seeming to have dissipated along with her amusement.

"Tell me when you became so serious about racing."

"I think most of the drivers at Middlevale are serious about racing, Slate."

"Not to the extent you and your brother seem to be."

"So? I told you Buck's and my ambitions go past Middlevale Raceway."

"Those are big ambitions, Trina."

"It doesn't pay to think small."

Slate's response was a frown.

"What about you, Slate?"

"What about me?"

"How long do you expect to stay in racing?"

"As long as it amuses me."

"Another season or so?"

Sensing her disapproval, Slate said seriously, "Look, Trina, I don't pretend to have you and your brother's dedication, but I *have* been interested in engines and cars since I was a kid. And I'm pretty proud that some of the parts for my car were hand tooled in my shop."

"You have a right to be proud."

And Trina meant what she said. Slate had a right to be proud of his accomplishments. Suddenly, Trina was ashamed of her own narrowmindedness. She could not expect anyone but Buck and herself to understand the compulsion that motivated them both. Slate was still uncertain how to take her comment, and in an effort to soften her words, she raised her hand to his cheek and smiled.

"Slate, I'm sorry. I'm so caught up in this racing thing that I sometimes forget other people view it merely as a sport, not a way of life." Lifting her lips to Slate's, she kissed him lightly. "But I do have to get up, Slate. It's already..." Glancing at her watch, Trina's eyes widened. "It's already ten-thirty!"

Warmed by Trina's show of affection, Slate responded hoarsely, "So it's ten-thirty! Do you have to catch a train?"

"No, but I want to get home.... I have some things to do before work tomorrow."

"Work on your car..."

"No, do my laundry, food shopping, clean my house just a little at least and..."

"And work on your car..."

Trina's lips stretched into a reluctant smile as she nodded. "And work on my car."

Slate nodded. This woman lying beneath him stirred more tenderness inside him with one vulnerable smile than he had ever thought himself capable of, and the experience left him shaken.

"Well, since the truth is finally out..."

Slipping to his side, Slate watched as Trina moved to the edge of the bed and stood up. His eyes followed her naked form, his stomach doing a little flop as she turned, walked smoothly toward the bathroom, and closed the door behind her.

Slate lay in bed, myriad emotions occupying his mind. The hiss of the shower sounded from behind the closed door. He swung his legs over the side of the bed and stood up. He stopped at the bathroom door, his hand on the knob. Trina was anxious to get home today. Two could shower faster than one.... Trina couldn't blame him for such rational thinking....

He turned the knob and walked in.

CHAPTER SEVEN

"I HAVE TO TALK TO YOU, Trina. It's important."

"Sure, Karen. I go out to lunch in an hour. Why don't you meet me at Otto's."

A tingle of apprehension moved down her spine as Trina absentmindedly hung up the phone. She shot a quick glance arouhnd the small boutique. It was well into the summer months, and the boutique had begun to see the midvacation slump. She could afford time off for a longer-than-usual lunch.

It was unlike Karen to call her at work. As a matter of fact, it was unlike Karen to call her at all. In the three years Buck and Karen had known each other, she and Karen had never gotten very close. It was not as if she disliked Karen; she knew Karen was perfect for Buck.

She had to smile. Buck and Karen sure were proof of that old bromide about opposites attracting. Big, brawny Buck...all dark hair and beard, dark eyes...outspoken and demonstrative. Fierce looking until he smiled and that pussy cat underneath shone through. And little Karen...small, petite, blond, light-complexioned, quiet, soft-spoken, really only blooming when Buck slung his great arm around her or smiled in her direction.

But in the time since Buck and Karen had been together, Trina had come to realize that Karen's soft, withdrawn exterior shielded a strong, determined mind that no amount of cajoling or threats could turn once she had set a particular course for herself. It was that aspect of her personality that presently gave Trina the most cause for thought after she called.

"That was your sister-in-law, Trina? It is unusual that she calls you for lunch, is it not?"

"Not quite my sister-in-law, Ingrid, but, yes, it *is* unusual that she call me for lunch."

Ingrid's observant eye did not miss Trina's pensive air. "You think it is trouble, Trina? If so, you must not hurry back from lunch. I will eat in the back room and..."

Trina could not suppress a smile. Ingrid was one of the sharpest businesswomen Trina had ever known, but her shrewd business sense did not interfere with her sympathetic and caring nature. It was times like this when Trina realized how very lucky she was to have fallen into her position at the boutique.

"Thanks, Ingrid, but I doubt if I'll be late. Karen's not very much of a talker...."

"I DIDN'T KNOW what else to do, Trina. You're the only other person who has any influence at all on him...."

Not much of a talker...Trina had all she could do not to laugh outright at her own statement of a short time earlier. In the time since she had arrived at the popular neighborhood restaurant, Otto's had filled and emptied of the twelve o'clock business lunch crowd, and was now well into the one o'clock group of customers. And during that time, Karen had carefully related the situation that had necessitated the call earlier in the day.

"Why did you wait so long to tell me these things, Karen? After all, Buck—"

"Buck would be angry if he knew I was here now. You know how he is. He wouldn't want me to worry you."

Trina nodded her head. That sure enough was true. Buck was overprotective...felt the need to shelter her. But Karen was still talking....

"He's so determined to make points champion this year...and he's behind by three races. Slate's win last week really did the job. He's determined to win this week, at any cost."

"What do you mean by that, Karen?"

"I mean...well, I think he's past the point where he considers his own personal safety first. Look at the way he drove last week! He was like a maniac getting through that pack! The only reason Slate managed to nose him out at the finish was because of Buck's tires. Slate had new tires on his car again last week, didn't he? Buck's are beginning to show signs of wear. So he bought four new tires for this week's race."

"*Four* new tires? I didn't think Buck could afford one! He said his credit was overextended."

"He can't, and it is, but somebody must've been a sucker for the Mallory Racing Family line, because he came home with four new tires last night. He's going over to your house tonight to work on the car. That's why I called you this afternoon, Trina. I thought you might be able to talk some sense into him."

"I'm afraid I'm not the right person to tell anyone not to overextend himself, Karen...not the way I've been spending money this season."

"Oh, I didn't mean...it's not the money I'm worried about. It's the desperation that I sense in Buck. He's..." Karen's head dropped to avoid Trina's earnest gaze. "It's just that I feel this whole thing is my fault. You know I never had a real family of my own; I never knew my parents. Maybe that's why I want to settle down so badly—have children, be a real family. But when I told Buck I couldn't wait another season for us to start our lives, wait another season for him...I didn't mean to put this much pressure on him. If I could take back what I said, I would. I can wait. It frightens me to see him pushing so hard to win."

Trina stared into Karen's eyes as they finally lifted to hers. She felt a strong surge of pity. There was no doubt Karen's fears were genuine and she felt a true pang of remorse that Karen's disinterest in racing had stood between their forming a more intimate friendship in the past. Determining to correct that oversight, Trina patted Karen's hand and offered a small smile.

"Karen, why don't you tell Buck what you just told me? It would ease his mind."

"No, I think it's too late for that. Buck would think I'm feeling sorry for him because he's behind in the points standing, and that would make him more determined than ever to win."

Trina nodded her head. Karen knew Buck far better than Trina had realized. Buck was proud...too proud.

"But I'm only his sister. What can I say to him?"

"Just tell him the truth. He respects what you say because you're a driver. Tell him that he won't have to worry about winning if he doesn't make it through the pack the next time on one of his wild runs...that he's just giving the championship to Slate if he totals his car or gets killed...."

At the last word Karen paled, and tears formed in her large brown eyes.

"All right, I'll tell him," Trina soothed. "I'll have a good talk with him tonight."

"And just so you know, Trina—" Karen's voice trembled but she looked directly into Trina's eyes "—I love Buck very much. I wouldn't have been able to write off these past three years even if Buck had chosen racing over me."

"I know, Karen."

"And I do want Buck to be happy, even if that means we stay in racing."

"I know that too, Karen."

Her innate shyness returning unexpectedly, Karen lowered her eyes and looked down to her plate at the cottage cheese that sat on a lettuce leaf, untouched.

"Guess I'm not too hungry this afternoon."

Trina looked down at her hamburger. She'd taken a couple of bites, then had lost interest.

"I'm not, either."

Nodding their heads, almost in unison, they both stood up and snatched at the check. Trina's hand was quicker and she smiled.

"This time it's my treat, Karen. Next time it'll be yours."

Karen grinned and nodded. Trina had always known Buck and Karen were made for each other, but now she knew why. It was simply a matter of Karen and Buck bringing out the best in each other. Karen brought out Buck's gentle, caring side, the side hidden from the world; Buck brought out Karen's strength, the strength that love had given her. Just thinking of it made Trina feel good. She gave a short wave as Karen rounded the corner of the street.

Trina turned in the direction of the boutique, thinking that Buck was a very lucky man.

"BUCK, DON'T BE SO damned stubborn!"

"You're a good one to call someone else stubborn!

Besides, it's none of your business!" Buck had arrived at Trina's garage only a half hour before, and was obviously in no mood for talking. Karen had been right. He was more tense than Trina had realized.

"Since when is your welfare not my business?"

"My welfare isn't threatened!"

"It isn't? You know as well as I do that you've been driving like a nut in the feature races these past two weeks."

"There haven't been any complaints from the track officials...."

"You haven't been roughriding...I didn't say you were. But you've been taking too many personal chances."

Buck was beginning to look suspicious. "You know, this conversation sounds entirely too familiar. Has Karen been talking to you?"

Trina avoided answering directly, but she did look him straight in the eye. "What's the matter? Don't you think I'm capable of some simple observation?"

Buck shook his head, his fierce expression softening only slightly. "No, it's just that I don't think you're capable of thought in that direction. You're too attuned to winning, like I am. And I've seen you cut some pretty mean circles around that track when you thought your lead was threatened."

Unable to deny the truth of his statement, Trina nodded. "You're right, Buck, but it's different. You're getting absolutely reckless. I don't think..."

"You don't have to think about *my* race. Concentrate on your own race."

"But I just don't think..."

"What's the matter? Think I'll be a threat to your boyfriend?"

Her response stopped dead on her lips as Trina saw Buck's expression. There was no sign of relenting there.

"That hurt, Buck."

"Why should it hurt, Trina? You've spent every weekend with Slate Montgomery since the season started. I think he can be considered your boyfriend, and since he is number one in the points standing—"

"I wish you were number one, Buck."

Buck's gaze was intense. "I *will* be number one."

Uncharacteristically, tears flooded Trina's eyes. Stepping forward, Trina wrapped her arms around her brother's waist and laid her head on his chest. "Buck, you do believe me, don't you? I really wish you were number one. Slate likes to win, but he's not at all serious about racing. He's just having a good time."

There was a moment's hesitation before Buck responded quietly, "Are you sure the same doesn't go for his relationships off the track, too?"

Trina stiffened. Her arms dropped to her sides and she stepped back. "That wasn't necessary, Buck. I think I'm capable of making my own judgements."

"Did you ever stop to think I might worry about you, too? I don't want you to suffer through another Spence."

Choosing to ignore his last comment, Trina persisted quietly, "What I just said to you deals with your personal safety on the track, Buck."

"And what I said is just as important."

Lifting her chin, Trina nodded. "Well, if it'll relieve your mind I'll let you know the situation as it stands. Slate understands the priorities in my life. He knows what I want to do in racing...that it comes first. I have the feeling it suits him just fine. And as long as he's satisfied, it's okay with me. We're just enjoying each other, Buck. I prefer it that way."

Buck tossed the screwdriver he'd been holding onto the workbench. "I just don't want you to get hurt, Trina. It's been eating at me since the beginning of the season. He came to Middlevale and hopped right up to the front of the pack. It was easy, Trina, just like everything seems to be for him. And when things come easy, sometimes a guy gets bored. When he's tired of the whole scene, he'll leave as fast as he came. I don't want you to get hurt, honey."

The old pain of rejection nudged at Trina's insides. "You don't have to worry this time, Buck. As far as Slate and I are concerned there's no threat. My only commitment is to racing, and he knows it. And as far as I know, he's very happy with the circumstances."

"Well, if you say so, Trina..."

"I do. And since I've listened to you very patiently, I'd like you to give me the same courtesy."

Buck folded his arms across his chest, his eyes on hers. His expression was noncommittal. "Go ahead ... shoot."

"You're letting all this get to you, Buck. You're getting too involved to think clearly on the track. I know there's a lot of pressure on you. Yes, Karen did come to see me, and I'm glad she did. We talked...really talked for the first time, Buck. She loves you and she's worried. She said she wouldn't leave you even if you didn't make it this year and decided to go for another season. She's afraid of the way you're driving, Buck. If I were you I'd go home right now, talk to her, and clear the air."

There were a few moments of silence as Buck considered her words. Nodding, he took a few steps forward and clamped his broad hands on her shoulders.

"You give good advice, little sister. I think I'll take it. But before I do, answer me truthfully. Did you mean what you said about Slate Montgomery? You know where you stand, and you're happy with it?"

Buck's concern caused a lump in her throat that Trina momentarily had trouble controlling. "Yes, don't worry about me, Buck."

His eyes took a moment longer to search hers, then Buck shook his head and grinned unexpectedly. "Now, home to my little 'mighty mite' so I can set her straight." He shook his head, his grin broadening. "How I love making up with that little blonde."

Trina nodded. "I kinda think she likes it, too."

Buck looked shocked. "She tell you that?"

"No."

"Oh, didn't think she would...."

Watching Buck as he walked to his car and drove away, Trina knew he was already feeling relieved. Unwilling to spend any more time in the garage that night, she turned back toward the house, fervently wishing she felt the same.

SLATE PULLED UP in front of Trina's small, familiar Cape Cod cottage and shut off his engine. He took a deep breath and frowned. He was glad to see that lights were on in the house and the garage was dark. He disliked working with Trina on her car at any rate. They always argued. Slate was not accustomed to making do with parts that were showing signs of fatigue, and his first inclination had been to simply buy the new parts she needed. But Trina's pride always got in the way and he ended up having to watch her race with unreliable used parts in her car. He kept on insisting that it was dangerous to drive under those conditions, and Trina kept on laughing at his concerns.

His philosophy was contrary to Trina's, in that his world did *not* revolve around his modified car. And since he'd met Trina, his world did not revolve around his company, either. As a matter of fact, he'd been neglecting his business recently. He had to be thankful for a dedicated partner who was great with details and paperwork. He had always been proud of the company's success, but lately, everything seemed to take second place to Trina.

Slate's frown deepened. Somehow, after all the time they had spent together, he had thought things would be different between Trina and himself. But this had been a long week—he had made several attempts to see her and been turned down each time. The previous week had been the same story. For Trina it was still a no-ties, no-commitment relationship.

Now, well into the season, the status of their relationship remained the same. He had begun to wonder just what would happen if he pushed Trina...told her he wasn't satisfied with the crumbs she chose to throw him on the weekends. But—and he was almost ashamed to admit it to himself—he was afraid to try. He didn't want to lose her.

Still frowning, Slate opened the door of his car and stepped out. Squaring his shoulders unconsciously, he started up the walk. He hadn't called ahead to say he was stopping by. He had known what the response would be. Too tired...too busy...working on the car...working late at the boutique... By midweek he was usually so disgusted with the situation that he was ready to turn his back on the irritating brunette who had turned his life around. But come Saturday night...when he held her in his arms again...he was lost. God, he was hopeless. All he needed was a glimpse of her and all his resolutions turned to dust.

Thursday...it was only Thursday. He had been traveling most of the week, settling a few government contracts. Now he needed to see her, to hold her in his arms. And no matter how strong her protests, he was certain of one thing. The moment she was in his arms the world stopped. When they were together, only they made the world move, and make it move they did. If there was another thing he was sure of, it was that when Trina was in his arms, she truly loved him. As for himself, the niggling thought that had begun at his subconscious had blossomed to a full-blown awareness.

He loved her. He loved Trina Mallory more than he had thought it possible to love a woman. And as certain as he was of the permanency of his love...that was how uncertain he was of hers.

Within a few seconds he was standing at the door, ringing the bell. What was taking her so long to answer?

The door finally opened and he smiled. She was dressed in a pale blue, short robe belted around her narrow waist and exposing the long length of her legs. She had pink slippers on her feet and her hair was a mass of black shiny ringlets. She must have just stepped out of the shower...the water always tightened those curls like that. Her face was devoid of makeup, with only the smooth tan she had acquired at the pits accenting the incredibly beautiful planes of her face.

He thought he saw a spontaneous flicker of warmth in her eyes before she frowned.

"Slate. What are you doing here?"

"I wanted to see you, and I figured the only way was to just show up on your doorstep. Now, are you going to invite me in?"

"I was about to go to bed, Slate."

"That's fine with me, too, Trina." Slate's grin was not returned and he felt it fade slowly from his lips as Trina spoke.

"If you don't mind, Slate, I'm extremely tired tonight..."

"You must be. You're not working in the garage."

His sarcasm was missed by Trina. She was obviously upset and Slate frowned. "Is anything wrong, Trina?"

"No, nothing's wrong. I'm just tired...like I said."

Slate tried another tactic. "Have you seen Buck this week?"

Trina's eyes jerked to his face. "Why do you ask? He just left here."

So she was upset about something that happened between Buck and her.

"No reason. I'm just glad I found you alone."

"You're wasting your time, Slate. You're not staying tonight."

Suddenly he was angry. "I don't remember asking to stay."

Trina's expression went blank. She blinked and turned to walk into the house. Slate's reaction was spontaneous: he closed the door behind him and caught up with her in a few strides. He turned her to him only to be startled by the tears that filled her great black eyes. Without hesitation, he pulled her into his arms, his hand moving in her hair as he held her tight against his chest. She felt so good...so right in his arms.

"Trina, honey, what's wrong?"

"Nothing...nothing's wrong...."

Slate gave a small laugh. "You're not going to convince me of that. Tell me, sweetheart. You said Buck just left.... Is it something he said?"

Trina's spontaneous stiffening was more revealing than words.

"What did he say? Tell me...come on, Trina."

"What my brother says to me is none of your concern, Slate."

"It is if he spoke about me...."

"He didn't."

"Liar."

Trina was starting to tremble. He didn't need that.

"Come on, honey." Releasing her, Slate slipped his arm around her waist and drew her to the kitchen. "You can make me some coffee. I've had a long ride."

"Forty-five minutes...Fort Lee isn't exactly the other end of the world, Slate. And I don't feel like making coffee."

Trina's response was typical, but she continued to walk at his side, and Slate felt a protective instinct overcome him. Damn that Buck Mallory!

"So I'll make the coffee."

Still refusing to release her, Slate reached for the automatic coffee maker and, drawing her with him, turned on the tap. Trina moved from his side and Slate followed her with his eyes, releasing a silent sigh of relief as she reached into the cabinet for the coffee. She filled the basket and slid it into the slot, her eyes averted from his. She was working something out in her mind, and Slate waited a few moments before asking, "Are you going to tell me what Buck said that upset you?"

"Buck didn't say anything that I didn't already know."

"And what was that?"

Trina raised her eyes evenly to his. "That your interest in me is like your interest in the track—temporary. That you're going to take off when the notion hits you, and that'll be that."

Every muscle in his body tensed and Slate responded stiffly, "And what did you tell him?"

"That I didn't expect to get burned."

Slate took a step closer. "And by that you meant that you had no intention of ever letting me get that close to you...."

"By that I meant that I have set my priorities and intend sticking to them."

"And what if I said I want you to change those priorities?"

"Then I'd say you'd better start looking up Sally again...."

The knot in Slate's stomach tightened painfully. "Just like that, Trina?"

"Yes. Just like that...."

Trina held Slate's stare, her frigid composure belying the trembling that had begun deep inside her the moment she had seen Slate in the doorway. Why had he come tonight, of all nights? Buck's warning had shaken her far more than she had realized. She could not seem to come to terms with the conflicting emotions assaulting her.

She also did not want to admit her increasing longing to be in Slate's arms. She would not acknowledge the many nights she lay alone in her bed, unable to sleep for the haunting memory of Slate's body pressed tightly against hers. But more frightening than her physical longing was her mental dependence on him. A number of times during the long week, she found herself wondering what his reaction would be to a particular situation. His casual smile, the amusement in his eyes that spontaneously sparked her own...she missed them. And in her lowest moments, like tonight, she longed for his low whispered encouragement, the consolation of his touch, the warmth of his arms....

She was tired of battling the inevitable lift that his appearance gave her, the instant high that surged through her veins whenever she saw him. But she dare not let him gain control. First there'd been Buck's warning, and now Slate was talking about changing her priorities.

Slate's expression had hardened. "But if I took you in my arms right now, it wouldn't be long before you'd change your tune, and you know it."

"Maybe..."

"Trina, I came here tonight because I wanted to see you...be with you. It's a long week from Sunday to Saturday, and I'm a little tired of being relegated to the weekend. I know you may find this hard to believe, but I would also like to think you enjoy being with me..."

"Slate, I told you I'm not in the market for that kind of relationship."

"Oh, I forgot. Weekends only, right? A few hops in the sack and then so long for another week...."

Trina stepped back as if she had been stung.

"What's the matter? The truth hurt?"

Slate stared at her, his gaze hard and unmoving. He wanted to hurt her...to make her experience some of the feelings that were tearing him apart.

Trina fought for control. Yes, Slate was right. This whole thing was wrong.... It had been wrong from the beginning. She wasn't ready for an emotional commitment. She was afraid...afraid of too many intangibles.... Slate wanted to know if the truth hurt.

"Yes, I guess it does." Her response was not what Slate expected, and he took a step forward, only to be stopped as Trina shook her head adamantly. "No, Slate. You're right. You deserve to be given fair treatment, and I can't give it to you. I'm too wrapped up in my ambitions and fears right now and you're coming up short."

Slate swallowed tightly. He sensed what was coming and he began to panic. He hadn't come here tonight for this...not to put an end to it.

"Trina—"

"You summed it all up very accurately just now. I've wanted it my way from the beginning. I've been selfish, taking and not giving to you, and you've had enough. Without realizing it, I almost turned myself into a carbon copy of someone I'd rather forget. You've had enough of it, and I can't say I blame you."

Damn his big mouth! She was wrong. Sure, he wanted more...but when it came down to the wire, he'd take what she was willing to give. Give her up? No...he didn't want that. He searched her face, only to see a smile forming. Dammit! What game was she playing?

"Trina..."

"This thing was all wrong from the beginning, Slate. I really have to thank you for setting it right."

Slate took the hand she held out to him. She withdrew it a few seconds later and walked toward the front door. He was dying inside but followed silently.

As he reached the doorway he turned to glance into Trina's face. She was still smiling, but the smile was a bit ragged at the edges.

"I'm sorry, Slate. I hope we can be friends...."

Slate gave a small laugh. "Now you're asking for too much."

"Well, whatever..." Trina shrugged, her smile wobbling. "Goodbye, Slate."

The door closed and Slate walked down the front path toward his car. He was a block away when he realized fully what had happened within the space of those few short minutes. It was over....

Inside the house, Trina was dazed as she walked back to the kitchen. The aroma of coffee permeated the room and she glanced absentmindedly at the pot. She felt strangely numb, as if she had purged all the feeling from her body when she had closed the door on Slate. She did not want to remember the look on his face. She just wanted to forget. Very carefully, she lifted the pot of coffee from the stand and poured it down the drain.

She flicked off the lights as she passed through the rooms on the way to her bedroom. She got into bed and closed her eyes. She had had enough...more than enough for tonight. She would go to sleep now and do the rest of her thinking tomorrow.

CHAPTER EIGHT

THE ROAR OF ENGINES was loud in her ears and Trina frowned. Another one of those headaches—the same that had given her little rest since Thursday night—beat heavily in her temples. Determined not to allow it to get the best of her, Trina forced herself to concentrate on the paper that Doug had just thrust into her hands.

"You hit the headlines again, Trina! Still number one in the sportsman points standing, and you look a hell of a lot better in your firesuit than Charlie Strong. I'll tell you, he's doing a slow burn at all the publicity you're getting."

Trina looked up into Doug's grinning face and made herself smile. She turned her attention back to the paper, her eyes skimming the surface barely reading the words. Her concentration had not been very good since Slate had left two days ago. She was not sleeping well; a familiar fair-haired figure invaded even her unconscious moments to interfere with her peace of mind.

It had ended so quickly. She had expected that she and Slate would finally call it quits as a result of an argument. But it had happened so quickly...so finally...and so amicably. Or so she'd thought until she had arrived at the track a short time before. One glance at Slate's cold expression and his brief nod had told her otherwise. She wished he was not angry with her. She would have liked to have walked over to talk to him.

The irony of her thoughts struck her. She had never wanted Slate to get too close. And now, when Slate wanted no more of her, she wanted to talk to him. She was just kidding herself. She still wanted it her way...to have Slate when she wanted him, but to be able to turn him off when he threatened to penetrate her defenses. No man would stand for being manipulated in that way for long...certainly not Slate.

Despite her good intentions, Trina continued to look out of the corner of her eye toward the blue and white rig parked at the far side of the pits. Slate was talking to Bob Mitchell, and the rest of his pit crew was standing beside them, listening. Trina knew Buck was going to have to go like the devil to beat Slate today.

"You're going to wear the print right off the paper at that rate, Trina." Doug's voice cut into her thoughts.

Bill Watson interjected, "Hell, if I was getting as much play in the papers as Trina is right now, I'd eat it up, too, Doug. Too bad your daddy can't be here to see his little girl make it big at his favorite track, Trina."

Trina's smile widened, and she was about to respond when Buck approached them and interrupted on a serious note.

"Did you finish that work on your steering, Trina? You complained last week that your car was handling a little rough...."

"No, I—" Suddenly realizing she couldn't tell Buck she had intended to finish it Thursday and Friday, but had somehow lost her incentive, Trina offered lamely, "I decided it could hold for another week. It wasn't that bad, and..."

Buck frowned. She wasn't fooling him. "Come on. I'll give you a hand. We'll look at it right now."

"No, it's okay for another week. We'll take a look at it on Monday."

"Trina..."

"I don't want to work on it now, Buck."

"Suit yourself." Hesitating just a moment longer to survey her expression, Buck turned and strode away.

Trina was puzzled at his prickly mood. She had thought his talk with Karen would ease Buck's tension.

Her eyes still on her brother as he walked away, Trina caught the small smile Karen shot in his direction. Evidently Buck had caught it, too. Changing direction in midstride he walked to stand towering over Karen. A smile breaking across his formerly sober features, he slid his arm around her shoulders and leaned down to whisper in her ear. A bright flush suffusing her face, Karen snapped her head up to Buck's face, her brown eyes wide. Buck's low laugh and the light kiss he pressed against her mouth appeared sufficient to soften Karen's shock, and she leaned full into Buck's embracing arm, a reluctant smile moving across her lips.

Trina felt both relieved and satisfied. She hadn't had time to talk to Karen since their luncheon date, but it was obvious that her discussion with Buck had come out all right. They were so obviously happy together.... Trina felt a small stab of envy.

"It's not polite to stare, you know."

At Doug's soft admonition Trina's eyes snapped back to his, and she flushed with embarrassment. So involved had she been in her thoughts that she hadn't even realized Bill had walked away.

"They look really happy, don't they, Doug? I only hope Buck will make it this year, and then..."

"If Buck wins, Slate loses. Are you ready for that?" Doug's eyes were fixed intently on Trina's as he awaited her response.

"Well, somebody has to lose, Doug."

"And you'd prefer it to be Slate? I admit I'm surprised. I got the impression the last few months that you two were a 'thing.'"

Trina's smile stiffened. "Well, if we were, we aren't any more. In any case, I would've wanted Buck to be points champion. He wants it more than Slate...."

The expression that came to Doug's face gave Trina momentary cause to regret her words, but Doug continued carefully, "I don't know. Slate looks pretty determined to me."

"Well, maybe I should have said that the points championship means more to Buck than to Slate. But in any case—" Trina smiled as she slipped her arm through his "—we'll just have to wait and see what happens today. The only thing I can tell you for sure is that I'm going to hold off Charlie Strong and Wally Tierney in the sportsman feature race, and you can plan on seeing me take that checkered flag."

Doug's smile broadened as he nodded. "I'm with you all the way, honey."

"Well, that's good to hear, but does that mean you'll spring for a cool drink? It must be a hundred degrees in the shade."

"You could coax me into it."

"Good. Let's find Bill and drag him along. I love the way he flatters me."

Doug's face dropped. Unable to suppress a laugh, Trina offered softly, "You wouldn't want me to play favorites, would you?"

"Wouldn't I?"

Refusing to take him seriously, Trina urged him toward the tall, gray-haired Bill as he ambled across the pits. "Come on. You're not going to get out of buying me a drink that easily!"

Slate's eyes followed Trina as she walked between Doug and Bill toward the refreshment stand. Finally, he forced himself to turn away from the picture that was always so effective in tying his stomach into knots. Taking the three steps up into his rig in one leap, he walked toward the parts carefully stowed in the rear and stood staring unseeingly down at them. A moment later he had to laugh at his own blindness.

Doug Frawley... He had delivered Trina right into Doug's waiting hands. And Doug was not going to let his opportunity pass this time, of that he was sure. A quiet desperation overcame Slate. He had handled everything wrong with Trina from the first. He had moved too fast. He hadn't given her a chance to get to know him.... But if he were to be honest he'd have to admit, given the same set of circumstances, he'd probably do the same thing again. He was so damn wild about her that it was tearing him apart. But Trina hadn't been ready to return the feelings she aroused in him. And now it was too late....

Slate ran his hand absentmindedly across the rack. He was sick with wanting her. *Trina...Damn it, Trina, honey, I love you. Why won't you let yourself love me back?*

"Slate."

Slate turned around at the sound of his crew chief's voice. "What is it, Bob?"

"You'd better suit up. The modifieds are going out on the track for warm-ups first today."

"I'll be right there."

Reaching for his firesuit, Slate nodded. He wasn't going to let her go like this. Tonight...he'd talk to her tonight, and he'd make her listen....

THE SPORTSMAN feature race was tight. Her mind intent on the cars jamming the track around her, Trina stepped on the accelerator and attempted to take number 32 on the outside. But it was no good. Damn! That was the worst thing about the position she now held on the track and the fact that she had won the previous week's feature. It necessitated starting last in the field, and although the last position had not been a hindrance in the past few races, today it was proving a real problem.

Ten laps...ten laps and she still hadn't progressed past the halfway point in the pack! In the meantime, Charlie was out in front and putting more and more distance between himself and the rest of the pack. If they didn't have a caution light to squeeze them together before the end of the race, she wouldn't stand a chance of catching up with him, even if she did manage to filter through this damned mess!

The first turn—they were rounding the first turn again. Suddenly Trina saw her chance. Accelerating sharply as those in front of her braked around the turn, Trina pulled to the outside, this time pulling clear of the aggravating number 32 who had remained persistently in her path for the last two laps.

Elation surging through her veins, Trina lessened her pressure on the accelerator as she veered sharply to the left in an attempt to catch herself the coveted spot on the inside. But something was wrong! The car wasn't responding! She was still going straight...straight toward the fence in the second turn! She was cutting across the track, directly in the path of the pack behind her. She was out of control! She braked, but it was too late! The fence...she was going to hit the fence! Abruptly she was struck from the rear, the force of the angle lifting her high into the air! The world was spinning...spinning beneath her...the scream of her own engine echoing in her ears, shrill and piercing.... The lights overhead blinded her eyes...she couldn't see... She could only hear the roar of the crowd...her own frightened screams...and then it was dark....

Fear paralyzing his throat, Slate watched as the pink and purple number 013 flipped high into the air. As if in slow motion, it struck the ground, the hood flying off as it flipped end over end two more times before it came to a final, shuddering halt on the far straightaway. And then he was running through the crowd that surged through the pits toward the motionless vehicle.

The tow trucks and ambulance were already at the car when he came to a breathless halt beside it. The attendants were struggling to loosen Trina's seatbelts...cautiously lifting Trina out of the seat. She was unconscious. There was a small trickle of blood coming out of the corner of her mouth, and Slate felt an overwhelming panic. She had to be all right...she had to be....

"Trina!"

He was thrust out of the way as corpsmen cautiously lifted Trina's limp body onto the stretcher and put it into the ambulance. Buck brushed past him, his face pale, and jumped into the ambulance to assume the place beside Trina. His eyes on Trina's still face, Slate was about to climb into the ambulance behind them when a hand jammed firmly into his chest.

"I'm sorry, sir. Only one person allowed."

He needed to be with Trina...he needed to know that she was all right. His eyes moved to her chest. Her breathing was shallow. Fear jarred him into motion. He attempted again to climb into the back of the ambulance, only to have the corpsman repeat insistently, "I'm sorry, sir."

"I'm coming with you...."

Buck's voice grated harshly through the melee surrounding them. "Get out of the way, Montgomery. You're holding us back."

The harsh truth of Buck's statement forced Slate to step away from the ambulance, and the doors slammed shut in his face. Racing back through the clusters of curious observers, he headed directly for his Porsche. He was behind the wheel and heading for the exit before the gates began closing behind the ambulance. The crowd was still roaring behind him, the revving engines adding to the din as he followed the screeching ambulance out onto the dark street.

SATURDAY NIGHT...the emergency room was filled to capacity. Slate was unable to sit still. Trina was in one of the treatment rooms. He had heard nothing since she had been taken inside a half hour before. Knowing he could stand it no longer, he took the arm of the first nurse he passed and questioned tightly, "The driver...the race car driver...which room is she in?"

The stout, gray-haired woman's gaze softened slightly as she looked into Slate's agitated expression. "I'm sorry, sir. I can't give you any information...."

"Look, either you give me information on how she's doing, or I'm going in there right now to find out for myself."

Shooting a quick look out of the corner of her eye toward the security guard at the entrance, the woman hesitated. "You know you'll only get yourself in trouble if you try that. Why don't you just sit down and relax? I'm sure someone will come out with information as soon as it's available."

Slate nodded and turned away. It was useless trying to talk to them. He waited. As soon as the rotund figure had disappeared through the outer doorway, Slate walked calmly through the waiting room and into the hallway. His eyes immediately touched on Buck. Still dressed in his stained firesuit, he was seated slumped on a bench, his hands covering his face.

Panic surging through his body, Slate rushed to Buck's side. His voice was hoarse as he stood over Buck's slumped figure.

"Is she all right, Buck? Is she conscious?"

Buck's head came up slowly. "They're working on her. She was still unconscious when I was in there last." He shook his head. "She didn't want to bother with that steering problem she was having.... She said it could wait until Monday night.... I should've forced her to check it...should've done it for her."

"She knew she had a problem with her steering? She didn't tell me..." Slate shook his head. No, Trina never told him anything about her car. She didn't want him to interfere.

Slate felt sick. When this was over, things were going to be different. He wasn't going to let her put him off. Hell, he was going to stick in there...not give up until she loved him as much as he loved her. And if she didn't want to hear the words, he would prove the way he felt without them. She was going to be all right. She had to be....

A sudden movement in the doorway of the room in front of them snapped Buck to his feet. Slate's eyes followed Buck's to the unsmiling doctor's face, and he waited breathlessly as Buck's deep voice broke the silence in the hallway.

"Is she all right, doctor? Can I see her?"

"She's conscious at the present time, but she's slipping in and out. We did some X rays...there's no fracture, but she has a severe concussion. Right now we're worrying about shock. Her blood pressure is back up to normal as well as her pulse, but we're going to have to keep her in Intensive Care tonight and watch her carefully. She has some nasty belt burns, but other than the concussion, she appears to be all right."

"Can I see her?" both men asked simultaneously.

The doctor's glance moved between the two men. "One of you can see her for a few minutes. I don't want her excited in any way...."

Buck did not hesitate. "She's my sister. I'm going in."

Slate stepped back and ran his hand anxiously through his hair as Buck followed the doctor inside the room. He didn't want to make a scene...Trina shouldn't be excited...but he had to see her. He wasn't going to leave until he saw with his own eyes that she was all right.

An eternity passed before Buck walked back into the hallway again, his brow still furrowed. The doctor was beside him. Unwilling to wait a moment longer, Slate stepped forward. "I want to see her, doctor."

"I'm sorry, she's in no condition..."

"I just want to look at her. I won't bother her...."

Aware that Buck was intently following the exchange, Slate continued quietly, his eyes trained on the doctor's reluctant expression. "Look doctor, I just want to see for myself that she's all right."

The doctor's wary eyes moved across Slate's anxious face for a few seconds. "Just a few minutes, and then out."

Slate swallowed hard. "Thanks, doc."

He suddenly realized he was trembling as he took the few steps to the doorway of Trina's room.

SHE WAS COMING BACK to the light again.... Where was she? Oh, yes...the hospital....

With frightening clarity she saw the track wall coming at her again! It was coming closer...it was almost upon her! She was flying...flying in the air, turning over and over... The lights...the screams...the engine roaring...!

Trina's eyes snapped open wide, only to drop closed once again. She was in a hospital and Buck had just left her. He had said she was all right...the doctor had told him she was going to be okay. But she felt so sick.... She ached all over. Her head...it hurt so bad.... It was making her nauseated. She was going to be sick. But no...she had already been sick...her stomach was empty. She felt so awful...so awful...

Her eyes opened again, and she fought to focus. There was someone standing beside the bed. Slate. It was Slate. He didn't look angry anymore. There was a funny little leap inside her. She wanted him to touch her...to hold her.

"Slate..."

"Trina, honey. How do you feel?"

He was holding her hand, and Trina tried to smile. "I hurt, Slate. Buck told me my car is totaled. But the doctor says..." She had to stop. The world was whirling dizzily and she held on tightly to his strong hand. She lost her train of thought. She opened her eyes again and made a greater effort to focus. Slate's brilliant blue eyes were trained on her face, and he was pale....

"Are...are you sick, Slate? You're so pale...."

A small, wry laugh escaped his lips. "I am? Well, there I was worrying about you and I'm the one who's pale. What do you know...."

In the next instant Slate's face was close to hers, only inches away. "Honey, you scared the hell out of me on that track. I have a right to be pale."

"Why, Slate?" It was all unclear.... Trina was having trouble getting her thoughts together. "You said we couldn't be friends...."

"I said that, did I? I guess I was a little angry."

"You're not angry anymore?"

Slate hesitated a moment before raising her hand to his lips and kissing it gently. "No, I guess I'm not."

Trina tried to smile, but her head...it was hurting her again. She was beginning to feel sick to her stomach.

"What's wrong, Trina?"

"I'm...I'm going to be sick, Slate."

Then a cool, impersonal hand took hers and Slate slipped from her sight. She was retching. Soon the darkness was assuming control again. It was good in the darkness. There was no pain....

"I DON'T WANT to stay here, Buck."

It was morning. Trina stared into her brother's worried face, her eyes flicking to Karen who stood silently at his side. She was starting to feel the surge of panic. She had awakened in the Intensive Care Unit of the hospital that morning. She had already been moved down to a semiprivate room and it looked like they were settling her in for a stay. She didn't want to stay. She could not explain the claustrophobic feeling that overcame her in this sterile atmosphere. She felt inexplicably alone and vulnerable here. Her heart was beginning to race. A faint memory stirred in the back of her mind. Her mother...had it been her mother who had lain in the hospital bed, pale and weak sounding...her voice hardly audible? She had died there.

Her father's death was much clearer in her mind. A heart attack... He was in the hospital.... They had said he'd get better, but he hadn't.

No. She didn't want to stay here...she didn't...

"Buck, I want to go home."

"Trina, be reasonable and calm down. You're not supposed to do anything that will raise your blood pressure. Listen to me. You have to have constant care. So far your blood pressure and your pulse are stable, but the doctor said there is danger of relapse for forty-eight hours...possibly even seventy-two hours afterward. You have to take it easy. That means no stairs, bending, lifting...for a week. You have to stay in bed at least that long and rest. You can't be alone in case something happens."

"I can take care of myself..."

"No, you can't..."

"I'll stay with her, Buck." Karen's soft voice interrupted the conversation, causing the others to turn in her direction. "I'll call in at work and tell them I can't come in for a week...."

Trina's response was immediate. "No, I can't let you do that, Karen." She attempted to shake her head, but it was too painful. "No, thank you...I appreciate your offer, but I know Piersall, Ltd. You won't be able to take vacation time on such short notice, and you'd end up losing a week's salary. You can't afford it."

"Then Karen will only take a few days off, and I'll take the rest of the week."

Trina could not help but smile. "Buck, it's the same pocket after all, isn't it? Besides, they'd never get a driver to take your route on such short notice, and they'd give you no end of trouble. I can't make you fall further behind."

"So, I guess that settles it. You'll just have to stay here for a few days, until they can be sure you're okay." Buck's voice was gruff, his expression stern.

"No, she can come home with me."

Trina's eyes snapped to the doorway and she watched as Slate walked into the room. As he looked at her, his concern was obvious, and Trina felt a momentary ray of hope that was dulled by Buck's unexpected reply.

"She's going to stay here until they release her."

Completely ignoring Buck's response, Slate walked to Trina's bedside, a small smile working across his lips as he leaned over to take her hand. A new sense of calm worked through her veins at his touch.

"Feeling better, Trina? I talked to the doctor before I came this morning..."

"You talked to the doctor!" Buck interjected.

Overriding Buck's comment, Slate continued evenly, "And he said everything went well during the night, but you had to be watched for forty-eight hours at least...."

"I don't want to stay here, Slate."

Her eyes reflecting her inexplicable fear, Trina clenched Slate's hand.

Trina's eyes were looking directly into his, and Slate swallowed hard at the appeal in her gaze. The first time...it was the first time Trina had allowed him even a glimpse of her inner feelings. She looked so vulnerable, so damned frightened, and Slate fought the impulse to take her in his arms and comfort her.

His response was low, consoling. "Don't worry, Trina. I'm taking you home with me."

"She's not going anywhere."

At Buck's adamant response Slate turned toward his unyielding face. "Look, Buck, Trina doesn't want to stay in the hospital. My condo has two big bedrooms and plenty of room for her. I have a woman who comes in every day. She cleans and has dinner ready for me if I want it. She'll be happy to stay with Trina, and should anything go wrong, my shop is close by—"

"She's not going home with you." Buck's response was unrelenting, and Trina closed her eyes against the confusion welling inside her brain.

"Buck..." Karen's soft admonition turned Buck's head in her direction.

"You're upsetting Trina. Besides, it's her decision to make. Why don't you ask her what she wants to do?"

"Because she's not responsible right now..."

Trina felt her panic rising. She didn't want to stay in the hospital.... She couldn't stay....

"Buck...I want to go with Slate...."

Suddenly realizing all eyes were upon her, Trina said softly, "I...I can't stay here, Buck. Please understand. And if you don't want me to go home alone, Slate is my only alternative..."

Slate winced inadvertently, and Trina closed her eyes momentarily. "I'm sorry, Slate. I don't mean to sound ungrateful.... It's just..."

"It's all right, honey. I'll tell the nurse you're going to leave."

Slate was on his way out the door before Buck could react. Trina's soft appeal stopped his protest.

"Buck, I'll tell Slate to give you his telephone number and you can call me...or come to see me if you have the time..."

"If I have the time?"

"Buck...Karen, please try to make him understand."

"Don't worry, Trina. Buck understands. He has an aversion to hospitals, too, and if he was in your place, he'd be trying to get out of staying just as much as you. Isn't that right, Buck?"

Hesitating only a moment longer, Buck walked the few steps to the bed and took Trina's hand. The gentleness of his touch and the sudden tenderness in his expression brought the heat of tears to her eyes.

"Trina, honey, I'm sorry. If you want to go with Slate, that's the way it's going to be. But he damned well better take good care of you."

Trina smiled and squeezed his callused hand. She closed her eyes. Her head ached and she was tired. She really just wanted to sleep....

THE BRIGHT AFTERNOON SUN had done its work well, transporting her to a state just short of sleep, as Trina sat with her head back against the car's headrest, her eyes dropping closed intermittently. It had been a long drive from the hospital, longer than she had expected, and despite the comfort of the air-conditioned Porsche, Trina was relieved to feel Slate pulling the car to a slow halt. Her heavy-lidded eyes drifted to the impressive brick apartment building. Abruptly, she was aware of Slate's scrutiny. Turning back toward him, Trina attempted a smile. But there was no smile in return as

Slate's eyes moved assessingly over her face before glancing up to the doorman who approached the side of the car.

"Harry, get someone to park my car. I won't be needing it anymore today."

"Sure thing, Mr. Montgomery."

Slate got out of the car and opened her door. "Slowly, Trina.... Stand up slowly...."

His expression tense, Slate waited only until Trina had risen to her feet on the curb before scooping her up into his arms and turning toward the entrance to the building.

"Slate, I can walk."

"No, you can't."

"Slate..."

"Be quiet, Trina."

Trina's frown at his brief command drew the first smile to Slate's lips. He walked through the entrance toward the elevator, stopping only after he had pressed the button. Lowering his head, he pressed a light kiss against her forehead.

"You hate being told what to do, don't you, honey? But this time you have no choice. We're both going to follow orders...the doctor's orders...and to the letter. So if you have any idea of having your own way for the next week, just forget it. You're going to stay in bed and rest."

The brilliant blue of Slate's eyes were close to hers...almost mesmerizing in her fatigued state. But Trina could not allow such a bald statement to pass uncontested. "The doctor didn't say you had to make an invalid out of me...."

Slate's gaze moved over her pale face, and he shook his head. "You can hardly keep your eyes open...you're as weak as a kitten, but you won't give in, will you?"

The elevator doors opened and Slate stepped out and walked down the hallway. Trina thought fleetingly that Slate carried her as if she were weightless. But maybe it only felt that way because she was so lightheaded....

Seconds after they stopped before the doorway, the door swung open to reveal a tall, gray-haired woman who smiled anxiously.

"Mr. Montgomery...I have your room ready just as you instructed."

"Thanks, Freddie...."

Trina was barely aware of the room through which she passed so quickly, merely managing to gain the impression of light and space before she was carried through the bedroom doorway and laid carefully on the oversized bed in the center of the room. Trina glanced around. Something was wrong...this room was too lived in. Slate's personal articles were on the dresser...there were keys and some spare change on the table near the bed....

Her careful scrutiny of the room did not go unnoticed. "Yes, this is my room, Trina. I thought you'd be more comfortable here. I'm going to be staying in the spare room...."

"But why? I don't mind using the other room. I don't want to inconvenience you any more than I am already...."

A faint trace of annoyance moved across Slate's expression. He sat carefully on the side of the bed and directed a firm gaze into her eyes.

"Look, let's get one thing straight, once and for all. You're not inconveniencing me. If I didn't want you with me, I wouldn't have offered to bring you here. It's as simple as that. This is not a magnanimous gesture. It's a purely selfish one. I'll be able to rest more easily knowing you're under my care until the doctor releases you."

Trina could not suppress a small smile. "So, you're a frustrated mother hen...."

Slate shook his head, and his grin was slightly lascivious as he said, "Honey, you bring a lot of things out in me, but none of them are maternal or paternal instincts."

A low cough from behind broadened Slate's smile. "And now that you've made me embarrass Freddie..."

"I made you embarrass Freddie?"

"Let me introduce you to Mrs. Fredericka Stern. I gave her a call from the hospital, and she was kind enough to rush over here and make the place ready for you." Turning toward the tall, slender figure who hovered uncertainly by the doorway of the room, Slate smiled warmly. "Freddie's been with me since...well, I guess it's five years now. And she's terrific...."

The narrow, lined face flushed under Slate's praise as Fredericka Stern walked forward. "Mr. Montgomery is a pleasure to work for. And I'm pleased to meet you, Miss..."

"Trina...please call me Trina, Freddie. I hope I won't be any extra trouble for you."

"Of course you won't! I'm pleased that Mr. Montgomery will trust me with you. He obviously thinks very highly of you—"

"Let's not give away any secrets, Freddie." Leaning over, Slate slipped Trina's shoes from her feet and pulled the coverlet up and over her denim-clad legs.

"Besides, Trina has to sleep for a while. She's had a long ride home from the hospital."

Leaning over, Slate pressed a light kiss against Trina's lips before she could mutter a protest. He cupped her cheeks with his hands and held her gaze tightly with his. "Go to sleep, honey. Freddie will have dinner ready when you wake up."

Supremely grateful for his understanding, Trina nodded weakly and allowed her eyes to fall closed at last. She felt Slate's mouth move lightly against hers once more and a sweet peace enveloped her. The panic that had overcome her in the hospital was dissipating....

A LOW, FAMILIAR RUMBLE of voices penetrated her sleep, sharply awakening Trina. Momentarily startled by the unfamiliar darkened room she felt a resurgence of panic and called out. The bedroom door jerked open as Slate moved quickly to the side of the bed.

His expression anxious, he inquired softly, "What's wrong, Trina?"

"Noth...nothing, Slate." Giving a small, embarrassed laugh, she continued hesitantly, "I woke up and didn't know where I was...." Unexpected tears sprang into her eyes and Trina swallowed tightly. What was wrong with her? She felt so weak...so alone. She longed to feel Slate's arms around her, holding her close. He was crouched by the bed, his eyes searching her face, and she turned to him in wordless appeal.

A low, inarticulate sound escaped Slate's lips as he moved his hand to cup her cheek. "Don't look at me like that, Trina. You know I have no resistance when it comes to you." Slowly lowering his head, he covered her mouth with a gentle kiss. He drew away at last, his eyes still intent on her face as he said slowly, "You have visitors already. Buck and Karen.... They brought you some clothes."

She smiled instantly. "Where are they? Why don't they come in?"

"They didn't want to startle you."

She was annoyed. "Do they really think I'm that fragile?"

"Yes...you are, and for the next three days you're going to be treated like glass...."

"Ughh! You don't really expect me to—"

"Trina, honey, behave yourself." Shaking his head, Slate turned toward the doorway. "Buck ... Karen ... come on in."

Slate was opening the blinds of the room to the setting sun as Buck walked through the doorway, his eyes intent on her face. Taking a moment to flash a smile in Karen's direction, Trina surveyed her brother's expression. It could not have been easy for him to come to Slate's apartment, but there was no trace of resentment on his face. Instead, he gave her a small smile as he leaned low over the bed and hugged her tightly. Suddenly the tears that seemed ever threatening spilled down her cheeks.

"Hey, what's this? Since when did you get so sloppily sentimental?"

Buck's voice was gruff, and Trina laughed, filled with warmth at his typical response. "I'm not responsible, Buck. That knock on the head seems to have turned on the waterworks, and I have trouble shutting them off."

"Just as long as you don't drown me...." His broad hand was smoothing the tears from her cheeks just as they had when their father had died, and Trina fought to control her tears.

Disgusted with herself, she moved to the side of the bed. "I'm going to get up."

"Oh, no you're not." Slate's protest was immediate.

"Yes, I am...."

Slate sat down at her side, blocking her exit before she could move an inch closer to the edge of the bed.

"Look, Trina. You're not to get up. Buck and Karen can make themselves comfortable and talk to you in here. I don't want you walking at all for three days.... I'll carry you where you want to go."

"And what if I have to go to the bathroom when you're not here? Will Freddie carry me?"

"Smart ass!" Buck's low ejaculation came from where he stood towering over the bed. "You'll do exactly what Slate says. You wanted to come here, and you're under his care. And if I find out you're giving him a hard time about obeying the doctor's orders, I'll take the week off like I said and take care of you myself!"

"Oh, no, sir, not that!" Raising her hands in mock horror, Trina smiled into her brother's angry face, but he was not to be mollified. "I want your word, Trina...."

Exhausted by her brief rebellion, Trina closed her eyes for a few short moments and nodded. Her gaze moved between the two stern faces that regarded her intently. "Okay. You have my word I'll behave."

Slate's nod and Buck's low grunt of acknowledgement brought a small, overly sweet smile to her face. "So...who's going to carry me to the bathroom?"

"Now?" Slate's question was wary.

"Yes, now, Slate. My bladder is about to burst."

Giving her a short, wry smile that said with great eloquence, "You're hopeless!", Slate scooped her effortlessly into his arms and walked to the bathroom door.

"You can walk three steps into the bathroom and back out again. That's all you're allowed."

Startled to find her legs wobbling beneath her as Slate stood her on her feet, Trina clutched at Slate's arm, immediately angry with herself for her weakness as alarm flashed across Slate's face.

"Don't worry, I'll make it. You're not going to lose your first patient...."

Slate did not look amused and Trina groaned inwardly as she closed the door behind her. It was going to be a long week.

TRINA OPENED HER EYES in the darkness and was suddenly afraid. It was still night, and she was in Slate's apartment. But fear was a colleague of the night. Her eyes flashed to the clock at her bedside, the luminous dials confirming that it was many hours yet until dawn. She was beginning to perspire despite the comfort of the air-conditioned room and, trying to relax, she thought about her situation.

Buck and Karen had left shortly after bringing her a suitcase full of the necessities for her stay. She was intensely relieved to be out of her jeans and into the comfortable shortie gown. And she was sure that as soon as this week was over and she was recovered from her injuries, she would be herself again. This strange panic that saw fit to visit her intermittently would disappear. But in the meantime—

A small noise at the door of the room alerted Trin to someone else's presence the second befo swung open and a lamp was flicked on n trance. Slate's face was almost indistinguish semidarkness as he approached her bed. He was still fully clothed, as if he had not yet been to bed and he ran a broad hand through his already tousled hair as he came.

"I thought I heard you twisting and turning in here. Can't you sleep, Trina?"

"I was sleeping, Slate. I just woke up. I don't know why...."

Slate's voice was concerned as he sat on the side of the bed and reached over to turn on the table lamp.

"Do you feel all right?" His hand went automatically to her forehead, and satisfied that there was no fever, he allowed his fingers to trail down her cheek to her chin.

"Yes, I feel fine. Please don't worry about me, Slate. Get some sleep or you won't be worth much in your office tomorrow." Her eyes slipping from his, she offered in a softer tone, "Please, Slate. If I thought I was going to be in your way, I would've stayed in the hospital...."

"Trina, honey, look at me...."

Following his soft plea, Trina looked up into Slate's face, only to be startled by the torment visible there. His voice, too, was affected by emotion.

"Trina, I haven't been able to make myself go to bed, yet. I...I want to be with you tonight."

Trina shook her head, her eyes clearly reflecting her thoughts.

"No...I don't mean to make love to you. I know that's not possible...not now.... But every time I close my eyes I see your car flipping over and over inside my mind. I just want to be with you. I want to know you're in bed beside me...safe...in my arms."

The need in Slate's expression struck a corresponding emotion inside her. Responding blindly, Trina hesitated only momentarily before nodding, her throat too choked to speak.

His eyes moving assessingly over her face, Slate slowly raised his hand to turn off the lamp. He stood up, and within moments had shed his clothes. The bed beside her moved under his weight, and Slate's strong, familiar arms reached out to draw her close against him. Trina sighed involuntarily. Slate's breath was warm against her hair; his hands caressed her gently. The anxieties so strong in her mind only moments before began to fade as she leaned full into his embrace. She closed her eyes. She was no longer afraid.

THE SUN STREAMED in the window behind Slate's desk, weaving a familiar slatted pattern across its surface and on the papers he scanned so dutifully. Initialing the last letter, Slate closed the folder and placed it in his out basket. Well, that was the mail taken care of for another day. Judy would remove it later and have the letters he had dictated an hour earlier ready to be signed when he came to the office tomorrow. He glanced at his watch for the fifth time that morning. Eleven o'clock. He just had time to go over the blueprints of the job for Hawthorne Associates before leaving.

In the three days Trina had been staying with him, Slate had slipped into a very comfortable pattern of coming to work in the mornings, while Freddie stayed with Trina, and returning home by twelve-thirty so that Freddie could leave. He then spent the rest of the day with Trina, and he had to admit the situation couldn't make him happier.

He glanced again at his watch. He found that he was increasingly impatient for the morning to come to an end so that he could go home to Trina. Home to Trina.... It had not taken him long to recognize the importance of that phrase...to realize he wanted things to stay just that way. He gave a small laugh. He had never thought he would come to the point in his life where he wanted one woman...one woman to go home to...one woman to love...one woman for the rest of his life. And that one woman was Trina. Of that fact he could not be more sure. The only problem was going to be in convincing Trina.

Somehow, he didn't believe that an accident, even as serious as the one she had suffered, was going to change her objectives. She had worked for one purpose for the greater part of her life, and he was certain she would consider this setback only temporary. He frowned. He was only too aware of Trina's deflated finances. With the hospital expenses she had incurred, and the doctor bills that would also come, he had no doubt she would be unable to raise the money for a new car this season. It would be senseless to offer to help. She'd never stand for it, pigheaded as she was. But he loved her, pigheaded or not. Oh, God, how he loved her....

Damn! Why did he have to fall for a career woman...and for one with a damned-near impossible career goal at that? For the first time in his life he truly knew what he wanted. He wanted Trina, as his wife, and he was certain the idea of a wedding ring would send her running. The thought of a commitment other than to racing seemed to scare her silly. He still wasn't sure what he had done to make her distrust his motives...or was it that she just distrusted men in general? Whatever, he was going to have to take it slow with her...ease her gently into the position where she was as lost without him as he was without her. He would just have to—

Raising his head at a sound at the door, Slate lifted his brow as Dave entered and closed the door behind him. Noting that his partner's face had that innocent look that usually preceded an avid round of personal questions, he suppressed a smile.

"What's the matter, Dave? Is your hand sore?"

"Is my hand sore...?"

"Well, since you didn't knock..."

"Since when do I have to knock on your door?" Looking sincerely offended, Dave shook his head. "The next thing I know you'll be asking me to make an appointment before I can have a few minutes to talk to you!"

"Come to think of it, that might be a good idea...."

"Oh, come off it, Slate, will you?"

Unable to suppress his amusement any longer, Slate drew himself to his feet and waved his hand expansively in the direction of the couch. "Dave, come in and make yourself comfortable. You know I'm always glad to see you walking through my doorway...."

"Oh, brother, I don't think I can stand it."

"Stand what?"

"You've been in such a damned good mood these last three days that it's driving me crazy."

A low laugh escaped Slate's lips and he shook his head. "You don't know what you want, do you, Dave? Aren't you the same guy who was criticizing me for my foul mood a little while back? So now I'm being pleasant...agreeable..."

"Sickening.... You're so damned content that you're making my stomach turn. Hell, you're like a satiated cat who just finished a big dish of cream. You're all but licking your lips...."

Slate's amused laughter brought another groan from Dave's direction. "You see, I can't even get a rise out of you anymore!"

"Dave, there's only one person who gets a rise out of me now...."

Slate's smirk elicited a responsive grin from Dave. "And damn if the man doesn't even admit to being stuck on the woman! I thought I'd never see the day!"

Refusing to comment on his partner's remark, Slate checked his watch again. "What did you want to talk to me about, Dave? I have to be leaving here soon, and I've got a few more things to do yet."

"Stop trying to change the subject. When am I going to get to meet this 'Wonder Woman'?"

"Oh, Trina would love to hear herself referred to as Wonder Woman."

"Stop trying to hedge. I think I've waited long enough. After all, I am your partner and your best friend...."

"Well, you're my partner, anyway."

"Damn it, Slate, you...!"

Laughing at his friend's response, Slate raised his hands in a gesture of compliance. "Okay, okay, you win, Dave. I've been thinking of showing her the machines we used to tool the parts for my car anyway. As soon as she gets the doctor's approval, I'll bring her in here."

"I was sorta thinking I could go home with you this afternoon...maybe for lunch or something... Oops!" Reacting to Slate's spontaneous frown, Dave shook his head again. "Don't give me an answer. I know what it is."

"No, Dave, I'm sorry. Trina's not really well enough, yet. I don't think she's ready for company."

"And it's obvious, neither are you.... Can't bear to share her yet, huh?"

"That's not the point. You know Trina's condition. She—" Stopping in midsentence, Slate suddenly grinned. "Yeah, I can't bear to share her yet. For the first time since I've known her she's all mine, even if she is too sick for me to do anything about it. And I sure as hell don't want you there taking up my time."

"Getting kind of possessive, aren't you, Slate? From the little you've let drop about her, I had the idea Trina Mallory might not respond to that kind of treatment."

"Well, she doesn't have much choice about it right now, does she?"

"And you're loving it...."

"And I'm loving it."

"Slate, you know you're in trouble, don't you?"

Dave's expression was suddenly serious, causing the grin to drop from Slate's face as he responded in a low tone, "Dave, I've been 'in trouble' since the first day I met Trina Mallory."

"You're not telling me anything I didn't know. I'm just surprised to hear you admit it, that's all."

"There might be a few more surprises in store if things go my way, Dave."

Dave looked startled, and he muttered in a disappointed voice, "Hell.... There goes my vicarious love life...."

Slate laughed. "Dave, get out of here, will you? I've got work to do."

Turning on his heel, Dave nodded as he walked toward the door. "Yeah, yeah...."

Slate shook his head in amused disbelief as the door closed behind his partner. Then his eyes dropped to his watch again, and he hesitated only a moment longer before reaching for his suit jacket. It was obvious he wasn't going to get anything else accomplished this morning. He was going home. Home to Trina...

TRINA FLICKED the remote control on the TV to another channel, and then another. Unable to stand the raucous buzzer and the resulting screams of the contestant who had delivered a correct answer on the game show, Trina switched off the set and dropped the control absentmindedly on the bed.

Her eyes moved around the large, beautifully decorated bedroom. It was by far the most impressive bedroom she had ever slept in. She had had plenty of time to survey the furnishings, and she had come to the conclusion that Slate had used an interior decorator when he had furnished the apartment. Certainly he couldn't have managed such a perfect, subtle blending of colors by himself. A masterpiece in beige and blue, the decor ran the full range of pale, harmonizing shades in an effect that was cool and relaxing.

The room itself was immense, which was fortunate since the bed in which she slept was also immense. Besides the fact that it was king sized, the headboard incorporated a massive wall unit that included a mirrored backdrop, cabinets, indirect lighting...the works! Soft, upholstered chairs were strategically placed amongst the matching furniture scattered around the room; a luxurious beige rug ran wall to wall, stretching to the bank of windows presently covered by vertical blinds. The bedroom had an adjoining master bath in matching colors, with which she had become quite familiar. It was the only other room she had seen since her arrival three days before.

Her eyes moved to the window blinds, against which a bright sun shone, and she frowned. She raised her hand and ran her fingers through her hair in an impatient gesture, grimacing at its touch. She hadn't washed her hair in three days, and she was beginning to feel less than clean. What she really needed was a nice shower instead of the pitiful sponge baths to which she had been limited.

Trina was feeling decidedly improved. The headaches that had plagued her were gone, and the frightening bouts of anxiety she had suffered had also disappeared. Turning away from the window, her eyes moved unconsciously to the pillow beside hers. She had no doubt Slate's presence beside her at night was responsible for relieving that problem. Such a large bed, and yet she had slept each night clutched tight in his arms, safe from the recurring, haunting flashbacks of the accident.

But she was beginning to feel well enough to chafe at her unnatural existence. She had been in bed for three days, and her muscles cried out to be used. But every time she made an effort to get out of bed, someone was there to stop her. She shot a quick look toward the clock on the dresser. Eleven-fifteen. Slate would be home in an hour or so. She'd talk to him then and see if she could get up and take a shower.

Wait a minute! Angry at her own compliance, Trina pulled herself to a sitting position in bed. Since when had she to defer to Slate for permission to do anything? Shouldn't *she* be the one to decide if she was well enough to do something as simple as taking a shower?

She glanced at the clock again. She could be showered, changed and back in bed by the time Slate returned. Then she could tell him that she had successfully accomplished the small feat and he need not worry about her any longer. She frowned. If she was going to do it, she'd better do it now. If Freddie kept to her schedule, she would be checking on her in fifteen minutes, and she didn't want to frighten the poor woman. She took Slate's directions so seriously....

Trina listened intently for a few minutes. Yes, Freddie was busy in the kitchen. She could be in the bathroom and back again before Freddie even realized she was out of bed.

Moving herself carefully to the edge of the bed, Trina slid her feet over the side and drew herself slowly to a standing position. She was decidedly unsteady on her feet, and she suddenly realized it was not going to be as easy as she thought. She began an uneasy path across the bedroom toward the master bathroom. Yes, the room was indeed large. It was a longer distance than she had realized to the bathroom door.

She stopped and took a deep breath. She was swaying unsteadily, but determination pushed her onward. She walked through the bathroom doorway toward the sink. She needed to splash some water on her face to clear her head. Reaching the sink at last, she managed to accomplish the task with more difficulty than she had considered possible. She turned toward the shower and reached inside. The low hiss of the water was soothing to her ears, and barely able to restrain her anticipation, Trina pulled the abbreviated nightgown over her head and slipped out of her brief bikini bottoms.

She was standing blissfully under the relaxing water when weakness assaulted her. Bracing herself against the shower wall, she took a deep breath and attempted to still her quaking frame, but it was no use. Her legs were turning to rubber, refusing to support her. Her heart was beginning to race; her breath was coming in short, labored gasps. She was sinking slowly to the floor of the shower when the door jerked open unexpectedly to reveal Slate's angry face. Assessing the situation immediately, Slate reached in, unmindful of the spray that soaked his head and shoulders, and scooped her into his arms.

The next thing she knew, the cool, dry surface of the bed was beneath her and Slate was wrapping her in the bedspread. His hands were moving roughly over the surface of her skin through the material, bringing back warmth that had seemed to desert her only moments before. A deep, silent gratitude suffused her. She forced her eyes open and attempted to speak, only to be stopped by the anxiety obvious on Slate's face. She closed her eyes again.

"Trina...Trina, talk to me. Are you all right?"

Slate's voice was tense, and Trina was swamped with guilt. She opened her eyes.

"Yes, I...I'm okay. I just felt a little weak...."

Slate's eyes held hers silently for long moments before he turned away from the bed. Returning a few seconds later with a large bath towel, he unwrapped her from the bedspread and proceeded to rub her carefully with its soft warmth. When he was finished he pulled a blanket up over her and began to work on her hair.

His voice was gentle when he spoke again. "Why did you take such a chance, Trina? I told you I'd help you. All you had to do was ask...."

"I—I didn't want to ask. I thought I could handle it."

"And how do you think I felt when I saw you in there ready to collapse? If you had fallen...hit your head again..." The thought was obviously more than he could bear, and he hesitated a moment before continuing, "Trina, honey, don't do this to me. If anything happened to you..."

"I know...I'm sorry, Slate."

But she was tired...suddenly extremely tired, and she allowed her eyes to drop closed for a few seconds. Slate's hand moved immediately to her forehead, and he frowned. He turned to the bedside phone and within minutes was talking in a deep, earnest voice to the doctor. When he was done, he turned back toward her and touched her cheek gently.

"Trina, how do you feel now?"

"I'm okay, Slate. Please don't worry...."

"Dr. Michaels said you probably didn't do yourself any damage if you don't feel any aftereffects. You *do* feel all right, don't you? You're not hiding anything from me?"

"Slate, I'm fine...really."

"Promise me, Trina. I want you to promise me you'll tell me if you start to feel sick...."

"I promise, Slate." Hesitating only a moment, Trina added softly, "I'm sorry, Slate. That was a very stupid thing to do."

"Oh, honey..."

Slate's gentle, lingering kiss was the last thing she remembered before she dropped off to sleep.

CHAPTER NINE

SLATE WAS UNUSUALLY SILENT as he guided his Porsche through the afternoon traffic. Trina was puzzled. She had expected to see a smile of relief on his face when the doctor finally dismissed her. But the exact opposite had occurred when Dr. Michaels had pronounced her fit only a short time before. She shot another quick glance in his direction. His strong profile was etched against the blurring flash of passing streets, and he was still frowning.

The week had gone exceedingly well. Determined to be the perfect patient after the fright she had given Slate, Trina had followed his orders without protest. Not that she had been given an opportunity to do otherwise. Freddie's observation had been more stringent after her aborted shower, and Trina still could not think about it without embarrassment. She had acted like a fool. But despite her stupidity, Slate had been endlessly patient and thoughtful.

Slate had not asked her permission to come to her bed after the first night. It had seemed natural to both of them that he should sleep beside her. She had come to rely on the security of his touch. The warmth of his body, the scent of his skin, had become warmly familiar to her, a sweet consolation during the night. The strength of his arms was a reality that continued to hold at bay ragged, frightening dreams. She had learned to welcome the gentleness of his touch, and finally, to smile at his ever-present concern and consideration. She had to admit, it was a side of Slate she had not even suspected existed.

Her week-long confinement had also succeeded in establishing a line of communication between Slate and Buck. Unwilling to allow a telephone call to suffice, Buck had come to see her several times during the week, and she truly felt the conflict between Buck and Slate had been resolved for good.

They had turned the car over to the doorman, and soon they were walking down the hallway toward Slate's door. Slate had not broken the silence he had maintained since leaving the doctor's office, and Trina was beginning to feel uncomfortable. He unlocked the door and allowed Trina to enter in front of him.

Nodding a quick hello to Freddie as she walked through the living room, Trina walked directly to the master bedroom and took her suitcase out of the closet. She had reached down beside the bed for her slippers and put them into the suitcase when Slate's voice at the doorway caused her to turn in his direction.

"What are you doing?"

He entered the room and closed the door behind him before coming to stand beside her.

"I'm packing my things, Slate." Trina forced a small smile as she fought the unexpected sense of loss the thought evoked.

Slate's expression tightened. "What's the rush?"

"I'm not in a rush, but it is about time I went home. After all, I've been here over a week. I have a lot of things to take care of at home, and I'd like to see the damage to my car."

"Buck and I both told you it's totaled, Trina."

"I know, but..."

"Trina..." Slate's hands moved to her upper arms to hold her still as he continued softly, "I...I don't want you to leave." At her startled expression, Slate continued quietly, "I've gotten accustomed to having you here, honey...I like the way it feels having you lying beside me at night. I like talking to you in the darkness, knowing I can reach out and touch you whenever I want. Stay with me, Trina."

The appeal in his eyes and his low supplication was more than Trina could stand. Her reaction to the need in his voice was spontaneous. Reaching up, she wound her arms around Slate's neck. Pressing her body tightly against his, she whispered against his ear, "Oh, Slate, you've been wonderful this past week. But I didn't really expect..."

She hesitated, and Slate continued as his arms closed around her, "You didn't expect what, Trina? You didn't expect me to care as much as I do? Didn't you realize how I feel about you, Trina? I love you, honey."

"No, Slate. You've just gotten used to taking care of me...."

"I love you, Trina." Drawing himself far enough away so that he might look into her face, he continued softly, "I don't want you to leave. Stay with me...."

"No, Slate, that would be a mistake...."

"It would be a mistake if you left."

"No. If I stayed you'd just go on feeling responsible for me. I don't know what it is about me that brings that out in some people. Buck still hovers over me like a mother hen...."

"Trina, believe me. I don't feel like mothering you...."

Still held close against him, Trina could feel the physical proof of Slate's statement and she could not suppress a grin.

"Yes...well, maybe that was a poor choice of words." Becoming more serious again, she persisted, "But the effect is the same. And I appreciate everything you've done for me this past week too much to allow it to slip into a situation you'll regret."

"The only regret I could have would be if you left."

"Slate, please, you think you mean what you say, but..."

"Let me prove to you how I feel, Trina. Trina, honey, I want you so much..."

It was obvious he had become tired of talking, tired of wanting. The mouth that closed over hers was no longer seeking her assent. Instead it was demanding her response, a response Trina offered willingly with no restraint. His mouth was loving, worshiping her lips, the innate sweetness of her mouth. It covered her face in a spray of warm, moist kisses even as his hands moved caressingly over her body. She could not resist the hunger in his touch, a hunger that matched her own, and she raised her arms as he pulled the lightweight shirt off over her head. His hands moved over the smooth flesh of her back, stroking her sides, cupping her small, rounded breasts. He circled the dark areolas with his tongue, stopping to nip at the swollen crests. He cupped the rounded curve of her buttocks with his hands and, suddenly impatient with the clothing that hindered his touch, his hands moved to the clasp of her jeans.

Within moments he had stripped them away, and sinking to his knees, he followed the line of her bikini briefs with his seeking mouth. The small, pink wisp was efficiently discarded a few moments later, and Trina emitted a low gasp as Slate's kisses moved to the curling nest between her thighs. Too impatient to linger long, Slate moved directly to the source of her building passion. Intensely aware of the trembling that had begun to assail her, Slate moved his mouth caressingly in the warm moistness beneath. It was sweet to the taste, warm and eager for his caress. He stroked her gently, delighting in her response, coaxing, drawing from her until she shuddered weakly under his heady administrations.

Raising his gaze, Slate looked into Trina's impassioned expression. Her eyes were half lidded, the lush fans of her lashes fluttering as she sought to control passions welling inside her. Her face was flushed, her lips separated to display a trace of perfect white teeth. She swallowed tightly, and he felt his own hunger grow. Her heated gaze met and tangled with his, and he whispered hoarsely, "I love every part of you, darling. Show me how you love me back. Show me how, Trina...."

Lowering his head again to the soft petals of her womanhood, he fondled the bud of her desire with a new urgency, tasting, seeking, drawing. His appetite insatiable, he persevered in his intimate quest until Trina's slender body began to heave in giving response, returning to him the homage he sought, freely, lovingly, without constraint. His own love flushing wild and strong inside him, Slate accepted her body's sweet homage, continuing his ardent caresses until her last convulsive shudder.

Still supporting her, he allowed her to slip to her knees. He held her close against him for long moments before lowering her to the lush carpet beneath them. Impatiently stripping away his clothes, he paused to crouch over the naked length of her, his gaze intense, before lowering himself into the warmth of her body at last.

Slate was too far lost to his emotions to pause more than briefly to savor the supreme ecstasy of possession. Plunging inside her again and again, he brought himself rapidly to the summit of the emotion that raged inside him. Pausing at the brink for a long, glorious moment, Slate gasped her name in the second before he brought them both to simultaneous, thundering reward.

Raising his head at last from the scented cloud of her hair, Slate whispered into Trina's ear. "How many ways can I say I love you, Trina?"

They were still lying in each other's arms when Trina gasped suddenly, "Freddie...I forgot she was here! What will she think?"

A flash of amusement flicked across the tenderness in Slate's expression. "Trina, Freddie knows the bed in the spare room hasn't been slept in all week. I kind of think she has an inkling that we..."

The flush that rose to Trina's face brought a small laugh as Slate lowered his head to press his mouth lightly against hers. "She's going to have to get used to the idea of seeing you here on a more permanent basis, anyway...."

Moving to free herself from Slate's arms, Trina drew herself to her feet. Her eyes darted away from Slate's alert blue-eyed gaze.

"No, she isn't, Slate."

Drawing himself to his feet beside her, his grip was less than gentle as he turned her back toward him. "What do you mean, Trina?"

"I mean...I can't stay, Slate. I have to go back home."

"You *can't* stay? You mean you don't *want* to stay."

"Slate, when I agreed to come...it was only until I was well again. I never said..."

Slate's expression was hardening. "And everything that's happened since...it's changed nothing...."

Trina felt a stab of despair. She had no desire to hurt Slate. Her feelings were quite the reverse. It would be so easy to succumb to the desire to have Slate continue to protect her, take care of her. She no longer had any doubts that Slate truly cared for her, or at least that he believed he did. But she wasn't ready for this. She needed her independence. She needed it desperately. She had to be able to think without Slate's influence, the drugging effect he had on her senses. She had to think...to think...

Her dark eyes filled with torment, Trina raised her hand tentatively to Slate's cheek. "Slate, I can never thank you enough for what you've done for me this past week..."

"Is that what you tried to do just now when we made love....thank me?"

"Slate, please." Raising her mouth, Trina pressed a light, lingering kiss against his lips. When she drew back, the anger had left Slate's face.

"Trina...what are you trying to do to me?"

"I'm trying to tell you that I can't stay, Slate.... That I care for you more than I've cared for any man for a long time, but...but it's not enough.... I can't get involved yet."

"You intend to race again...is that it, Trina?"

"Yes...."

"And you're afraid living here will interfere...."

"Wouldn't it?"

Refusing a response, Slate questioned instead, "And what do you expect to race? I told you...Buck told you...your car is finished. There's no way you can save it."

"I'll get another...."

"How? You said your credit is already exhausted."

"I don't know, but I'll get another car."

"And in the meantime I wait...."

"Slate." Trina's eyes pleaded for his understanding. "I didn't say we had to stop seeing each other. I just said I couldn't stay here."

"So, I'm back to seeing you on weekends again...."

"Slate, I do...I really do care for you."

"Do you? Do you really, Trina?" Slate's expression was one of frank disbelief.

A rush of unexpected tears brought a quiver to Trina's voice as she replied softly, "Yes, I do. Please don't ask me to choose between—"

Slate's response was quick, delivered with a spontaneous frown. "No, I wouldn't ask you to choose between me and racing, Trina, because I know I'd come out the loser. So what if I tell you Wright-Montgomery can afford to sponsor another car...a sportsman model..."

"No."

"You don't want my help, do you? That hasn't changed."

"I'd feel like a bought woman."

"Thanks. That says a lot for me. I only want to make it easier for you, Trina. I know I'd be putting my money on a sure thing. You could be points champion this year!"

"No, not this year.... It's too late now. But next year..."

"Next year!"

"Slate, I'm not proposing that we stay apart that long. We can be together as often as we like. Slate, please..."

Brilliant, intense blue eyes moved over her face and Trina waited as a multitude of emotions washed over his face.

When he spoke, his tone was flat, without feeling. "All right, we'll play it your way." Abruptly turning away, Slate reached for his clothes. "Come on. We'll get dressed and I'll take you home."

Nodding, not quite understanding the ache deep inside her, Trina turned toward the bathroom door.

CHAPTER TEN

THE LATE AUGUST SUN was hot on his head, but Slate was oblivious to the intense heat. He felt too good. Street stock cars roared loudly around the track surrounding the pits, almost drowning out the conversation of the small, informal group that had gathered spontaneously between the cars while the drivers waited out the first of the qualifying heats. He laughed absentmindedly at one of Bill Weston's droll comments and leaned back against the fender of his modified car. A small, amused snort escaped his lips as Bix Morley brought a fresh round of laughter from the group. Casually reaching out, Slate slid his arm around Trina's waist and pulled her back against him. She relaxed against the support of his body, leaning full against him with intimate spontaneity.

It had been almost a month since Trina's accident, and although he'd had a period of desperation when Trina had moved back to her own house, she had not proceeded to withdraw from him as he had feared. Instead, she'd consented to see him with few exceptions when he called. Freed from the obligation to her car, she had agreed to spend the weekends with him at his apartment.

And he had actually convinced her to be late for work one Monday morning so that he might take her into Wright-Montgomery, on the pretext of showing her the machine which had tooled the parts for his car. Trina had been dressed for work in a pale-pink linen sheath dress, and Dave's eyes had all but bugged out of his head. She had been openly enthusiastic about the work the machine produced. He had explained the Computer Numerical Control basis on which the machines worked, and she had proceeded to ask several astute questions that had even surprised him. Dave hadn't stopped talking about her since.

Trina's black, gleaming curls were resting against the side of his cheek, and he turned his head to press a light kiss against them. His heart did a small flip-flop in his chest as she turned around to shoot him a small smile in reaction to another comment Bill had made. She missed the short, revealing glance Doug Frawley had shot in their direction.

In the past month, Slate had become more familiar with Trina's group of friends at the track, and he had to admit that Doug was a nice guy. But he was glad that Doug was finally getting the message that Trina belonged to Slate. He was continually surprised by the scope of his feelings for Trina. He hadn't realized it was possible to love so hard and so completely.

He had faced another truth about himself in the past month...the truth that he was glad Trina's car had been wrecked in the accident. He was also glad she had not accepted his offer of another car financed by his company. He found he was actually dreading the thought of again sharing Trina with racing, and he was beginning to think Trina knew him better than he knew himself.

He was also aware that he had to come to terms with the fact that, sooner or later, Trina was going to get another car. Ingrid had started the full round of fall shows, and Trina had worked in every one. He knew she was also actively seeking out sponsors. She was determined to have her car ready for the spring season, and she was already beginning to develop plans with Buck.

As the group stood together, Slate was aware of Buck's silent perusal. The truce necessitated by Trina's accident a month before was still in effect, but it was obvious Buck was still withholding final judgement. Karen was another story entirely. The small, quiet blonde had approached him only the week before and offered him her hand. She had told him she wasn't as stubborn as Buck and afraid to admit she was wrong. It had meant a lot to him to have her say that.

Suddenly Slate realized Trina had slipped her hand over his and was holding it against her waist. He gave a small, wry snort. He had unconsciously moved his hand up to cup her breast and she had carefully sidetracked him. He needed to be sidetracked sometimes when it came to Trina.

"Damn it, Trina, can't you get this fella to leave you alone long enough for you to participate in an intelligent conversation? Here I am giving you some good information on the value of hard tires versus soft, and he's got something of an entirely different nature on his mind!"

"Bill!"

Trina flushed, and Slate let out a low laugh.

"Well, I'll put it to you this way, Bill. Would you be thinking about tires if Trina was your girl?"

There was no hesitation as the gray head shook from side to side. "Hell, no!"

"But you could be a little more generous and share her a bit, Slate. We only get to see Trina once a week."

Doug's interjection was delivered with a smile, but Slate's reaction was spontaneous.

"Doug, I don't expect to share Trina with anyone or anything."

Meeting Slate's eyes for the space of a tense thirty seconds, Doug finally gave a small laugh. "No, I don't suppose I would either if I were you."

A call on the pits' audio system interrupted the conversation moving around the small group.

"All right, gentlemen, lineup for the modified heat. Let's get started: Numbers sixteen, forty-two, three, eighty-one, double zero eight, twenty-two..."

The list of numbers continued, the call efficiently breaking up the impromptu gathering as the men moved to their respective cars. Waiting only until the rest of the drivers were out of hearing, Trina turned toward Slate.

"That wasn't necessary, Slate. You made Doug's simple comment appear like a challenge. He didn't mean anything by it."

"Trina...you and I both know there's only one woman on Doug's mind. Just because he's been throwing a few crumbs to Helen this past month..."

"That's a terrible thing to say, Slate!"

"It may be terrible, but it's the truth. Crumbs are all he has left to give her. He's stuck on you, and you know it."

Trina lowered her gaze from his, and Slate's words trailed to a halt. He raised her chin gently and was startled to see tears glistening in her dark eyes.

"I never meant to lead him on, you know that, don't you Slate? Helen would be great for Doug if he ever gave her a real chance. I've told him that a few times."

"He'll give her a chance. He just needs a little time....and a little nudge from me now and then...."

Blinking away the sudden tears, Trina said softly, "No more nudges, Slate. Doug's my friend...."

"Mine too, Trina. And I want him to stay that way."

The audio system blared its call for drivers once again, bringing Bob Mitchell walking rapidly toward the car.

"Well, what do you say, Slate? Are you going to get into this heat or not?"

Giving Bob a brief nod, Slate turned back toward Trina and winked unexpectedly. "Well, who are you going to root for today, honey? Me or Buck?"

Trina attempted to shake her somber mood, responding with a forced smile, "Buck, of course! Need you ask?"

Slate reached out and cupped the back of Trina's head in his broad hand, holding her steady under his visual assault. His smile faded ever so slightly. "We'll see, honey...we'll see."

He dropped a light kiss on her lips, zipped up his suit and climbed into the car.

Trina was so intent on following the blue and white modified to the lineup that she was startled by Bob's low voice at her shoulder.

"It's a good thing Slate's got me, Bix and Sid to work on his car. We used to be able to depend on him two or three times a week to work with us on what needed to be done before the next race. But he's got only one thing on his mind these days...and her initials are Trina Mallory...."

Uncertain how to take his comment, Trina turned toward Bob's somber gaze. "That almost sounds like an accusation, Bob."

"I never thought I'd see the day Slate would be so wrapped up in one woman..."

"Bob..."

But Bob was intent on speaking his piece. "You know, at first, I thought it was kinda funny the way meeting you seemed to knock Slate flat on his backside. In all the time I've known him, it was always the other way around, with women chasing him. I figured it was about time he got his due. But it's different this time with him. He's not playing anymore. He's putting everything he has into this thing with you—"

"Bob, I don't need—"

"I know...you don't need my advice, but I'm going to give it to you anyway, Trina. Unless I miss my guess, you're holding back on him and he knows it. I don't know your reasons, and I don't want to, but I'd think things over very carefully if I were you."

A small frown worked between Trina's brows. "I'm not the femme fatale you seem to think I am, Bob. I think you overestimate me...or perhaps underestimate me...."

"Maybe so." Pausing only for a few moments in silent scrutiny, Bob nodded. "In any case, I've had my say." Mumbling a quick excuse, he turned back toward the rig and walked away.

Watching his wiry form until he disappeared inside, Trina turned and started in the direction of the refreshment stand. The race progressing around her was the furthest thing from her mind.

A few moments later, standing in the shade of the refreshment booth, Trina clutched the large paper cup and took another quick sip of soda. Perhaps she was more transparent than she thought. In any case, Bob had sensed her disquiet with the direction her life had taken in the past month. She wasn't ready for this kind of total absorption into someone's life. The demand was too much, and it made her too vulnerable.

But whatever she thought when she was apart from him, a paralyzing languor overtook her when she was with Slate; it felt so good in his arms. It felt too good. She needed an escape...a place to go in case things turned sour. She needed to keep her perspective.

"Trina...Trina Mallory!"

Trina's head snapped up toward the distinguished-looking man who smiled into her face. Something about him was familiar, but she just could not place—

"You don't remember me, do you? That *is* a blow," he said ruefully.

Trina frowned. She just could not seem to place him. There was an air about him...perhaps the way he spoke or moved. It was distinctive...

Reaching out a large, manicured hand, he took Trina's and raised it to his lips theatrically, his smile broadening.

"The last time I did this, you were wearing a black negligee and you gave me a dazzling smile."

It came to her in a flash and Trina laughed spontaneously. "Of course! Ingrid's show at Pierre's Restaurant! You were with that large group.... How could I have forgotten? It isn't often that a man kisses my hand so gallantly."

"Oh, I can hardly believe that...."

Trina's expression was a bit wry. "Whether you believe it or not, the racing scene isn't really conducive to such gestures."

"Well, then, I'm pleased to have brought a little diversion into your life. In any case—" he seemed to become suddenly serious as he continued "—it's time I introduced myself. My name is Kent Henning. I've been avidly following your career through the sports pages, Trina. The writers seem to love you. And I'll admit to being a bit more than surprised when I saw your picture for the first time about a week or so after the show. As a matter of fact, I couldn't believe my eyes."

"I'm not really certain how to take that...."

"It's only that it seemed so incongruous to me at the time...the lovely, sophisticated model who had stolen the whole show...."

"The strictly amateur model, Mr. Henning. As a matter of fact, I'm the only nonprofessional Ingrid uses in her shows and I sometimes wonder why."

"Please call me Kent. Her reasoning is perfectly obvious to me. You're a beautiful woman, Trina."

Trina's laugh was spontaneous. "Kent, please. I'm not accustomed to such blatant flattery. You'll turn my head."

"I can't believe that, either. But in any case, I was terribly sorry to hear about your accident. I was concerned. I even had my wife, Marie, call Ingrid to find out how you were."

"Ingrid never mentioned it."

"It must have slipped her mind. I read a follow-up story only a few weeks ago. I understand your car was destroyed in the crash and you're out of racing."

"Only temporarily. I'll be back as soon as I can finance another car." Trina laughed wryly. "Unfortunately, that may not be for some time. My finances are in a pretty poor state."

A subtle flicker of something indefinable passed over Kent's expression. "Then perhaps my offer may be even more opportune than I had hoped...."

"Your offer?"

Kent Henning was suddenly extremely serious. "Yes. I didn't come here to see the races. I came here specifically to see you, to make you a business proposition."

"A business proposition?"

Trina was intrigued as he reached into his pocket and withdrew a card from his wallet. She accepted it and read aloud, "Kent Henning, Executive Vice-President, GTB Foods."

"One of many executive vice-presidents, I'm afraid, but I do pride myself on being one of the most enterprising."

"I have no doubt.... But what did you want to see me about?"

The abrupt acceleration of racing engines coming off the fourth turn drowned out his words, and Kent Henning's brow wrinkled in a frown. "Is there somewhere we can go where I won't have to shout over the roar of an engine, Trina? I'm not as accustomed to the pits as you. I find the noise very disconcerting."

Trina hesitated only a moment. "How about the park a few blocks over. They have picnic tables and shade...."

"Perfect. My car is parked in the lot outside the gates. We can pick up my briefcase on the way."

The din of the track behind them had dulled momentarily and Trina shot a quick look to the pole on the third turn. The light was red...full stop on the track. Her eyes flashed to the first turn. Yes, an accident...a group of cars had collided, tying up the track. No, Buck and Slate weren't involved. As expected, they were at the head of the pack, awaiting the signal to proceed.

Trina made a quick decision. "We can probably get out now if we hurry...before the track starts moving again."

"Let's go, then."

Aware that the distinguished man who had been a stranger to her only moments before followed at her heels, Trina ran toward the exit gate. The gates closed behind them just as the cars again began moving around the track, and they headed toward the park.

A few minutes later Trina searched Kent Henning's face in disbelief. The shouts of a group of children playing on the swings nearby went completely unheard. Instead, Trina was conscious only of the pale eyes that soberly held hers.

"I have to admit, I'm stunned!" Glancing down once again to the papers in the roughly-hewn picnic table in front of her, she allowed her eyes to move over the formally typewritten proposal Kent had stopped to retrieve from his silver Mercedes.

"You want to offer me a contract...."

"That's right. Unfortunately, it took me almost the full month since I last saw notice of your accident to convince my board of directors how perfect you are for our product...."

"Spirit...a diet soft drink...!"

"We...GTB Foods...will be introducing it next month. We expect it'll make us a lot of money, Trina, if it catches on. That's where you come in...."

"But I'm a nobody! How could I..."

"You're a natural, Trina. I don't suppose you realize how much publicity you've gotten lately in the sports pages. I have, because I've been following your coverage with intense interest since I recognized your picture. When you had your accident, your exposure doubled and there were several follow-up stories that were picked up by other papers. You're perfect! Not only are you beautiful, you're poised, slim, articulate; and your interests are diversified to such an extent as to make them outrageously appealing to the American public...the American woman in particular. You work for a living, you model clothes—"

"But I'm only an amateur model...."

"That's of little significance. You're of a professional quality, and immensely more memorable than the average model. And you race cars for a hobby! You're the epitome of the active, modern American woman...the American woman with an adventurous spirit who drinks Spirit soft drink! What woman reading about your exciting life wouldn't wish to emulate it?"

"Kent, if you only knew how far off base that assessment is!"

"Why? Do you mean to tell me it isn't exciting to race cars?"

"Of course it is!"

"Well?"

"But it's a few minutes of racing as opposed to endless days and nights of tedious, dirty work in the garage. I've had to do without things that the average woman would consider a necessity, just to finance the car in the first place...."

"Then why do you do it?"

"Why do I race?"

"Yes."

"Because I love it."

"Well?"

"But, Kent, I don't have a car anymore. I haven't raced since my accident. My car was demolished. I'm going to have to start from scratch again...build a new car...as soon as I get the money together."

"Oh, no...we'll do that for you."

"You'll what?"

"I said GTB Foods will build the car for you...to your specifications...."

Trina was suddenly grateful she was sitting down.

"Are you all right, Trina? You're very pale."

"It's the shock...."

Kent smiled, relieved. "A pleasant shock, I hope."

"More than pleasant."

"Then you find the offer appealing?"

"Kent, I'm drooling...."

Kent's smile widened. "Of course, once the car's built, we'll supply the pit crew and take care of the maintenance."

"Pinch me. I must be dreaming...."

"But there are a few conditions...."

Trina's spirits took a quick dive. "That figures. What are they?"

"You have to change your racing colors to the Spirit colors—yellow and green...."

"No problem."

"And you have to agree to a certain amount of publicity and articles to be written about you...."

"Okay."

"And to dispense with all your other sponsors...."

"You don't know how easy that'll be."

"And you have to qualify and race in the Syracuse Schaefer 200 this year. I've learned enough about dirt-track racing to know that it's the biggest race of the year, and it'll be a perfect follow-up to the kickoff of our product."

"That'll be in October. Will the car be ready?"

"The car will be ready if you are."

Trina took a deep breath. Her heart was hammering loudly in her ears, and she wasn't sure she could speak coherently.

"It's a deal!"

"You're sure you don't want to think it over?"

"Are you crazy?"

Kent nodded. He extended his hand across the small table and clasped hers tightly in a businesslike handshake. "I can see it all now.... Full page ad and promo shots of you in different outfits, blurring into action shots of you racing...."

Trina's smile began to fade. "When is all this promo work supposed to be done, Kent? I work for a living, you know. There's a limit to the amount of time I can take off...."

"Of course we won't expect you to do all this extracurricular work without compensation...."

"You mean you'll pay me, too?"

"Reasonable compensation...."

A sudden thought struck Trina. "The racing purses. How will they be split?"

"Whatever you win will be yours."

"I don't believe it...."

"Believe it, Trina."

Trina became sober, Buck's long struggle for sponsorship flashing into her mind. "And all this because I'm a woman...."

"All this because you're a beautiful woman, involved in racing...exactly what we need, when we need it."

"I still can't believe it...."

"Then I can have our lawyer draw up the contracts?"

"Yes! And in the meantime I'll draw up the specs and plans for the car."

"We have them all done. They'll just need your approval."

"I *must* be dreaming...."

"I hope not." Kent was obviously enjoying her candid reactions. "I'm looking forward to the reality of the next few months."

"So am I...."

THE DIM LIGHTING of The Last Pit Stop was not dim enough to obscure the frown that moved across Slate's expression as Tom Harper gave Trina a sound hug.

"I'm telling you, Doc, it's going to be good to see you back on that track again. I kinda missed the sight of you in your firesuit, squeezing into the seat of your car. But you're probably going to have a custom-made suit now, aren't you...? Spirit colors? What did you say they were?"

"Yellow and green." Trina smiled as Tom winced at her response. "Don't be smart! I'd wear purple and orange if it got me a new car."

"Don't kid yourself, Trina. So would the rest of us if it brought us a sponsorship like yours." Buck's quick interjection brought a grin to her face. There was no doubting the pride in his expression as he slid his arm around her shoulders. "But I have to admit, you're the only one of us here who could handle a purple and orange firesuit."

Trina leaned full into Buck's embrace for a few seconds. She had returned to the pits after her conference with Kent Henning, extremely happy that he had chosen to leave rather than return with her. She had been too excited to contain her joy and had burst out with the details of her Spirit sponsorship. Buck's reaction had been a spontaneous hoot as he had lifted her high in the air. It had taken her long moments to realize that Slate's reaction fell somewhat short of exuberance.

The unending stream of congratulations she had been receiving all night long had done nothing to improve Slate's strained smile. She was still unable to comprehend his reaction.

Trina scanned the bar around them. There was no privacy here where they could talk. Looking up, she suggested quietly, "Let's dance, Slate."

Nodding, Slate ushered her out onto the floor, his arms closing around her with more strength than was needed as he drew her close against him. But she couldn't afford to submit to the magic of Slate's touch. She had to talk.

"What's wrong, Slate? Everyone seems to be happy for me except you."

"I'm happy for you, Trina...."

"You aren't."

"I am.... I know it's something you always wanted."

"Well, I really don't have it, yet. I have to qualify for the Syracuse 200 or the contract will be null and void."

"You'll qualify."

"I wish I had your confidence in me. I've just started to realize I'm scared to death that I might blow it when I have it all in my hands at last."

"You wouldn't have had to be afraid or uncertain if you had accepted my offer."

"Your offer?"

"For Wright-Montgomery to sponsor your car."

"Is that why you're angry?"

"I'm not angry."

"Well, maybe not angry, but you certainly aren't very happy for me."

Slate's brow creased into a frown. Hating himself for his next words, he offered with a shrug, "Maybe I'm a little suspicious of this whole thing.... Maybe I'm the only person who is looking at this fairy tale with my eyes open."

"What are you trying to say, Slate?"

"Doesn't it look a little strange to you that you'd be approached here at the track, by a man you've never seen before? He handed you a card. Anyone can get cards printed up."

"He wasn't a total stranger to me, Slate."

"He wasn't?"

"No, I met him informally once before...at one of Ingrid's shows."

"And that's a recommendation of his character?"

Trina was beginning to get annoyed. "I think I'm capable of making a sound judgment by myself, without your help. And I choose to believe Kent Henning is a—"

"Kent Henning?"

"Yes.... He's a charming, intelligent man..."

Slate's eyes were focused on her face. To all intents and purposes, they could have been completely alone instead of on a crowded dance floor.

"Which show...where did you meet him?"

"The show at Pierre's."

Slate's eyes narrowed. "The big, dark-haired guy, the one with the large party on the side of the room...the one who fell all over you and kissed your hand?"

"You're exaggerating...but yes, that was Kent Henning."

"Now I understand...."

"Are you trying to insinuate that Kent has a personal reason for offering me this contract? Because if you are, you're wrong."

"If you want a car, Wright-Montgomery will build it for you."

"GTB Foods will finance my car."

"You won't let me do this for you, will you?" Slate's voice was a low, angry murmur.

"Slate, please. This is no place to argue about it."

"Then let's get out of here. I've had enough of this place tonight."

"I can't go home with you tonight, Slate."

"What?"

"Kent... He said he was going to call me first thing in the morning to set up an appointment on Monday. He wants all the paperwork cleared up so we can proceed immediately."

"He's going to call you on a Sunday morning?"

"He said something about dinner."

"Did he say something about breakfast, too?"

Trina's face flamed. "Slate, you're insulting!"

"Am I? I thought I was being realistic."

"Not all men think like you! Besides, he's married."

"Oh, he got around to telling you that, did he? Did he also tell you he has a wife who doesn't understand him...?"

Glancing around, Trina realized they were drawing curious glances from the other couples on the floor. Jerking herself out of Slate's arms, Trina walked off the floor. But she didn't make it far before Slate's hand closed over her arm, drawing her into a corner as he turned her to face him.

"I know you'll find this difficult to believe, but Kent Henning thinks I'll be a perfect spokesperson for Spirit! And if you were really as fond of me as you say, you'd be happy for my good luck."

"Oh, so now my feelings for you are suspect." His voice was calm, but the spasmodic tightening of his hand on her arm betrayed his deep anger. "Are you trying to tell me something, Trina? What's the matter? Are you afraid I'll get in the way of your contract with Kent Henning?"

Trina's eyes held Slate's sober gaze unflinchingly. Her response was low and even. "I don't think I deserved that, Slate, but I guess it's all in your viewpoint. The funny part of it is, I really didn't think you had such a low opinion of me."

"Trina, I didn't mean..."

"Yes, you did. Maybe you didn't mean to say it, but the truth came out before you could stop it. You wouldn't be acting this way if you didn't think..."

"I don't believe anything of the sort. I just want you to tell Henning you don't want any part of the contract. You don't need his backing."

"You're wasting your breath." A deep, heavy ache had started inside Trina's chest.

"Trina..." Slate's eyes moved over Trina's expressionless face. He attempted to move her toward the doorway, but she remained motionless, no longer caring if they drew curious glances. "Trina, we have to talk...."

"We've already talked."

"We have to talk in private...alone...."

"No. That's our problem, Slate. When we're alone, we forget about talking. No, I think the truth is finally out...."

"The truth is that I'm not going to give you up, but you were right when you said to me a long time ago that I wouldn't like playing second fiddle to a car."

Something dawned on Trina then, and her eyes widened. Her tone was incredulous as she said, "You...you were glad when my car was totaled, weren't you? You were happy that I wasn't racing anymore. You knew what racing meant to me, but you didn't really care. I didn't have a car to occupy my time anymore, and you had a full-time playmate. God! How could I have been such a fool?"

"Trina, it wasn't that way, honey. Really, it wasn't. All right, I admit it. I *was* glad your car was totaled. It got in the way.... You were so damned tied to that thing and I couldn't compete. But I would've sponsored another car for you if you had agreed..."

"Yes, you would've liked it that way...you still would. Because then you'd have control of my car and me." The pain in her chest was so intense she could barely stand it.

"No, Trina... Honey, come home with me now. We'll talk this thing out."

Trina's eyes held his. "No, you don't mean that, Slate. You mean you'll make me forget everything that's been said...for a little while. No, I don't think so. Thanks for the offer, but Buck will take me home tonight. I'll sleep in my own bed, where I belong."

"You belong with me."

"No, I don't think so."

"Trina..."

"Goodbye, Slate."

"Trina, please..."

"I'll see you on the track."

"Trina...honey..."

Steeling herself against the plea in his voice, Trina turned away and walked toward the bar. Twelve steps. They were twelve of the most difficult steps that she had ever taken in her life.

CHAPTER ELEVEN

CRYSTAL CHANDELIERS; white linen tablecloths; sparkling stemware and silverware; soft, subtle background music; lavish service; rich, delicious food dishes, the names of which Trina found difficult to pronounce; a circle of unfamiliar faces around the table, their eyes assessing; and endless questions...polite but pointed questions.... It was a scenario to which Trina had become accustomed in the last few weeks.

She shot a quick smile at the waiter who poured her yet another glass of champagne, then returned her attention to Kent Henning. The elegant French restaurant in which they sat was the perfect backdrop for his cosmopolitan charm. He had confided to her only two nights before that he felt she had been born to this type of social whirl, and she had laughed. Nothing could be further from the truth. But the final contract had not yet been signed and she was committed to these social affairs with the members of the Board of Directors of GTB Foods. She knew she was being tested to determine her feasibility as the embodiment of the Spirit woman.

Well, she couldn't really blame GTB Foods for being cautious. It was obvious from the start that although Kent Henning was well respected by his colleagues, his judgement still needed to be confirmed. And so had begun the past three weeks of frequent business dinners to which Kent had been her dutiful and charming escort. She had been informed by Kent just prior to their arrival that this particular evening would be the last of her informal interviews. She had passed all the tests with flying colors, had charmed the board members completely, and could just about consider herself home free. She supposed she should be elated, but somehow her emotions fell somewhere short of that mark.

The only thing that had caused her to endure the horrendous trial to which she was being subjected was the fabulous machine she had watched emerge piece by piece in the well-equipped garage rented by GTB Foods. If anything, ever, was a dream come true, the Spirit car was it for her. Perfection... A powerful 467 cubic inches of engine; a sleek, uniquely painted body; an interior built to fit her specific proportions. She had been consulted right from the design stage and had suffered through fittings for a custom-made firesuit.

She had been introduced to the men who would eventually become her pit crew and had been impressed. They had graciously carried out her one request for a change in the tires. Doug had approached her after her contract had been signed and volunteered his services as part of her pit crew, and for that she was grateful. She hadn't realized how much she would need a familiar face among all those new, assessing gazes. She was well aware that a few of her crew thought that she was sleeping with Kent Henning and the thought burned her clear through. As if an attractive woman couldn't be considered worth anything outside of bed! If she had been fat and ugly she supposed they would have thought differently. But in truth, if she had been fat and ugly she wouldn't have gotten the job, no matter how well she drove. It was a vicious circle!

But she would prove herself to all of them...including Slate. She winced inwardly at the memory of the look on his face as she had said goodbye. In the three weeks since they had parted at The Last Pit Stop, Slate had attempted to see her on several occasions. But the obligations on her busy "social" calendar, which were subject to change almost without notice and which were more in the manner of command performances than social engagements, had saved her from herself.

The preliminary publicity had already begun, extending itself to the track on racing Saturdays. The attention she had been receiving at the track had been an embarrassment, but it had served as an effective buffer between Slate and herself.

But in the long, dark hours of the night, she had been unable to steel herself against the thoughts that haunted her. She had begun to suspect she'd never be free of the memory of Slate's touch; the tenderness in his gaze; the sweet, enduring beauty they had created in each other's arms. It was only now, isolated from him, that Trina came to realize the true extent of her feelings for Slate.

She remembered fleetingly her time with Spence. It was truly a wonder to her now that she could have considered the pale, limited emotion she had felt for him to be love. But Slate's motives were as self-centered as Spence's had been. There had been no room for her own hopes and ambitions, only Slate's desire for her. He had expected her to live in the void he would create for them. If he had truly cared for her he would have been happy for the stupendous stroke of luck that had turned her life around.

She felt a sharp pang of jealousy as she thought of how Sally had been hanging around Slate's car in the past weeks. The dear girl was so accommodating.... *Trina, Trina, pull in your claws.*

Her attention returned to the present as Kent said, "So we'll be ready within the week. And Trina, here, is the star...."

Acutely aware that all eyes at the table were turned toward her at the conclusion of Kent's informal speech, Trina offered a smile. She hadn't been listening, but Kent had obviously just rendered another of his flattering monologues.

Trina moved a trifle uneasily under the heavy, speculative gazes. Despite the fact that she knew she looked exceptionally good, she did not bear the intense scrutiny with as much grace as she appeared to. She was fortunate to have Ingrid's outfits to borrow for all these dinners. She had not wanted to accept Ingrid's offer at first, but Ingrid had been insistent, stating that Trina was a walking advertisement for her store. Trina had to agree when the advertising agency had advised her that they intended using Ingrid's Boutique in some background shots for her first layout.

Trina ran her hand over the skirt of the simple, white gauze dress Ingrid had suggested she wear this evening. Understated, elegant...the secret of the success of Ingrid's fashions. This dress was no exception. The effect of the yards of filmy material was to call attention to her narrow waist and her long, slender legs. But most impressive of all was the manner in which the white, diaphanous fabric contrasted with the honey tan she had acquired so effortlessly in the unsheltered pits. Against the white of the dress, her gleaming hair cascaded in unruly curls, appearing even darker.

Flushing under the unwavering scrutiny of the three gentlemen at the table, Trina could not withhold a small laugh.

"Gentlemen, I'm afraid Kent is a bit biased on my behalf. He's sure he's come up with the advertising gimmick of the century for Spirit."

Of the three men still studying her so avidly, Trina had least expected a comment from Herb Winslow, the small, unassuming fellow on her left.

"I think I can speak for Jack, Wilson and myself when I say we're truly impressed with Kent's idea but..."

Trina held her breath. The big little word "but."

"But I, for one, would appreciate a little confidential honesty here. Is it really true that you built your original car yourself...I mean, actually assembled it and put it together...?"

Whatever secret she had been expecting to be asked to reveal, it had not been this. She was unable to stifle a spontaneous laugh, and was totally unaware of the appeal of her dimpled cheeks. "Yes, it most certainly is true! My brother and I built both his car and mine from the frame up; welded the roll cage and insulated it; traced a pattern and cut the steel panels for the body; bolted it to the chassis. The engine...everything.... The only thing we didn't do was paint and letter it ourselves. We hired a local artist to do that."

"And you maintained the vehicle yourself?"

"Certainly...."

"But Miss Mallory...Trina...your hands. My son works on his car and it shows on his hands.... Your hands are perfectly groomed."

"You don't get grease under your fingernails if you use surgical gloves when you work on your car."

"I can vouch for the truth in that, Herb. Her nickname at the track is 'Doc' Mallory."

Herb Winslow's small features squeezed into a tight wince. "Well, we'll have to keep that little secret from our greatest competitor." There was a twinkle in his eye. "Yes, Dr. Pepper would love to hear that...."

The remaining four at the table groaned spontaneously. The sheer comic burlesque of their expressions seemed to strike all of them at once, causing a round of laughter to sweep the table.

When the last jovial snicker had died away, Kent shot Trina a quick glance of satisfaction that said it all more clearly than words. "You're home free, Trina...home free!"

"BEAUTIFUL, simply beautiful..."

Trina nodded, her eyes following Doug's enraptured gaze as it stared down at the engine of the partially completed Spirit car. She had just returned from a miniconference and had asked Kent to drop her off at the garage so that she might see her crew drop the engine into the chassis of her car. It was, after all, a milestone in her career. Doug and the other mechanics had just lowered it into the body. But while the other two mechanics had returned routinely to their jobs, both she and Doug had remained, worshipfully awed by the power it represented.

"This little beauty is going to do it for you, Trina. You're going to burn up that track in Syracuse."

"I sure hope so, but just between you and me, I'm starting to get stage fright. So much hinges on that race."

Doug turned a small frown in her direction, his expression concerned. "You only have to qualify for the race to fulfill your contract...isn't that what you said? You shouldn't have any problem doing that with this baby."

"I know. I guess I'm just a little out of sorts. I hardly know who I am lately, Doug. I haven't raced in so long. And with all this publicity, I'm starting to feel like public property whenever I go near the track. The only time I can really believe what's happening is when I'm here, and I can actually touch this machine."

A sympathetic smile softened Doug's concerned expression. "You just need to relax a little, honey. Your blood sugar's probably a little low, too. Come on. I'll drive you home and we'll stop at Maude's Diner for something sweet." Doug picked up a rag and began wiping his hands clean as his eyes moved to the two mechanics working knowledgeably around the car.

"George...Art... You don't need me anymore tonight, do you? Trina and I are going to take off."

"No, go ahead. We're not going to stay much longer, either."

George's reply was delivered with a suspicious glance, and Trina fumed inwardly. She had been prepared to turn down Doug's suggestion, telling him she'd take a cab the short distance to her house, but she changed her mind. If George and Art thought she was double-crossing Kent with Doug, then let them. She'd give them something to think about.

Trina tossed an absentminded smile in Doug's direction as he opened the door of his Mazda and ushered her inside. She waited until they were on the road before she spoke.

"You don't have to take me anywhere, Doug. Really, I'll be all right. I'm just tired."

"It sure must be hell being famous."

Trina flushed at Doug's quick remark. "Not you, too, Doug. I thought you were on my side."

Doug's dark eyes flashed warmly in her direction. "I am, honey. I was only teasing you. And I'm not going to let you off the hook. We're stopping at Maude's. I need a cup of her coffee to keep me up tonight."

Trina closed her eyes and nodded. She was too tired to argue. "Okay, Doug. Whatever you say."

Doug's eyes touched on her once again. "You know, Trina, a statement like that could get you in trouble."

"Even with you, Doug?"

"Especially with me."

"Then I take it back. A cup of coffee and a Danish. Is that specific enough for you?" Trina's spirits were beginning to pick up with Doug's light kidding.

"Too specific. I always did have a big mouth."

"A big mouth and a big heart.... That's what I like about you, Doug."

Doug turned to flash her a quick smile. "Well, at least there's something you like about me. We're heading in the right direction." His broad hand covered hers. "Now be quiet, lean your head back against the seat and relax. We're almost there."

Doug had been right. She had barely had time to get comfortable before they were pulling into the lot of the small diner. A few minutes later they were in a booth and their coffees and Danish pastries were on the way. Trina looked up as Doug's hand again slid to cover hers.

"I thought I'd give those two boys something to talk about. You do know they think you're Kent Henning's chick, don't you?"

Trina gave a small laugh. "Of course. How else could somebody like me get this big chance? I'd have to be sleeping with the boss, wouldn't I?"

"And there you are, sleeping alone in your bed each night." Doug took a swallow of his coffee before returning his gaze to her face. "You are sleeping alone these nights, aren't you, honey? I mean, this thing with Slate...it's all over, isn't it?"

"Doug..."

Doug's face was suddenly intensely sober, his dark eyes holding hers steadily. "Don't tell me it's none of my business, Trina. It might not be, but I sure as hell want it to be. I'm not going to be cute or clever. What I feel for you is too close to the surface for that. You and Slate, are you finished for good? You're the only one who can say.... It's obvious he can't keep his eyes off you whenever you're at the track."

"Come on, Doug. Slate amuses himself very well. Sally hangs all over him, and he was never one to turn her down."

"Slate doesn't even see Sally when you're around."

"Doug..."

"Just like I don't see Helen..."

"Doug, don't say that! I thought Helen and you—"

"Helen's a great girl, Trina. She just isn't you, that's all."

"Doug—" Trina's eyes filled unexpectedly with tears "—what do you want with me? I'm all messed up. There's only one thing I know I really want right now, and that's the chance to take that car out on the track at Syracuse."

"I want you to answer my question, that's what I want. Are you and Slate finished or not?"

Trina let out a small sigh and dropped her gaze to their hands. "Yes, we're finished. I can't see a way in the world we can make it together."

"And you, Trina? Is that the way you want it? Tell me the truth, honey. I need the truth now."

"I'm not sure. I think I wish it could be. I...I don't really know, Doug." Trina raised her eyes to his once again. "See what I mean? I'm all screwed up. Don't get mixed up with me, Doug."

Doug's eyes moved slowly over her face, his expression unrevealing. Reaching unexpectedly across the small table, he slid his hand around the back of her neck and drew her across to press a light kiss against her lips. He smiled at her disturbed expression.

"Don't worry. That doesn't mean I intend to press you. It only means that I care about you, Trina. But I care enough to want you to be happy. So I'll wait around, sweetheart, just like I've been doing. I'll wait until you have this race at Syracuse under your belt and your head clears a little bit. But in the meantime, I want you to know I'm here. If you need me, just give me a call. You don't have to worry that I'll take advantage of it."

Trina felt a thickness in her throat. "But what about Helen, Doug? I thought you and she—"

"Sweetheart, I've got my problem and Helen's got hers." He patted her hand lightly. "I'm trying to work on mine."

Trina gave a small, choked laugh. "So I'm a problem to you, too...."

"Hell, yes. But I'll straighten you out." The light tone of his voice didn't quite match the look in his eyes, but Trina's heart warmed at his effort to set her mind at rest.

"Now, drink up your coffee and finish your pastry like a good girl, and I'll get you home. I have just so much willpower when it comes to you, and you're stretching it to the limit tonight."

"I'm more trouble than I'm worth, aren't I, Doug?"

"I wouldn't say that, sweetheart. No...I wouldn't say that at all...."

CHAPTER TWELVE

THERE WOULD BE NO CLOUDS of dust hovering over the track today. Trina shot a quick glance at the threatening sky above her and shook her head. It had been raining all week, and the track was a mess. Clay tracks turned to brown mud when they were wet. She shuddered in apprehension.

September... the last official race of the season at Middlevale Raceway, and Buck and Slate were still neck and neck in points. There was still fierce competition between them, but the anger and ill will was gone. In its place had developed a reluctant admiration for their mutual skills as drivers. Trina smiled at the irony of it. Most of the time when she and Slate had been close, the animosity between Slate and Buck had caused considerable strain. But now the discomfort remained only between Slate and herself—Slate and Buck appeared to tolerate each other quite well.

Trina shook her head again. Now it was Doug who suffered under Buck's watchful scrutiny. There was no doubt in her mind that Buck liked and respected Doug, but she knew he sensed her vulnerability and wasn't about to let anyone pressure her, no matter how good his intentions. Doug's reaction had been typical.

"Buck's like a bull mastiff when it comes to protecting you, Trina. I get the feeling if I take one step out of line, he'll attack."

"You know Buck, Doug. He's worried about the pressure I'm under and..." Trina hesitated, not quite knowing how to continue.

"And he thinks I'll take advantage of it, and maybe you'll do something you'll be sorry for." Trina had flushed slightly and Doug had looked slightly hurt. "Doesn't he know I'd never hurt you?"

"Oh, Doug..." Sincerity had rung in his voice and shone in his eyes, and she had reached out to touch his cheek lightly with her fingertips. "That's the kind of pressure I think he has in mind, Doug. The kind that's hardest to resist."

Doug had looked thoughtful for a second before a small smile claimed his expression. "Does that mean you're finding me hard to resist, Trina?" She had become flustered, and Doug had been unable to suppress a rueful laugh. "I only wish..."

The caution light flicked off once again and Trina's mind returned to the track, her stomach twisting into knots. Her eyes shot to the back of the pack where Slate's number 008 and Buck's number 82 had resumed their spots in the lineup. The pace car, which had been leading the anxious pack around the track as tow trucks had worked anxiously to remove the tangle of cars partially obstructing it, turned into the pits at the third turn. The lead car suddenly accelerated, and the accompanying roar was almost deafening as thirteen powerful modified engines followed suit. A surge of adrenaline rushed through Trina's veins as the starter dropped the green flag and the race commenced.

The jockeying for position was frantic as drivers pressed their cars to the ultimate to attain maximum speed before the necessity to brake at the third turn. Holding her breath, Trina watched as a muddied blue and white car shot from the back of the pack to take a phenomenal five cars in the straightaway. Trina marveled! Slate had advanced almost to midpack in that one strategic push! He was going into the turn at full speed, his tires barely gripping the slippery track as he slid sideways, holding to his course by an almost unbelievable combination of skill and pure unadulterated luck.

The ordeal was not yet over. Spotting a momentary opening in the pack, the red and white number 82 shot forward through the sliding cars surrounding it, securing the coveted inside spot on the first turn. With blurring speed, Buck shot around the first and second turns, his car completely sideways as it negotiated the hairy corners, only to straighten out in a roaring burst of power as it stormed down the far straightaway.

Trina's eyes moved to the front of the pack, then backward as she counted mentally. Seventh and ninth! Slate and Buck were seventh and ninth, and still moving evenly through the pack! Karen, standing on the flatbed beside her, screamed sharply, jerking Trina's eyes toward Buck's car as he narrowly missed a serious collision with the eighth-place car. But he was still gaining...both he and Slate were still gaining, as the crowd roared its wild appreciation.

Two more laps to go! The race seemed endless, with caution and red flags extending it. But one thing had been firmly settled. Slate and Buck were the leaders, and the race was solely between them.

Two more laps, and the lead was switching almost from moment to moment as each man juggled and strategized his position in the final wearying minutes of the race.

Close to tears, Trina watched as the two cars raced around the first turn side by side, each straining to gain a line around the second corner that would turn them out onto the far straightaway in a better position than the other. She was holding her breath when she felt the first drop of rain. No! Not rain! She absentmindedly jerked the hood of her raincape over her head. The race was almost finished! There was no possibility of calling it unless there was a downpour so intense that the drivers could not finish the final two laps, but track conditions were already at the danger level! She was only too keenly aware of the racing mentality that wouldn't allow either Slate or Buck to assume any caution that might cost him the race.

The rain pelted down as Slate and Buck shot under the white flag. One more lap...only one more to go. Trina surveyed the field. Slate and Buck were at least a half a track ahead of the remaining cars in the race. The only threat that remained to them, other than the track itself, was each other!

The track was already a muddy swamp when Buck approached the third turn, barely nosing Slate out as he secured the inside lane. He was rounding the fourth and final turn when Trina saw the first sign of a slide. Her eyes jerked to Slate, only a fraction of a second behind Buck, and Trina saw his car holding the track well. Of course...Buck's tires. Doug had commented that Slate had bought new tires for this race, while Buck had been forced to make his much-used tires do one last time. Equipment was proving to be the turning point in the head-to-head competition finally come to a close before the eyes of the screaming crowd.

Holding her breath, Trina watched as Buck miraculously regained control of his vehicle just before it careened out of control, bringing it back into line only a few lengths behind Slate's. But it was too late—too late to regain the front spot as Slate accelerated once again, flashing under the checkered flag only a hairbreadth ahead of the quickly pursuing 82.

Slate had won! The final glory of points champion belonged to Slate. He drew his car up in front of the starter's stand and slipped out of his car to wave to the screaming crowd. As abruptly as it had started, the rain had stopped. Trina pushed the hood of her raincoat back and found herself following the tide of people in the pits as it surged toward the presentation ceremony. She stopped as Buck's car pulled into the pits and moved slowly toward them. Karen's petite figure flashed past her into Buck's arms as he slipped out of his car.

Karen threw her arms around Buck's neck and whispered something to him, and Trina was startled by the grin that flashed across Buck's bearded face as he finally nodded. Slipping his arm around Karen's waist to draw her to him, he approached Trina with a slow, weary step.

"A damned good race, wasn't it, Trina?"

"Damned good, Buck!" Her eyes filling unexpectedly with tears, Trina threw her arms around her brother's chest and hugged him soundly.

"Hey, hey, what's all this? Waterworks again? This track is wet enough!"

"It was your tires, Buck. They couldn't hold the wet track as well as Slate's...."

Buck's smile softened. "This time it was my equipment that didn't get me through, honey. Next time it could be something of Slate's that breaks down.... That's racing. But I'm proud of the race I ran, Trina. And my position here at Middlevale gets me automatic qualification in the Syracuse 200. I'll have *new* tires for that race, and we'll see who wins that one!"

Trina took a deep breath and sniffed hard. She was so damned proud of Buck that she was almost bursting.

"You're going to have *real* competition in that one, Buck. I'll be right beside you in that yellow and green beast that's waiting for me!"

"And it'll be my greatest pleasure to take you on, Trina."

Slipping his arms around her momentarily, Buck gave her a tight hug. She was just stepping back out of his quick embrace when a deep, familiar voice caused her to catch her breath.

"What about me, Trina? Do I get congratulated, too?"

Her heart began to thud in her chest as Trina turned slowly. Swallowing tightly, she forced a smile to her lips. Slate's face was smeared with mud, but the touch of his gaze as it moved over her face was almost physical in intensity. Trina steeled herself against the spontaneous warmth it evoked inside her.

"Of course you do, Slate. Congratulations! You ran a beautiful race. And congratulations on your points championship...."

Nodding, Slate took a few steps closer, coming to stand directly in front of her. His expression tightened.

"Thanks. But I was thinking of a little more enthusiasm than that. Buck got a hug.... Don't I get a kiss?"

Slate's expression was entirely sober now. His gaze was still holding hers. Its appeal stimulated a longing so strong inside her that Trina could not think beyond its simple truth. Her eyes gave him the answer he needed, and Slate cupped her chin as he lowered his head to press a light kiss against her mouth.

But the contact, once made, was too sweet to be broken quickly. Before she realized it had happened, Slate had drawn her close against him, his strong arms all but swallowing her slender frame as his mouth claimed hers. There was a hunger, a desperation in his kiss that struck a similar chord deep within her, and Trina felt herself opening to its warmth like a flower under the sun. All their differences were momentarily erased by its healing glory, and Trina was deeply enthralled when a strained voice invaded the sheltered world of their kiss, shattering its fragile beauty with a return to reality.

"Trina, the PR men want to take a few more shots of you by the refreshment stand. They have a couple of cases of Spirit set up as a backdrop."

Trina's eyes snapped to Doug's tight expression. She turned back to Slate, but all trace of the need she had glimpsed so briefly in his eyes had fled. Had it really been there at all?

"Go ahead, Trina. I know you have your priorities." Turning to Doug, he emphasized quietly, "You do know that Trina has her priorities, Doug."

"Trina's priorities are her own business. She knows what she's doing."

"Well, I just hope you remember those words at the appropriate time in the future."

"What I do or don't remember is *my* business...."

The exchange was getting heated. Shooting a quick look between the two men's darkening expressions, Trina turned toward Doug and took his arm.

"Come on, Doug. They're waiting for me. I think they want you over there, too."

Her eyes intent on Doug's tight expression, she missed the deep flush on Slate's face as he turned sharply on his heel and walked away.

CHAPTER THIRTEEN

"I THINK THEY'RE ALL CRAZY!"

A rare smile flashed across Trina's face as she experienced again the restrained excitement of the New York State Fairgrounds during racing season. She had attended the Syracuse Shaefer 200 many times and never failed to be amused by the racing fever that swept the fans during the five-day event. Her eyes scanned the crowded grounds, the packed grandstands, and fixed on the scores of campers settled comfortably in their allotted section of the crowded infield of the mile-long track. If there was a crazier group, she hadn't seen it. Most of the fans crammed the immense grandstand, some reserving their particular seats as far as a year in advance to ensure a perfect view, but these particular fans watched from their own unique versions of the catbird seat.

High scaffolding, constructed laboriously by their own hands, held some spectators towering above the track. Others sat leisurely on the roofs of their campers in deck chairs, drinks in hand, while others lined the rails and sides of rigs equipped especially for the occasion. Outside one camper truck stood an immense Christmas tree, completely decorated, with lights flickering brightly in the sharp October morning. No doubt its owner considered that the end of the week was going to be like Christmas when his favorite driver won the big one.

Banners bearing the names of favored drivers were in abundance, decorating cars, trucks and campers in a haphazard display. Bonfires were plentiful, with newfound friends whose racing interests formed a strong bond between them, celebrating the crowning event of dirt-track week. Refreshment stands hosting a wide array of edibles provided an endless supply of food for drivers and spectators. Specialty booths stood ready with all manner of racing paraphernalia and souvenirs.

Overhead a helicopter circled, its doors open to allow the passengers inside the pleasure of seeing the scene from the air for a nominal fee. And high above it all, on a tower constructed specifically for the purpose, ESPN TV recorded on video tape the races progressing around them as well as the incredible spectator scene for a waiting TV audience.

It was a scene Trina had witnessed many times and which always managed to tap a special well of pleasure within her. Four days into dirt-track week, and she had qualified for the big one...two hundred laps around the mile-long track for the prize of $45,000 and contingencies. Considering that there was lap money also involved, with the leader of each lap receiving additional sums, Trina realized that this could be a profitable week indeed.

She had made a great hit with the Spirit car. It was a beauty, the dream of a lifetime. Coverage had been ample and favorable, with TV eagerly picking up on the Cinderella story of which she was the heroine. She was grateful for the diversion of Jack Higgins, the bright, impersonal agency man who was assigned to her as part of the Spirit promotion. He kept her busy with pictures and interviews during the hours that might have lagged and allowed her to think about a certain blond-haired man. Somehow she had a feeling too much thinking would be a mistake right now.

Both Buck and Slate were featured in the printed program as guaranteed starters. Their pictures and full-page spreads on their racing history were on facing pages. Buck's spirits were high. He and Karen had a room down the hall from Trina's in a local motel. Doug had arranged to share a room with the other members of her pit crew in the same motel. She had been disappointed to see that Slate was also staying there. She had run into him on several occasions, each time with the buffer of Doug's or Buck's presence. The formality between them had been no less than numbing; and now, four days into the week, Trina was truly uncertain how she felt about anything.

It was the day before the final race and the moment she had waited for all her life. She was only too aware of that fact as she allowed her eyes to move once more over the crowd and listened to its roars as the consolation qualifying race progressed at a breathtaking pace. She glanced a few feet into the pits. The Spirit rig was perfection, bigger and better than any she had ever seen before. Six new tires graced the racks and a full supply of emergency parts lined the interior walls. Her own uniformed pit crew worked over the last-minute details in her car. Doug looked up with a speculative gaze before flashing an encouraging smile.

God, how had it all fallen so flat? The smile she wore for the public was tenuous, her witty responses forced. She had made it...or almost made it, and it was all so empty!

She was tired...that was it. It was the strain. She wasn't sleeping well. A multitude of memories saw fit to inundate her mind each time she closed her eyes. Brilliant-blue eyes haunted her. She glanced toward her car again. Her pit crew was totally efficient and competent. They didn't need her here now. Buck and Karen had gone back to the motel. She might as well go back, too, and try to grab some sleep before the party tonight in the motel.

Jack Higgins had come up with a last-minute party to celebrate her fantastic qualifying time. She had been instructed to look her best and had been provided with a ridiculous gold silk pants suit to impress the press. Wearing a fabulous outfit like that when the uniform for the week was usually jeans and T-shirts would make her feel like a fool.

Hesitating only long enough to give Doug a quick shout and tell him she was leaving, Trina turned toward the underground exit. Yes, the rest would do her good.

She was walking down the motel hallway, her key in her hand, when the excited babble inside Buck and Karen's room caught her ear. Curiosity mingled with a dread of facing her lonely room, and Trina hesitated outside the door. She knocked. Bounding steps sounded inside in the few seconds before the door was jerked open and she was faced with Buck's exuberance.

Giving a loud whoop, Buck scooped her up into his brawny arms and whirled her around. Laughing genuinely for the first time in days, Trina held on tight, aware that Buck had kicked the door shut behind them as he finally settled her on her feet and stood before her with a broad smile on his face.

"Don't keep me in suspense! What happened? You're grinning like a contented ape!"

Buck's grin widened. "Contented ape, huh? Trina, you see before you the new driver of the Thompson Auto Products car, fully sponsored for the upcoming racing season...signed, sealed and delivered!"

"Buck! No! I can't believe it!" Elation sweeping her senses, Trina shot a quick look toward Karen's ecstatic face. "It's true, isn't it?" At Karen's quick nod, Trina turned around, her arms circling Buck's broad chest for a strong, spontaneous hug. "Buck, I can't believe it! It's wonderful!"

"Of course, the sponsorship isn't on the same scale as yours, Trina; but, hell, I'm not as pretty as you are. But I'll be where I belong next year, behind the wheel of a car, and you'd better believe I'll prove myself!"

"And that means..."

Buck shot a quick look toward Karen. He extended his arm in her direction, the tenderness that suffused his expression bringing tears to Trina's eyes as Karen moved into the curve of his arm. Buck pulled Karen close against his other side. "And that means Karen and I have already set a date. We've decided to get married this Christmas, Trina. Now that I know I could support Karen—if I had to," he said with a wink, "with the expense of the car off my back, we're home free."

Momentarily unable to speak past the emotion blocking her throat, Trina's eyes moved between Buck's and Karen's radiant expressions.

"I'm...I'm so happy for you."

Stepping forward, Trina gave Karen a tight hug.

"You will be my maid of honor, Trina, won't you? It won't be a big wedding, but Buck and I want you to be a part of it."

"Of course...of course...."

Swallowing tightly, Trina backed toward the door. "Well, I think I'll go to my room now before I make a complete fool of myself. I promised myself a nap before tonight. You will be at the party, won't you? I'll need someone there to back me up. It's going to be an ordeal. But at least it's paid for, and we can do some celebrating of our own once the formalities are over."

"Not too much celebrating. Tomorrow's the big one." Buck's expression sobered momentarily. "Neither one of us wants to blow it now."

Trina nodded and turned toward the door. "I'll stop by at six to pick you up on the way down...in my 'racing silks'."

The sudden depression that hit her was overwhelming as she walked swiftly to her room. She inserted the key into the lock and had only time to close the door behind her before the sobs began. Walking slowly to the bed, she sank down and rolled to her side. Covering her face with her hands, she allowed her tears full rein.

TRINA CAME AWAKE SLOWLY. Her mind still drugged from sleep, she was momentarily startled by her surroundings. Oh, yes, the motel. The race was tomorrow.... The time! Her eyes shot to the travel clock on the night table. Five-thirty! Oh, no! She still had to shower and wash her hair. Her eyelids felt as if they had sandpaper under them and her eyes burned every time she blinked. That's right. She'd been crying...hadn't been able to stop....

Trina sat up abruptly and stole a look in the dresser mirror. It was worse than she had thought! She wasn't going to go downstairs looking like a drab and make a complete mess of things. No! She wasn't going to let

Kent Henning down and waste all the time and money GTB Foods had already spent on her.

Trina jumped to her feet beside the bed, swaying momentarily as a pain struck her in the top of her head. Damn! Her head was pounding. All she needed was a headache.

Emerging from the bathroom fifteen minutes later, Trina unwrapped her hair and toweled it vigorously. She plugged in the dryer and shot it absentmindedly over her hair. The special diffuser needed for her curly hair seemed to lengthen the drying time, and Trina became impatient. It would have to dry while she dressed.

She moved quickly to the mirror. The cold water had eliminated most of the puffiness from her eyes, and makeup could do the rest.

Within fifteen minutes Trina was knocking at Buck's door. He opened it and Trina was about to speak when Buck's spontaneous exclamation interrupted her.

"Wow!"

Trina smiled. "So I guess you like my 'racing silks,' huh?"

Buck's eyes moved appreciatively over her slim figure, covered by gold silk pants and a tailored shirt. The outfit clung to her delicate curves as if it had been made for her. He smiled at the gleaming curls that covered her head and cascaded down just past her shoulders. She must have just come out of the shower. He remembered that look. From the day Trina was born her hair moved into dark, silky springs in dampness. Tonight she had light shadows under her eyes that made those huge black orbs seem even larger and brighter than ever. She had probably been crying. He wasn't really surprised. She hadn't seemed truly happy for a long time. Not since she had broken up with Slater Montgomery.

Realizing Trina was still standing on the doorstep, waiting for his response, Buck grinned encouragingly. "Trina, you're going to knock them dead!" He turned back to Karen who was putting the last finishing touches to her makeup. "Come on, shortstuff. We don't want to keep this celebrity waiting."

TRINA'S HEADACHE was beginning to return. She had made a noble effort and was proud of the fact that Jack seemed more than pleased with it. Trina looked around the large, dimly lit reception area. Their party actually took up only a small section of the rear corner, adjacent to the entrance. She was relieved that all but one of the photographers had put down their cameras. She was tired of clicking cameras and flashbulbs. And despite the great number of pictures that had been taken, Jack had told her only a few would ever be printed. What a waste of time!

Trina's eyes moved around the room assessingly. There was a pretty healthy representation of the press here...two racing papers, a local daily, a women's magazine, and a monthly news magazine. Spirit posters lined the walls, and sample bottles of the soft drink were on each table. A large floor display filled one corner. The ad agency reps wore ridiculous straw hats with Spirit bands around the crown, and free coupons for the drink were being distributed to passersby. Trina knew the same scene would be repeated tomorrow, and many times after that.

Trina smiled when she saw Doug, George and Art sitting together at the bar. It seemed that it had finally gotten through Art's and George's heads that she hadn't slept with the boss in order to get the offer from Spirit. If she didn't miss her guess, Doug had a lot to do with that. In any case, she had sensed a marked change in their attitude toward her, and she was relieved. She just wasn't ready to handle any more discomfort in her life.

Trina's eyes snapped back to the last photographer as he recounted aloud, "Well, let me see. We have some pictures of you with your pit crew...some pictures of you with your brother, who's second in the points standing at your home track... Hey, wait a minute!"

The photographer's keen eyes moved to the doorway. Trina's gaze followed, only to have her heart drop somewhere into the vicinity of her shoes as they touched on Slate's tall figure. He was wearing a pair of fresh jeans that rode low on his hips, emphasizing his trim waist and the muscular length of his thighs. The simple white knit shirt he wore fit his well-developed chest snugly, drawing attention to his broad width of shoulder. His hair seemed to gleam a burnished blond under the bright light of the outer hall, and Trina swallowed hard against his reaction on her senses.

Slate's eyes tangled with hers for the space of a short second, the electricity in his glance sweeping a familiar longing through her veins. His eyes moved abruptly from hers to shoot around the group.

"Sorry. I didn't mean to intrude into a private party."

He was about to turn away when the photographer called out unexpectedly, "Say, you're Slater Montgomery, aren't you?" At Slate's short nod, he gestured familiarly with his hand. "Come on in. How about a picture with Trina here? After all, you're the points champion of her home track."

Slate looked as if he was about to refuse when suddenly he seemed to reconsider. He stepped into the room and walked directly to Trina's side. "Sure, how do you want it?"

Trina stiffened as Slate slid his arms around her waist. His fingers splayed widely. She could feel their warmth against the side of her breast, and she moved uncomfortably.

"That's fine. Don't move, Trina."

Slate inched her closer against his side until his firm grip forced her to lean against him. Her heart was pounding and she needed to get away. She hadn't eaten anything since breakfast, and the two drinks she had consumed were beginning to affect her strangely. What other excuse was there for her desire to turn into Slate's arms?

"All right, that's fine. I'd like to take one more. How about—"

But Slate's hand had dropped from around her. He stepped back as he shook his head. "No, I think that's enough."

Her eyes, diverted from his face, missed the flash of pain in Slate's eyes as they flicked toward her for the briefest second. "I'll see you later."

His tall figure had barely cleared the doorway when the photographer turned back to Trina. "You two make a great couple, you know that? Maybe we could work a little human interest story in here. Jack, what do you say we..."

Ignoring the conversation that continued on between Jack and the photographer, Trina went to the bar and picked up her drink. She took a deep gulp and placed it back on the bar. Almost immediately a familiar hand moved to cover hers. She turned to Doug's scrutinizing gaze.

"You okay, Trina?"

"Sure I'm okay." Trina gave a small laugh that didn't quite make it.

"Miss Mallory..."

Trina turned toward the reporter who rudely interrupted them, deciding she should be grateful for the opportunity to escape Doug's knowing gaze.

"Could you give us a little background, please? Now, what would you say was the most powerful influence on your decision to move seriously into racing?"

"Do you mean you've never heard of the 'Mallory racing family'?" Trina shook her head disapprovingly. "For shame.... Well, let me enlighten you...."

SLATE WALKED INTO his room and slammed the door behind him. He had been walking for two hours, and he still hadn't been able to work it all out in his mind. Running a hand impatiently through his hair, Slate sat down on the bed and shook his head. Nothing had changed in the time Trina and he had been apart. She still knocked him for a loop. His hands were trembling. Hell, he was a basket case. Nothing was any good without her. It was all he could do to keep from forcing himself into her room right now and begging her to give him another chance.

A knock on the door interrupted Slate's disturbed thoughts, and he frowned. He really didn't feel like talking to anyone just now. The knock sounded again. Hesitating only a moment longer, Slate walked to the door and pulled it open, his frown deepening as Buck Mallory stared unsmilingly into his face.

"What are you doing here, Buck?"

"To tell you the truth, I really don't know what I'm doing here. I don't usually stick my two cents in where it isn't wanted. But after spending two hours with my sister and that happy act she's putting on, and then seeing you come trailing back to the motel with that hang-dog look, I figured it was about time I found out what really makes you tick."

Backing up to allow Buck entrance, Slate closed the door behind him and shook his head. "I don't really have to make a comment on how ridiculous your interest is right now, do I? When Trina and I were close, you all but ignored the fact that I was alive, and now, all of a sudden, you're interested in what makes me tick...."

"I thought I had you figured out, Montgomery. I could see Trina cared for you, and I didn't want to influence her one way or the other. She keeps telling me she's old enough to take care of herself, and I try to respect her independence."

"So what are you doing here now?"

"I'm trying to find out if you're a good actor or just a damned fool."

Making a deliberate attempt to control his annoyance, Slate questioned quietly, "And what's that supposed to mean?"

"It means that I've spent the whole week watching Trina put up the best front I've ever seen. Nobody could criticize her for the effort she's putting into this Spirit thing."

"I haven't heard anyone who has...."

"But she's damned miserable, and I'm sick of seeing that look in her eyes."

"What look?"

"That same look you're wearing, damn it! I came here tonight to find out if it's really an act on your part...the way you look at my sister like the world revolves around her."

"For me it does...."

"Then why in hell don't you do something about it?"

Slate was starting to get angry. "I don't have to give you any explanations, Buck."

Buck shook his head. "No, you don't. I just can't understand how two intelligent people who love each other can make themselves so miserable. It doesn't make sense that you'd *want* to be unhappy."

But Slate was no longer listening. "You said...you think Trina really..." Slate couldn't suppress the spark of hope that came alive inside him. "No, Buck, you've got this thing all wrong. Trina's the one who broke things up between us. I've tried...I called her, tried to talk to her since, but she always had someone running interference for her. And now she's just about the happiest driver at the track. She has everything she always wanted, and I'm not included in that package."

"So, you're just a damned fool after all."

"What are you talking about?"

"So Trina's really taking you in with that act she's putting on."

"What act?"

"That happy 'Spirit Girl' act! Man, are you blind? Don't you see the way she looks at you? She's so damned miserable.... If you're too stupid to go upstairs and tell her how you feel—"

"Look, Buck, I don't need you to tell me what to do. For your information, I've told Trina how I feel about her. She knows I love her. The problem is she doesn't love me back."

"What makes you think that?"

"It's easy. She's never said so."

"What's the matter? Do you have to have everything spelled out for you? She was burned once. She's afraid to take the chance of saying the words." Looking directly into Slate's eyes, Buck added in a softer voice, "I don't suppose I helped the situation much with my attitude toward you at the beginning, but I was afraid she was going to get hurt again."

"Again?"

"Spence Morgan...you've heard of him...hotshot racer. Look, I don't want to go into old history. I just came here to tell you that if you really care about Trina, you're a damned fool if you don't go upstairs right now and straighten things out between you."

Slate stared for long seconds into Buck's adamant expression. "You know, I was arguing with myself about doing just that when you knocked on the door."

"Yeah? You trying to tell me that I've been wasting my breath?"

"No, I wasn't saying that at all. I'm glad you came, Buck."

Nodding in silent response, Buck abruptly extended his hand toward Slate. "Look, while I'm at it I might as well apologize. I was wrong about you. You're a straight racer. You earned your championship, and I have to admit you're a damned good driver. Whether or not you fix this thing up between you and Trina, I want you to know that I enjoyed racing against you this year."

Accepting his hand, Slate returned the pressure of Buck's strong grip. "Thanks, Buck...for everything."

Nodding his head, Buck turned toward the door and left Slate alone.

Slate gave himself only a few minutes longer to fully digest Buck's advice, then also turned toward the doorway and strode purposefully down the hall.

CHAPTER FOURTEEN

TRINA STEPPED OUT of the shower and toweled herself dry. Another shower.... If she kept this up, she'd dry up like a leaf and blow away. She jerked off her shower cap and threw it onto the vanity, shaking her hair down around her shoulders. But she had needed a hot shower. After that incident with Slate in the bar only a few hours before, every nerve in her body had been tight as a drum.

The reception had broken up shortly after Slate had left but she had stayed downstairs a little while longer with Buck and Karen. If she had to make an assessment, she would say she had done a good job of putting on a cheerful facade. After all, she had had no right to impose her unhappiness on them. They had waited too long for the realization of their dreams. But she had been relieved to be able to escape to the privacy of her own room.

Trina reached for her pink terry robe and shrugged it on, padding out into the bedroom as she belted it tightly around her. Nine forty-five.... Was that all it was? It felt so late...as if she should have been in bed long ago.... Tomorrow was the big day.... She had no doubt that most of the other drivers were out whooping it up....

Once again a deep hunger overwhelmed her. But it was a hunger that had nothing to do with physical appetite. It had more to do with need. She needed someone, and that someone was Slate. Trina gave a small, rueful laugh. This week had been a real eye-opener for her. She now had everything in the world she thought she had always wanted and she...

Trina's head snapped up toward the doorway as the sound of a heavy knock echoed in the silent room. She frowned.

"Who is it?"

The deep male voice in response was muffled. Doug... He had told her that he didn't want her to spend the evening alone...that she needed to have some fun to break the tension. She hoped he wasn't going to make the mistake of pressing now. She didn't need the added stress at this point, and she didn't want to hurt him. As she unlocked the door and started to pull it open, she pleaded in a low voice, "Doug, I really want—"

But Trina's statement got no further as her eyes touched on Slate's stolid face.

"No. It isn't Doug, Trina."

Trina took a deep breath. "What are you doing here, Slate?"

A muscle in Slate's cheek ticked as his eyes moved over the soft pink robe belted around her slender waist, the long, bared legs.... His eyes flicked up to touch on the gleaming tousled curls, moving to her hairline where wisps formed tight spirals against her cheek and forehead. He swallowed tightly as he saw the black, intent eyes searching his face.

Suddenly realizing Trina awaited his response, Slate gave a small, rueful laugh. "As usual, when I look at you I forget..." He abandoned his statement midway. It would do no good to put her on her guard, however true it was that he forgot everything except how much he wanted her when he looked into her eyes. Instead, his face sobered.

"I have to talk to you, Trina."

Her mouth tightening, Trina took a firmer grip on the door as she muttered ineffectually, "I...I was just about to go to bed. I want to get a good night's rest for tomorrow...." She started to close the door, but Slate's foot, strategically placed, impeded her attempt. Trina's eyes snapped back to Slate's face.

"May I come in?"

"No."

"Please, Trina." Slate's light eyes were direct, unwavering. "There are some things we have to settle between us, and there isn't much privacy in this hallway."

As if reenforcing his statement, a laughing couple turned the corner, only to be followed by two men conversing amicably as they walked past the door. Both shot them curious glances, finally forcing Trina to step back and allow Slate entrance. She was intensely aware that Slate closed the door firmly behind him.

"What do you want, Slate? I thought everything was settled between us."

"Did you, Trina? That's hard to believe. As far as I'm concerned, everything happened too fast that night. I just stood there and let you run me off. Even when I look back on it now, I wonder how I let it happen."

"But it did happen, and...and it's for the best after all...."

"It's only for the best if you're happy, Trina. Are you happy?"

Unable to meet his direct gaze, Trina averted her eyes, affixing them on the clock on the dresser as she responded quietly, "Of course I'm happy. And it is getting late, Slate."

She didn't see him reaching for her and was startled as his hands gripped her shoulders unyieldingly. "Look at me, Trina. Come on, honey. Look at me and tell me you're happy without me, and then I'll go away. But I have to see it first in your eyes."

Trina refused to meet his gaze, and he repeated softly, "Trina...look at me."

The dark eyes that finally moved up to his were suspiciously bright, and he swallowed at the emotion he saw there.

"It's time for honesty now, Trina, so I'll say it all...everything I should've said that night. I love you, Trina."

"I...I've heard those words before, Slate."

"I know, but you've never heard them repeated more sincerely than they are now. I love you. I've never said that to another woman before. I never truly knew the full meaning of those words until I met you, Trina. You taught me a lot of things, honey. You taught me how much I could love...how deeply I could love. And then you taught me how worthless everything is without that love."

"Oh, Slate..." He was saying it all for her...the thoughts that had been running through her head, demanding to be acknowledged...the same thoughts she had driven away, but which had returned to haunt her so relentlessly.

"But everything you said about my racing—"

"I didn't mean anything the way it came out, Trina. When your car was demolished in the accident, I *was* happy, but only because it gave me the opportunity to have you to myself for a little while. I was so damned insecure when it came to you. All I knew was that I was falling deeper and deeper in love with you every day, and except for the times when we made love, you didn't seem to care any more for me than you did for any of the other guys at the track. The only thing you gave your undivided attention to was your car, and I was jealous."

"Jealous of my car?"

"Jealous of the time you spent on it. Sounds stupid, doesn't it? But I knew you wanted to race again, and when the Spirit offer came, especially from Kent Henning…"

"Slate, I've hardly seen him at all since the approvals for the campaign were settled."

"I think I knew that. I just kind of went off the deep end for a few minutes. I panicked because I was afraid things would slip back the way they'd been before. In looking back on it, Trina, I realized all this could have been avoided if I had put my cards on the table, and demanded an answer one way or the other."

"An answer…?"

"Trina, honey, I love you. I've known that for a long time. If I'd had more courage that day when you moved back to your house…after the accident…I'd have told you then that I wanted you with me for the rest of my life."

"Slate…"

"So I'll say it now instead. Trina, I want you to marry me so we can be together the rest of our lives. It doesn't make any difference to me if you're the 'Spirit Girl,' in the Grand Nationals, or if you never race again…just as long as you're *my* girl."

His arms came around her, holding her close. Trina surrendered to his embrace, her heart so full of love that she could barely speak. He was pressing light kisses into her hair and his hands moved against her back in hungry caresses. Finally he pulled far enough away that he could look down at her face. His eyes were bright with hope as he whispered softly between the light kisses.

"So, what's your answer, Trina? I need to hear it now. I can't wait any longer...."

Swallowing against the thickness in her throat, Trina whispered hoarsely, "I've missed you, too, Slate. Everything...everything you said...it's true for me, too. I finally had it all...good equipment...a custom car...a real chance to make it, and all I could think was how much I wanted to share my happiness with you." Overcome with emotion for a few seconds, Trina hesitated. Finally spurred on by the hope gleaming brilliantly in the startling blue of Slate's eyes, she continued in a hushed voice, "And I found out something else, too. I love you, Slate. And I want to share my future with you, because...because it's no good anymore without you."

Slate was still...almost afraid to move. Then his face suddenly came to life. He grinned and began to laugh, his arms squeezing her so tightly against him that she almost lost her breath.

"Oh, God, Trina, I feel so good!"

He kissed her, his mouth devouring hers as she responded with a hunger of her own. He was trembling, but he pulled away to whisper between eager kisses, "I promised myself when I came here I wouldn't touch you until we could talk. Only, I realized as soon as I saw you that it was going to be a lot harder than I thought to keep that promise. You look so beautiful, Trina...all pink and soft. And I've missed you. I've missed you so much. Every time I see you I think I couldn't want you more than the last time...and every time I'm wrong...."

He kissed her again, and his heart leapt at Trina's total response. They were both trembling as Slate pulled his mouth from hers. He was breathless, struggling to maintain the last shred of his control, when he noticed the smile that tugged at the corners of Trina's mouth.

Intrigued by the curve of her lips, he trailed his mouth across hers, the light contact only eliciting a desire for more as he mumbled almost inaudibly, "Come on...tell me what's so funny...."

"Oh, nothing...just that..." Trina's response faded away to a light gasp as Slate trailed warm kisses across her cheek to the fragile shell of her ear where his tongue played erotically in the delicate hollows.

"Just that...?"

"Some drivers don't believe in strenuous exercise the night before a big race...."

"I wouldn't want to knock you off your training the night before the big one, honey, but right now..."

His mouth was claiming hers again, and Trina's arms tightened around his neck. The physical proof of his desire was warm and firm against her when he withdrew his mouth from hers. Trina's voice was the first to break the breathless silence.

"But right now racing is the furthest thing from your mind?" At Slate's short nod, Trina gave a small, shaky laugh. "Mine, too, Slate. But I was thinking, we can't afford to compromise our concentration tomorrow, can we, darling?"

Slate's smile grew more tender as it lowered to hers. "Never, Trina...my darling...never..."

"So I was thinking, maybe we should—"

But Trina was not able to finish her statement as Slate's mouth moved to cover hers. And for the longest time, they were not thinking at all.

EPILOGUE

A BRILLIANT SUN beat down on the heads of the thousands who had witnessed the running of the grueling Schaefer 200. The crowd thundered its applause as the winner stepped jubilantly to the microphone to accept the trophy. He jerked off his helmet, pausing only long enough to wipe the perspiration from his brow with the back of his arm before accepting the trophy. Turning a dirt-smeared face to the crowd, he grinned widely, holding the trophy high as the whistles and cheers sounded again.

Finally raising his hand, he signaled the crowd to a halt. His voice was exuberant.

"I can't tell you what it means to me to win this trophy again! I wasn't going to let that crash last year beat me! I just want to thank Harry Sloan and all the boys at Hillsdale Motors for..."

The acceptance speech was blaring loudly over the loudspeakers as the three weary drivers observing from the pits were joined by a small blond woman. She slipped her arm wordlessly around the waist of the tall, bearded driver and smiled up into his face as the other two exchanged brief glances. Once again the crowd applauded thunderously, signaling the end of Clipper Harvey's acceptance comments. The Schaefer 200 was over for another year!

Sober glances moved between the three drivers before smiles stretched over their faces.

"Well, what do you say to me buying you both a drink? It looks like you need it."

Trina's voice was the first to respond to her brother's invitation. He had startled her before the race by accepting—with an expression that bordered on relief—the fact that she and Slate had settled their differences at last.

"You don't look so great yourself, Buck, even if you did manage to come in ahead of both of us!"

"Yeah..." Buck's grin widened. "Who'd ever expect a poor, privately financed car to beat out the high-powered Spirit car *and* the Wright-Montgomery big bucks vehicle?" Answering his own question, Buck said proudly, "Nobody...nobody but me...."

"And me!" Karen's prompt interjection was unexpected and stimulated a low round of laughter.

"All right, don't rub it in, Buck." Trina shot a glance into Slate's weary but pleased face. "I would've done much better if I hadn't had trouble with the stagger on my car. Once it's adjusted, nobody'll be able to catch me! So, what's your excuse for coming in eighth, Slate?"

"I haven't thought up one that would sound at all plausible yet. I guess I'll just have to concede that Clipper Harvey had the fastest car, and that you two were luckier than I was today...."

"Luckier!"

"Yeah, luckier!" Slate's arm closed more tightly around Trina's waist as he shot her a quick wink. "I used up all my good luck last night."

The look that passed between Slate and Trina spoke for itself. Buck's dark eyes were quietly assessing, and he shook his head. "Something tells me the Mallory racing family is going to be developing another branch on its family tree...."

"And it's going to have to be a strong one, considering all the trophies it's going to have to support!"

Buck growled good humoredly at Trina's quip. "Oh, really!"

"Yeah, *really*!"

Trina's and Slate's responses came in unison, and they laughed aloud.

Then Slate's gaze became serious as he held Trina's eyes with his own. "But no matter which way I look at it, I figure I'm a winner today, Trina."

Realizing the truth in Slate's statement, Trina nodded and whispered in return as she raised her mouth for his kiss, "We're both winners, Slate...."

Oh, yes, victory was sweet...it truly was....

Following the success of WITH THIS RING and TO HAVE AND TO HOLD, Harlequin brings you

JUST MARRIED

SANDRA CANFIELD
MURIEL JENSEN
ELISE TITLE
REBECCA WINTERS

just in time for the 1993 wedding season!

Written by four of Harlequin's most popular authors, this four-story collection celebrates the joy, excitement and adjustment that comes with being "just married."

You won't want to miss this spring tradition, whether you're just married or not!

AVAILABLE IN APRIL WHEREVER HARLEQUIN BOOKS ARE SOLD

JM93

New York Times Bestselling Author

Sandra Brown

Tomorrow's Promise

**She cherished the memory
of love but was consumed
by a new passion too
fierce to ignore.**

For Keely Preston, the memory of her husband Mark has been frozen in time since the day he was listed as missing in action. And now, twelve years later, twenty-six men listed as MIA have been found.

Keely's torn between hope for Mark and despair for herself. Because now, after all the years of waiting, she has met another man!

**Don't miss TOMORROW'S PROMISE by
SANDRA BROWN.**

**Available in June wherever Harlequin
books are sold.**

TP

MEN: MADE IN AMERICA

Fifty red-blooded, white-hot, true-blue hunks from every State in the Union!

Beginning in May, look for MEN: MADE IN AMERICA! Written by some of our most popular authors, these stories feature fifty of the strongest, sexiest men, each from a different state in the union! Favorite stories by such bestsellers as Debbie Macomber, Jayne Ann Krentz, Mary Lynn Baxter, Barbara Delinsky and many, many more!

Plus, you can receive a FREE gift, just for enjoying these special stories!

You won't be able to resist MEN: MADE IN AMERICA!

Two titles available every other month at your favorite retail outlet.

MEN-G

Where do you find hot Texas nights, smooth Texas charm, and dangerously sexy cowboys?

Crystal Creek

WHITE LIGHTNING

by Sharon Brondos

Back a winner—Texas style!

Lynn McKinney knows Lightning is a winner and she is totally committed to his training, despite her feud with her investors. All she needs is time to prove she's right. But once business partner Dr. Sam Townsend arrives on the scene, Lynn realizes time is about to run out!

CRYSTAL CREEK reverberates with the exciting rhythm of Texas. Each story features the rugged individuals who live and love in the Lone Star State. And each one ends with the same invitation...

Y'ALL COME BACK...REAL SOON!

Don't miss WHITE LIGHTNING by Sharon Brondos. Available in June wherever Harlequin books are sold.

If you missed #82513 *Deep in the Heart*, #82514 *Cowboys and Cabernet* or #82515 *Amarillo by Morning* and would like to order them, send your name, address, zip or postal code along with a check or money order for $3.99 for each book ordered (do not send cash), plus 75¢ ($1.00 in Canada) for postage and handling, payable to Harlequin Reader Service, to:

In the U.S.	In Canada
3010 Walden Avenue	P.O. Box 609
P.O. Box 1325	Fort Erie, Ontario
Buffalo, NY 14269-1325	L2A 5X3

Please specify book title(s) with your order.
Canadian residents add applicable federal and provincial taxes.

CC-4

HARLEQUIN SUPERROMANCE®

HARLEQUIN SUPERROMANCE NOVELS WANTS TO INTRODUCE YOU TO A DARING NEW CONCEPT IN ROMANCE...

WOMEN WHO DARE!
Bright, bold, beautiful...
Brave and caring, strong and passionate...
They're women who know their own minds
and will dare anything...
for love!

One title per month in 1993, written by popular Superromance authors, will highlight our special heroines as they face unusual, challenging and sometimes dangerous situations.

Next month, time and love collide in:
#549 PARADOX by Lynn Erickson
Available in May wherever Harlequin Superromance novels are sold.

If you missed any of the Women Who Dare titles and would like to order them, send your name, address, zip or postal code along with a check or money order for $3.39 for each book ordered (do not send cash), plus 75¢ ($1.00 in Canada) for postage and handling, payable to Harlequin Reader Service, to:

In the U.S.
3010 Walden Avenue
P.O. Box 1325
Buffalo, NY 14269-1325

In Canada
P.O. Box 609
Fort Erie, Ontario
L2A 5X3

Please specify book title(s) with your order.
Canadian residents add applicable federal and provincial taxes.

WWD-MY